D0892093

DANTE'S DIVINE COMEDY

PARADISE

Journey to Joy, Part Three

Dante Alighieri
Gustave Doré

DANTE'S DIVINE COMEDY

PARADISE

Journey to Joy, Part Three

Retold, with Notes, by

Kathryn Lindskoog

Read Dante. . . .
Down to the frozen centre, up the vast
Mountain of pain, from world to world,
he passed.

C. S. Lewis

MERCER UNIVERSITY PRESS
MACON, GEORGIA
1998

©Mercer University Press
6316 Peake Road
Macon, Georgia 31210-3960
1998

Jacket art: Botticelli's *Sacred Nativity*
Book Jacket Design: Jim Burt
Book Design: Marc A. Jolley

Library of Congress Cataloging-in-Publication Data

Lindskoog, Kathryn Ann.
Dante's Divine Comedy/ Paradise, retold, with notes,
by Kathryn Lindskoog.
p. cm.
Includes bibliographical references.
Contents: v. [1]. Paradise. Journey to joy, Part three
ISBN 0-86554-584-7 (alk. paper)
1. Dante Alighieri, 1265–1321 — Adaptations. I. Dante
Alighieri, 1265–1321.
Divina Comedia. English. II. Title.
PS3562.I5125D36 1998
813'.54 — dc21
97-4270
CIP

MUP / H401

Contents

Frontispiece ii

Dedication vi

Preface vii

Acknowledgments ix

Introduction xi

Paradise 1

Further Reading 231

PREFACE

To read Dante is a joy.
To write about Dante is a pleasure,
for it is impossible to write about him
without reading him again more closely…
Etienne Gilson

People visit ancient cathedrals for all kinds of reasons. Some marvel at them because they are almost supernatural feats of engineering genius. Others go to contemplate marvelous stained glass windows. Some are intrigued by fascinating sculptures. Some spend days studying the tombs and their inscriptions. Some attend concerts there. Many explore cathedrals out of curiosity, and others have merely ducked inside to escape the weather. Some go because it's the thing to do. Some people know all the terms and what they mean: naves, apses, transepts, flying buttresses, facades, portals, wings, piers, vaults… Others know none of the terms, but thrill at the beauty. A few look at a cathedral as a gigantic stone history book.

Some go there to worship.

Reading Dante's *Divine Comedy* is much like visiting a cathedral. Visitors who try not to miss anything in a cathedral are apt to defeat themselves because it is too much, and readers of Dante who try not to miss anything also defeat themselves. There is far too much to take in at once.

To begin with, *The Divine Comedy* was written in rhymed poetry, not plain prose, and in Italian, not English. C. S. Lewis said that Dante is the most translatable of poets, but this guide is not exactly a translation. It is a faithful sentence-by-sentence restatement of Dante's spectacular Italian poetry in today's clear English prose (based on the work of many translators), for the sake of the story that Dante has to tell us about our journey to joy.

Many love Dante best as an Italian poet. Some love him as a spokesman for the medieval world. Some love him as a philosopher. Some love him as a builder of intricate intellectual systems. Some love him as a critic of the Medieval Church.

But those who love him best as a Christian storyteller and spiritual teacher for all people may say this book is the glimpse of Dante we have been waiting for.

ACKNOWLEDGMENTS

Thanks to the many *Divine Comedy* translators and commentators mentioned in this book. Thanks to the many world literature students who have ventured through Dante's mysterious realms with me. Thanks to John Bremer of the Institute of Philosophy, kindliest of encouragers. Thanks to Marc Jolley, the Dante lover at Mercer University Press who met me midway on my journey to publication and guided me there. And to my husband John, who deserves at least a canto of terza rima, I can only say thanks for everything.

To Father Richard and Marjorie Avery,
friends from Blessed Sacrament Episcopal Church,
Placentia, California

INTRODUCTION

C. S. Lewis and Dante's *Paradise*

C. S. Lewis read Dante's *Inferno* when he was in his teens, and he read *Purgatory* when he was in a hospital recovering from wounds received in the inferno of World War One.

When he was twenty-three he mentioned in his diary that he disbelieved in immortality and that Dante's "facts" were outdated. (At that time his brother Warren was reading Dante.) Six years later, in the spring of 1929, Lewis reluctantly decided that there is a God; but he did not yet believe in Christianity or an afterlife.

In early January 1930, C. S. Lewis visited his friend Owen Barfield for a few days, and the two did "some solid reading together." After lunch they would take a walk, then read Dante's *Paradise* (in Italian) the rest of the day.

Afterward, Lewis described this experience to his friend Arthur Greeves: "[*Paradise*] has really opened a new world to me. I don't know whether it is really very different from the *Inferno* (B. says it is as different as chalk from cheese—heaven from hell, would be more appropriate!) or whether I was specially receptive, but it certainly seemed to me that I had never seen at all what Dante was like before. Unfortunately, the impression is one so unlike anything else that I can hardly describe it for your benefit—a sort of mixture of intense, even crabbed, complexity of language and thought with (what seems impossible) *at the very same time* a feeling of spacious gliding movement, like a slow dance, or like flying. It is like the stars— endless mathematical subtility of orb, cycle, epicycle and ecliptic, unthinkable & unpicturable yet at the same time the freedom and liquidity of empty space and the triumphant certainty of movement. I should describe it as feeling more *important* than any poetry I have ever read."

Lewis suggested that Greeves might try it in English translation, but warned him "If you do, I think the great point is to *give up any idea* of reading it in long stretches... instead, read a small daily portion, in rather a liturgical manner, letting the images and the purely intellectual conceptions sink well into the mind.... It is not really like any of the things we know."

Six months later, Lewis told Greeves he had visited Barfield again and they had finished *Paradise*. "I think it reaches heights of poetry which you get nowhere else; an ether almost too fine to breathe. It is a pity I can give you no notion what it is like. Can you imagine Shelley at his most ecstatic combined with Milton at his most solemn & rigid? It sounds impossible I know, but that is what Dante has done."

The year after he first read *Paradise*, C. S. Lewis became a believing Christian, and he was clearly influenced by Dante for the rest of his life. There are traces of *The Divine Comedy* throughout his writing, from *The Pilgrim's Regress*, his first Christian book, to *Letters to Malcolm*, his last.

CANTO ONE

Toward a Golden Target

The glory[1] of the One who moves all things[2] permeates the universe and shines forth more in one part and less in another.[3] I have been in that heaven radiant with His greatest light, and I have seen things that one who returns from there cannot remember or cannot describe.[4] For as our awareness approaches the object of its deepest desire,[5] it goes so deep that memory is left behind. Nevertheless, whatever treasure my mind retains from that holy kingdom shall now become the subject of my song. [6]

---

[1] As Jeffrey Burton Russell points out, the first two words of *Paradise* state the theme of the entire book. But I propose that in another sense the theme of *Paradise* is 2 Corinthians 4:17-18: "For this slight momentary affliction is preparing for us an eternal weight of glory beyond all comparison, because we look not to the things that are seen but to the things that are unseen; for the things that are seen are transient, but the things that are unseen are eternal" (RSV).

[2] Dante's First Mover does not change or move, yet all things He created move and change because of their love for Him (which is like the instinctive love of a baby for its mother). Aristotle occasionally called the First Mover "god," but it was Dante's mentor Aquinas who identified Aristotle's First Mover as God in the Christian sense of the term.

[3] The light (glory) of God's nature shines on all things and re-shines, reflected with varying degrees of intensity. The mind-boggling diversity of things in the cosmos is one of Dante's themes, along with God's single light and its countless reflections.

[4] According to Joseph Gallagher, on an average Dante used some form of the verb "to see" eight times in each canto of *Paradise*.

[5] The object of our deepest desire is God; we are born with that spiritual longing. C. S. Lewis noted in his sermon "The Weight of Glory," "Now, if we are made for heaven, the desire for our proper place will be already in us, but not yet attached to the true object, and will even appear as the rival of that object."

[6] In her mid-century essay "The Meaning of Heaven and Hell," Dorothy Sayers speculates "It may even be that for some of the younger

O good Apollo,[7] for this crowning task make me an adequate channel of your power, worthy to receive your precious laurel. Until now one peak of Parnassus sufficed; but now I need both peaks as I struggle in this final arena.[8] Enter my heart and breathe, as you did when you pulled Marsyas out of his body's sheath.[9]

O Divine Power, if you inspire me so I can describe the shadow of the blessed realm stamped on my brain, you shall see me come to your favorite tree and crown myself with leaves, made worthy of them by my subject and and by you.[10] So

---

people in Europe to-day, the theology of Hell will seem more acceptable than the theology of Heaven. We have seen in our time the abyss of wickedness yawn open at our feet: school-children have witnessed things which to our Victorian forbears would have seemed quite unthinkable, though they would scarcely have surprised Dante. However that may be, the *intellectual* understanding of Three Kingdoms must begin with Heaven..."

Geoffrey Nuttall observes wryly in *The Faith of Dante Alighieri*, "In the sixteenth century, it might be said, men gave up believing in Purgatory; in the eighteenth century they gave up believing in Hell; and in the twentieth century they are giving up believing in Heaven." In *A History of Heaven*, Jeffrey Burton Russell says, "To the modern mind heaven often seems bland or boring, an eternal sermon or a perpetual hymn. Evil and the Devil seem to get the best lines. Dante knew better; nothing could possibly be as exciting as heaven itself. The human idea of heaven is a complex tapestry shot with flashes of glory."

[7] Until now Dante appealed to the Muses of mythology for help with his story. Now he is taking his appeal higher: to the Sun-god, the god of music and poetry.

[8] There were two peaks on Mt. Parnassus. Dante thinks of one of them as the site of the Muses and the other as the site of Apollo. For Dante to describe Paradise, he needs the aid of both.

[9] According to Ovid, after Marsyas challenged Apollo to a music contest and was defeated, Apollo skinned him alive for his arrogance. In contrast, Dante seems to me to be inviting Apollo to free his creative intellect from his human limits because of his humility.

[10] In 1319 a young poet and lecturer at the University of Bologna who had read Dante's *Inferno* and *Purgatory* wrote twice to Dante, saving copies of his two letters and Dante's two replies. Dante said that he was writing *Paradise* and hoped it would win him the poet's crown in

rarely, Lord, are they gathered for an emperor's or a poet's triumph (the fault and shame of human aspirations!) that the branch from Peneus must please the happy god of Delphos when it whets anyone's thirst for itself.[11]

A mighty flame can spring from a tiny spark; so, after my attempt, perhaps better voices will offer prayers and the god of Cirrha will respond.[12]

The lamp of the world rises for mortals by various routes; but from the one which joins four circles and three crosses it rises with a better course, linked to a happier constellation,[13] and warms and stamps our earthly wax to be more like its own nature.[14]

Florence.

[11] According to Ovid, Cupid shot Apollo and Daphne with his arrows, causing Apollo to love her and causing her to recoil from him. As she fled, she called to her father, Peneus, to protect her, and he changed her into a laurel tree. Leaves of the laurel were woven into crowns of honor for rulers and the greatest poets, "poets laureate." Thus the laurel wreath is from the favorite tree of Apollo, god of the town of Delphos, and it pleases him when a poet craves that wreath.

[12] The first part of this statement has become a well-known proverb. In the second part Dante suggests rhetorically that after his attempt to describe Paradise better poets may follow suit and Apollo (god of Cirrha, the second peak on Parnassus) will help.

[13] The sun rises at different points on the horizon as seasons change, and as it rises in the Vernal Equinox (in spring), it is at the beginning of the zodiacal sign of the Ram, the constellation of Aries. Dante refers to four great astronomical circles. The first three are the equator, the ecliptic, and the colure (a great circle that intersects both poles and which is the longitudinal circle of a given place (here Florence). These all cross the fourth circle, the horizon; hence, three crossings. At the spring equinox the three crossings actually take place at the same point on the horizon. With this display of scientific learning, Dante is alluding to the four cardinal (human) virtues and the three theological (divine) virtues. I think this in turn alludes to the human and divine nature of Christ.

[14] The warmth of spring stirs the earth to new life. Dante likens this to the human practice of melting a piece of sealing wax and stamping a symbol of identification, a seal or insignia, on a document. I think this image foreshadows the fulfillment of 1 John 3:2 in Dante himself at the

Thus it was morning on that side and evening on this; one world was all aglow when the other one was darkening.[15] And I saw Beatrice turn around and look to the left to see the sun.[16] No eagle ever looked into the sun like this.[17]

And even as a reflection always springs from a primary beam of light and rises back upward (as a pilgrim's goal is to return home), so from her action—which entered my mental imagery through my eyes—my own action sprang; and I looked at the sun more fully than ever before.[18] Much more is possible to our senses there than here, because that place was created to be the home of the human race.[19]

I could only stare at the sun briefly, but long enough to see it sparkle all around like molten iron pouring from a furnace. And suddenly it seemed that the daylight was doubled, as if the One who can do all things had given heaven a second sun.[20]

---

end of Canto 33.

[15] Dante's entire journey began on Good Friday, March 25, 1300. One week later, on April 1, he begins his journey through Paradise.

[16] Dante and Beatrice are still in the Garden of Eden (the Earthly Paradise, not the Middle East), where they were at the end of *Purgatory*. It is noon there and night in Italy. Because they are in the Southern Hemisphere facing east, Beatrice turns to the North to gaze at the sun. Throughout *Paradise*, the sun is a metaphor for God.

[17] Eagles were supposedly equipped to look directly into the sun, but they had never done it with the intensity of Beatrice.

[18] Dante likens the way he reflected Beatrice's action to the way a beam of light is reflected from a shiny surface.

[19] In the Garden of Eden Adam and Eve had physical capacities that they lost when they became sinners and had to leave the Garden. Their greatest loss was their direct contact with God.

[20] As Irma Brandeis says, "We are lifted from firm ground and set down on, surrounded by, discoursed to by light... Surely [Dante] meant to press the reader beyond the commonplace, saturate him with light, force him to struggle with difficult symbols and interlocked analogies, to feel it as energy and delight in the innumerable splendours, sparklings, whirlings, brightenings, with their musical quality and their dancing motion." At this point Dante has unknowingly soared beyond the earth's lower atmosphere. The ionosphere is an electronically conductive layer of upper atmosphere that encircles the

The eyes of Beatrice were gazing at the revolving heavens, and when I lowered mine from there I set them on her. Then as I stared at her I had an internal experience like that of Glaucus when he ate the herb that transformed him into one of the sea-gods. Transcending human consciousness this way is indescribable; anyone who has not had the experience yet will have to be satisfied with the story of Glaucus.[21]

Love who rules heaven, you know if at this point I was only that part of me which You created last; it was your light that lifted me up.[22] When the Great Wheel (which you make eternal with its longing for you) captured my attention with the harmony that you tune and modulate, I saw so much of heaven blaze with the sun's flame that rains and rivers never made a sea that wide.[23]

Never before had I felt so keenly a longing to understand a cause as I did now in response to the new sound and the great light.[24]

---

earth at a height of roughly 20 to 90 miles above the clouds, and Dante is evidently passing through it.

[21] According to Ovid, Glaucus was a human fisherman who ate magic salt-meadow grass that turned him into a god with a consuming desire and ability to dive to the ocean depths. After drinking water from the river of Eunoë in the final canto of *Purgatory*, Dante says, "I came back from the most holy waters born again, like trees renewed with new foliage; now I was pure and prepared to rise to the stars." After tasting magic grass, Glaucus could dive to the ocean floor; and after drinking supernatural water, Dante could soar to the stars.

[22] In retrospect, Dante knows his spirit had this experience, but he doesn't know if it was in or out of the body. (The part of a person created last is the spirit that God breathes into the body.) Dante is echoing St. Paul's description of his own visit to heaven in 2 Corinthians 12:2.

[23] The Great Wheel is the entire array of nine ever-revolving transparent heavenly spheres, one within the other, moved by their longing for God. Pythagoras (sixth century B.C.) taught that the energy of their motion produced music, and some of the cosmographers who followed him agreed.

[24] Sheila Ralphs observes in *Etterno Spiro: A Study in the Nature of Dante's Paradise*, "The human tendency to wonder and question arises

To put my mind at ease, she who knew me as well as I knew myself opened her lips to answer before I asked my question. She began, "You make yourself obtuse with a false assumption, and so you fail to see what you would see if you were rid of it. You are not on earth, as you believe. Lightning, speeding to its proper place, never reached the speed with which you are ascending."[25]

If I was freed from my first perplexity by these few smiling words, now I was even more entangled in another perplexity. I said, "I'm already content and over the shock of amazement. But now I'm bewildered about how my body can soar above lighter entities."

After a sigh of pity, she gazed at me with the expression of a mother looking at a delirious child[26] and began: "Every single thing has its own inherent order, and this is the way the universe resembles God.[27] In this way the highest creatures bear the imprint of Supreme Good, which is the goal that this very inner order was made for.[28] In the order I refer to, all things tend to move, in various ways and more completely or less, back to their source.[29]

"Thus they move to various ports on the great sea of being, each given innate impulse as its guide. Instinct directs fire

---

from man's being created capable of enjoying ultimate Truth." As John Bremer has observed, both Plato and Aristotle say that all philosophy begins in wonder.

[25] In *Inferno* Dante's heaviness often weighed him down. In *Purgatory*, as he was gradually cleansed, he became increasingly able to ascend with less effort. In *Paradise* he soars, unimpeded, higher than air and fire, faster than lightning or comets. If Dante had known about the speed of light, he would no doubt have used that term.

[26] According to Joseph Gallagher, someone has compared Beatrice to an older sister with a Ph.D.

[27] In his book *The Prince of Darkness: Radical Evil and the Power of Good in History* Jeffrey Burton Russell remarks, "In the *Comedy*, the physical universe is a metaphor for the ethical cosmos rather than the other way around."

[28] The highest creatures are angels and humans.

[29] God is both the origin and the goal of all creation.

toward the moon.[30] It is the mover in the hearts of everything mortal; it draws the earth together and holds it together. From its bow instinct shoots not only the brute creatures that lack intelligence, but also those that have both intellect and love.[31]

"The Providence that causes all of this sustains with its light the heaven in which the fastest sphere whirls. There, to that destination, the power of the bowstring is carrying us, the bowstring that points everything toward a golden target.[32]

"It is also true that just as an artisan's product often fails to turn out right because the material is resistant, so a creature that is able to do so sometimes goes off course and swerves toward a different destination—just as fire sometimes darts down from a cloud[33] if the first thrust is wrenched aside to earth by some fallacious pleasure.[34]

---

[30] According to Beatrice, instinct draws lightning upward from the clouds, part way toward the moon.

[31] Natural instinct is like an archer. Knowledge and love are the transcendent virtues that humans and angels share with God.

[32] God's providential will causes instinct to draw everything upward toward the ninth and fastest moving heaven, and then clear on out of our space-time continuum into the golden light of the highest heaven of all, the Empyrean.

[33] Lightning naturally darts upward from the clouds rather than downward, and when it strikes the earth something has attracted it there inappropriately. The scientific basis for this outmoded assumption has not appeared in previous *Paradise* commentaries because it was not discovered until the 1990s, when it was announced to the public in two articles: "Heaven's New Fires" by Carl Zimmer in *Discover* (July 1997, pp. 101-107) and "Lightning between Earth and Space" by Stephen Mende, David Sentman and Eugene Wescott in *Scientific American* (August 1997, pp. 56-59). According to the latter, "Indeed, scientists now realize that electrical discharges take place regularly in the rarified air up to 90 kilometers above the thunderclouds. It is remarkable that these events, many of which are visible to the naked eye, went undiscovered for so long. In retrospect, the existence of some form of lightning high in the atmosphere should not have come as a surprise to scientists." In fact, all reports of this unusual lightning, even those from responsible pilots, were dismissed as apocryphal by today's scientific community until the phenomenon was accidentally recorded by a new low-light video camera that some

"As I see it, you should be no more bewildered by your ascension than by a stream dropping down from a mountain's heights to its base. It would have been a marvel if, freed of all encumbrances, you had remained down below — as if on earth a living flame stood still." [35]
At that, she turned her gaze back toward heaven.

---

physicists were testing. In lay terms, some lightning bolts are attracted upward to the ionosphere rather than downward. Scientists promptly labelled the major forms of reverse lightning as blue jets (sometimes 20 miles from earth), red sprites (sometimes 40 miles from earth), and elves (sometimes 60 miles from earth).

[34] C. S. Lewis explained this principle in his sermon "The Weight of Glory." "If a transpersonal, transfinite good is our real destiny, then any other good on which our desire fixes must be in some degree fallacious, must bear at best only a symbolical relationship to what will truly satisfy." Thus whatever diverts us from our greatest pleasure is in the long run a deceptive pleasure, as in the saying "The good is the enemy of the best."

[35] The foregoing monologue has been referred to as Beatrice's Hymn to Divine Providence.

CANTO TWO

The First Heaven: the Moon

All you in little boats who have been following my ship that sings on its way, eager to hear my story, turn back to your own shores now.[1] Don't venture out on the open sea, because if you can't keep up with me you will be left behind.[2] The ocean path I take has never been followed before. (Minerva blows me forward, Apollo pilots me, and the nine Muses show me the Bear constellations.)[3]

You other few, who have already raised your heads for the bread of the angels which sustains life but is never filling,[4] you

---

[1] At the beginning of *Inferno.* Dante likened himself to a shipwrecked traveler. At the beginning of *Purgatory* he wrote "the little ship of my story-telling talent hoists her sails to glide across better waters, leaving behind that cruelest sea. And I will sing about a second kingdom, in which the human spirit is cleansed and becomes ready to go on up into heaven." Now he confidently likens his story-telling to "my ship that sings on its way," warning his readers that they can't keep up with him in little skiffs unless they follow very closely. (He does not really want readers to give up. He is luring them on with beautiful lines of Italian poetry.)

[2] According to John Ruskin "This is the part of the poem that is less read than the *Inferno* only because it requires far greater attention, and, perhaps, for its full enjoyment, a holier heart." John Ciardi admits that although Dante's language is usually simple, his thought is usually complex. "But if the gold of Dante runs deep, it also runs right up to the surface. A lifetime of devoted scholarship will not mine all that gold, yet enough lies on the surface — or just an inch below — to make a first reading a bonanza in itself."

[3] Minerva (in Greece Athena), goddess of wisdom, inspires and empowers Dante. Apollo, god of poetry, steers him. And the nine Muses enable him to keep his bearings with a view of the constellation that includes the North Star.

[4] See Psalm 78:25, "Man ate of the bread of the angels; he [God] sent them food in abundance." On the surface, this psalm refers to the manna

may safely trust your vessel to the deep sea if you keep close inside my wake, before the water smooths back down. The great men who sailed to Colchis were not so amazed at the sight of Jason plowing as you shall be at what you see.[5]

Humanity's permanent inborn thirst for the godly realm carried us up almost as quickly as you can see the sky. Beatrice was gazing upward, and I was gazing at her; and about as fast as an arrow lands and flies and is shot from the bow,[6] I found myself in a place where a wonderful thing absorbed me. She from whom I could hide nothing promptly turned to me and said, with as much joy as beauty, "Think of God with gratitude, because He has brought us to the first star."[7]

It seemed as if a cloud enveloped us, but it was shining, solid, dense, and polished like a diamond struck by sunlight.[8] This eternal pearl received us into itself much as water receives a ray of light without being broken.

If I was a solid body (although we can't imagine how one solid object could indwell the same space as another, that must be the case if one can enter another) this fact should increase our longing to reach that state in which we will see human and divine natures become one. There what we now believe by

---

that God provided to wanderers in the wilderness (Exodus 16), but Dante is referring allegorically to truth, especially the truths of philosophy and theology. I suspect that Dante is also alluding to the way Christians raise their heads and open their mouths to receive the consecrated bread in a traditional Communion service (Mass). In that sense the bread of the angels is Christ, who is the Way, the Truth, and the Life (see John 14:6).

[5] In Colchis Jason's crew in search of the Golden Fleece saw him capture two fire-breathing oxen and forced them to plow for him. Dante is now as daring as Jason.

[6] There are several reversals of phrasing like this in *Paradise*, suggesting reflections and mirror images.

[7] Dante uses the word star for the stars, the sun, the moon, and all the planets. Thus the first star (closest to the earth) is the moon.

[8] In Dante's day astronomers assumed that the surface of the moon was smooth and shiny.

faith shall be seen,[9] not merely made manifest, but directly experienced, like other basic truths all men believe.

I answered: "Lady, as devoutly as possible I thank Him who has lifted me out of the mortal world. But tell me, what are the dim spots on this heavenly body that cause people on earth to tell the fable about Cain?"[10]

She smiled a little and said, "If people accept a false explanation when their five senses can't unlock this truth, you should certainly not be pierced by arrows of surprise; because even when your senses help, you find that the wings of reason are too short. But tell me what you, on your own, think about it."[11]

I answered, "I figure that the apparent variations are caused by variations in the density of the material involved."

She answered, "Believe me, if you listen well to my argument against your theory you will see it sunk in falsity. The eighth sphere shows many lights to you, which in quality, as in quantity, have different appearances.[12] If diluteness and concentration alone produced that variety, then only one substance, in varying quantities, would be in them all. But their different influences have to be caused by formal principles, and accord-

---

[9] Hebrews 11:1 "Now faith is the substance of things hoped for, the evidence of things not seen."

[10] There was a fable in Dante's day that the dark patches on the moon were a sign that Cain was being punished there for killing his brother Abel. (We call the dark patches the man in the moon.) Dante is puzzled because up close there are no patches; the moon is like a perfect pearl lit by sunlight.

[11] Beatrice will use this as a springboard to teach Dante about the nature of God's material creation. Her teaching technique is often to draw out her pupil's ideas and correct them; in this process she uses the physics and philosophy of Dante's day. Barbara Reynolds assures readers, "Though the *information* conveyed by this passage is outdated [and thus obscure], its *relevance* to the reader's enjoyment and understanding of *Paradise* is as vivid and pointed as it ever was."

[12] The eighth sphere is the highest one with heavenly bodies in it, so it contains all those beyond our solar system.

ing to your theory there would be no reason for more than one kind of substance to exist.[13]

"Also, if diluteness of substance causes the dim patches you asked about, either the diluteness runs all the way through or else the moon is like a piece of meat with layers of fat and lean interspersed, like a book with both thick and thin pages.

"If the first idea were true, that would be made obvious during an eclipse of the sun by the sunlight shining through the dilute parts as light does when it passes through anything else rarefied. This is not the case; therefore we have to consider the alternative. And if by chance I disprove this also, your idea will be refuted.

"If the dilute substance does not run clear through the moon, there has to be a place inside where more solid substance blocks sunlight from passing on through; but at this point the sun's rays would be reflected back, as color is reflected by a mirror which hides lead behind the glass.

"Now you may argue that light is dimmer if it is reflected from the interior instead of from the surface, because it is farther away. But experiment, which is the spring from which flows the river of science, will free you from this concept if you try it. Take three mirrors, and set two the same distance from you. Between them set the third, farther from you. Face them, with a light behind your back that shines on the three mirrors and then reflects light back toward you. Although the size of the more distant reflection is less, you will see that it shines just as brightly.[14]

---

[13] Beatrice likens the variation of brightness on the moon to the variation of brightness among stars. In both cases variations in luminosity are due to an object's basic nature rather than to how concentrated (or large) the object is. Medieval scholastic philosophers' terms for these concepts were "material principle" and "formal principle."

[14] The two closer mirrors represent reflective substance on the surface of the moon, and the more distant mirror represents the supposedly recessed reflective substance of the moon. Because of faulty scientific expertise of Dante's day, Beatrice is inadvertently refuting erroneous theory with erroneous proof.

"Just as the stroke of the warm rays strips the ground beneath the snow of its whiteness and coldness, so with your intellect stripped of error I will instruct you with light so lively that it will shimmer as you look at it.[15]

"Within the heaven of divine peace there whirls a sphere that is the source of the essence of everything it enfolds.[16] The next lower heaven, which is full of heavenly lights, separates all of creation into varieties of existence, which it designates and contains.[17] The next lower spheres variously dispense their characteristics according to cause and effect. These organs of the universe function, you see, from one level to the next, receiving from above and endowing those below.

"Now note carefully how I wend my way to the truth you long for, so that in the future you know how to cross this river without me. As the hammer's skill comes from the metalsmith, so the movement and the power of the sacred circling comes from the Blessed Movers. And so it is that the heaven made beautiful by so many lights comes from the Deep Mind that turns it, and it is bound to receive that likeness and also impose it in turn.[18]

"And as the soul within your dust is distributed through different organs designed for different functions, so that Mind deploys its goodness, multiplied through the stars, yet still

---

[15] The forgoing exercise in scholastic reasoning (bewildering to twentieth-century readers) has been an elaborate preface to the point Beatrice really wants to make. By discussing the inconsistent appearance of the moon she is preparing Dante to learn about the human souls assigned to that lowest sphere of Heaven. They will be the subject of Canto 3.

[16] The Heaven of divine peace is the motionless Empyrean, the abode of God. Within it whirls the ninth sphere, called the *primum mobile* or the Crystalline Heaven. All the visible universe is encircled, engendered, and energized by the Crystalline Heaven.

[17] The eighth sphere, which contains all the constellations, is the source of all the diversity in the solar system.

[18] The Blessed Movers are the angelic orders related to the nine spheres. (The angels of the starry sphere are the Cherubim, which receive the imprint of the Seraphim in the ninth sphere and in turn imprint the spheres below them.)

revolves in its own unity. Each different power blends with the precious planet it enlivens to form a different compound. Because of the joyful nature of its source, the many-faceted power shines through a star much as a glad soul shines through a living eye.[19]

"This reality, not concentration and dilutedness, causes the difference between one light and another; this is the formative principle that produces dimness and brightness according to its own excellence"[20]

---

[19] "Your dust" is your mortal body. Just as your soul enlivens a variety of organs in your body yet remains one, so God's undivided power enlivens a variety of stars and planets. According to Oelsner-Wicksteed notes for Canto 2, the many-faceted power that shines through a star is the personality of that Angel mingled with the creating and inspiring power of God.

[20] Again Beatrice emphasizes that the myriad variations in the universe (in contrast to some kind of cookie-cutter creation or primordial soup) are manifestations of spiritual reality. Barbara Reynolds concludes her notes to Canto 2 by observing, "In her answer to Dante's question, Beatrice has extended his range to a consideration of the organization of the whole of Heaven and of existence. Everything else that Dante hears and experiences in the remaining cantos has been, ultimately, anticipated and prepared for by this discourse."

The physical and metaphysical structure of Hell was nine descending and constricting levels of darkness, and despair. The physical and metaphysical structure of Purgatory was nine ascending and narrowing levels of purification and expectation. The physical and metaphysical structure of Paradise will prove to be nine ascending and expanding levels of light and joy.

CANTO THREE

Piccarda's Face

That sun which first warmed my heart with love[1] had thus unveiled for me, by proof and refutation, fair truth's sweet face; and I lifted my head to confess myself corrected and convinced, as was fitting. But instead I saw something that seized my attention so that I forgot my confession.

The many faces I saw that seemed eager to speak were as faint as that of the reflection of our faces in clear, clean glass or in smooth, clear water almost too shallow to reflect—similar to the indistinctness of a pearl on a white forehead.[2] This caused me to make a mistake the opposite of that of the young man who fell in love with a pool of water.[3] As soon as I was aware of them, thinking them reflected images, I turned around to see whose faces they were; but I saw nothing and turned back to my dear guiding light, whose holy eyes grew radiant as she smiled.

"It's no wonder that I smile at your childish thought processes," she said, "since instead of setting your feet on the truth, as usual they lead you astray. You are looking at true substances[4] assigned here because they failed to keep their

---

[1] Beatrice is the sun that first warmed Dante's heart with love (when he was only nine years old). That was his discovery of spiritual love, not erotic love.

[2] In Dante's day women sometimes draped pearl pendants upon their foreheads.

[3] In Greek mythology Narcissus was so beautiful that when he saw his reflection in a pool he thought it was a real person and fell in love with it. (This is the source of the name of the flower and the source of the term narcissistic.) In contrast, Dante saw real faces but thought they were reflections.

[4] In scholastic philosophy a "substance" is something external that exists on its own, in contrast to something internally experienced, like a belief or a concept. The "true substances" in Canto 3 are real souls who

vows. Therefore speak with them, and listen, and trust them; for the true light that fulfills them does not allow their feet to wander off."

I turned to the spirit who seemed most eager and began like one who is overawed, "O spirit created for goodness, who in the sunlight of eternal life drinks in the sweetness which is unimaginable unless it is tasted, it would please me greatly if you would favor me with your name and your fate."

At that, with smiling eyes she replied at once, "Our love will never lock its gates to a just wish, any more than Love Himself would do so, who wants all His retinue to be like Himself. In the world I was a nun. If you search your memory well, my increased beauty will not disguise me and you will recognize me as Piccarda.[5] I am placed here with these other blessed souls, blessed in the sphere that moves most slowly.[6]

"Our hearts, which are kindled only in the pleasure of the Holy Spirit, rejoice in being conformed to His order.[7] And this location, which seems so lowly, is assigned to us because our vows were neglected and in some way not fulfilled."[8]

At that I said to her, "In your wondrous visage something divine shines out, transforming your former appearance. Therefore I was slow to recognize you; but what you tell me enables me to place you clearly. Now tell me, you who are

---

are relegated to the lowest heaven because they did not keep their religious vows.

[5] Piccarda was the sister of Dante's friend Forese Donati and Dante's enemy Corso Donati. In *Purgatory*, Canto 24, Forese informed Dante that Piccarda was in Heaven and Corso would soon end in Hell.

[6] Every 24 hours, the sphere of the moon and all the other heavenly bodies appear to revolve around the earth. The moon is the closest to the earth and thus its apparent circuit is smaller, which would mean that it moves through the sky most slowly.

[7] Barbara Reynolds says, "It has been said that the joys of Heaven would be for most of us, in our present condition, an acquired taste. In a sense, Dante's *Paradise* is a story about the acquisition of that taste."

[8] The only identified spirits Dante sees in the First Heaven are two passive females who were forced to change their vocations. That is obviously in keeping with characteristics traditionally associated with the moon: passivity, femininity, and changeability.

blessed here, do you desire a higher location in order to see more truth or to experience more love?"[9]

She smiled a little with her fellow spirits first, then answered me with such joy that she seemed to burn with love's first flame, "Brother, the quality of love quiets our will and makes us long only for what we have; we thirst for nothing else. If we desired to be any higher our will would differ from His who placed us here, and there is no room for that in these circles—if living here means living in love, and if you consider the nature of love.[10]

"No, the essence of this blessed life is to dwell within the divine will, with which our own wills all become one. And so this arrangement, from station to station throughout the realm, is a joy to all the realm and to the King who draws our wills to what He wills. In His will is our peace.[11] Everything that is created and that nature produces moves to that sea."[12]

---

[9] In Purgatory all the spirits were rightly longing to ascend, and Dante associates ascension with increased understanding and more of the love of God.

[10] This famous encounter with Piccarda in the third canto of *Paradise* reflects and reverses Dante's famous encounter with Francesca in the fifth canto of *Inferno*. In both cases Dante finds himself in a strange new realm, and the first inhabitant he interviews is the spirit of a woman connected with his life in Italy. Both women had been forced into marriages they abhorred, and both died young. Francesca was consigned to her level in the afterlife by Minos and hated it; Piccarda was consigned to hers by the will of the King and loved it. (Francesca told Dante that the King of the Universe was not her friend.) Francesca is consumed with self-pity and anguished love for Paolo, and Piccarda is consumed with gratitude and burning love for God. Francesca is weary and buffeted; Piccarda dwells in radiant rest. Francesca endures pain and misery; Piccarda enjoys the bliss they both should have.

[11] This is one of the most famous quotations in *The Divine Comedy*. As Allen Mandelbaum notes, it echoes Ephesians 2:14, "For He is our peace," and St. Augustine's *Confessions* (xiii, 9), "In thy good will is our peace."

[12] In the *Inferno* Francesca mentioned water flowing to the sea, "The town where I was born is at the shore, where the River Po and neighboring streams find their rest in the sea." At the end of Canto 1 in *Paradise* Beatrice likened Dante's spiritual ascent to "a stream

Then it was clear to me that everywhere in heaven is Paradise, even though the grace of the First Good does not rain there equally for all. But just as sometimes we are satisfied by one food yet still hunger for another, and while giving thanks for one we ask for the other, so I asked with gesture and word about that web through which she had not drawn her shuttle all the way.[13]

"Up higher there is a lady[14] whose perfect life and great worth have enshrined her there," she said, "by whose rule down in your world some clothe and veil themselves so that until death they may wake and sleep with that Spouse who accepts every loving vow that conforms with His good pleasure.[15] When I was still a girl I left the world behind to follow her, and dressed in her habit and pledged myself to her order. Later, men more acquainted with evil than with good tore me violently away from that sweet cloister, and what my life was after that, God knows.[16]

"And this other splendor, who reveals herself to you on my right and shines with all the light of our sphere, understands for herself what I tell you about myself. She was a nun, and her head was taken away from the shade of the sacred veil. Although she was forced back into the world against her will and

---

dropping down from a mountain's heights to its base." Now Piccarda suggests that all of God's creation *(ex nihilo)* and its continuation through natural processes moves (upward) toward an ocean of rest where it originated.

[13] The vertical threads on a loom are the warp, and the weaver pulls other threads through them horizontally with a shuttle to form the woof. Dante wants Piccarda to complete her personal story about how she failed to fulfill her sacred vow.

[14] St. Clare was a friend and disciple of St. Francis. She founded the Franciscan Order of Poor Clares.

[15] Nuns consider themselves wed to Christ. Putting on the veil is a symbol of perpetual chastity.

[16] Piccarda chooses not to name her guilty brother Corso, who for selfish reasons compelled her to leave her convent and marry a man with bad character. Whether the violence she suffered at their hands was both physical and moral or only moral, she did not live long after that.

common decency, she was never stripped of her heart's veil.[17]
This is the splendor of the great Constance,[18] who from the
second hurricane of Swabia gave birth to its third and final
power."[19]

So Piccarda spoke to me, and then she began to sing *Ave
Maria* and vanished as she sang, like something heavy slipping
away into deep water.[20]

My sight followed her as far as it could, and when it had lost
her it returned to my greater desire, focusing again on Beatrice.
But her brilliance dazzled me so that at the first my eyes could
not bear it; and this delayed my questioning.

---

[17] Although Constance was deprived of her physical virginity, she
never lost the purity of her commitment to Christ.

[18] It is significant that a woman named Constance should be the one
to shine so brightly in the sphere of the moon, because the moon is
traditionally associated with the human trait of inconstancy.

[19] Empress Constance inherited the crown of Sicily and Southern
Italy. In 1185 she married Henry VI, second great prince of the Swabian
(German) dynasty. She was already about 32 and he was 22. Nine
years later she gave birth to Frederick II, the third and last emperor of
the Swabian dynasty. In Dante's day it was commonly believed that
before her marriage she was a nun.

[20] The two spirits in the sphere of the moon who are identified to
Dante, Piccarda and Constance, were both taken away from the
convents where they had hoped to live peacefully, focused on God all
their lives. In Heaven they find themselves living eternally in the perfect
prototype of all convents. Piccarda's face had resembled a reflection on
the surface of shallow water, and now it recedes like a face slipping
under deep water. Dante seems to be alluding to her words about the
Empyrean, "that sea to which everything moves."

The Moon
Gustave Doré. (Canto 3)

CANTO FOUR

The Sacred Stream

Set between two foods that are equally close and equally appealing, a man with completely free will would die of starvation before he got a bite of either one. Similarly, a lamb between two equally close and equally terrifying wolves would freeze in place, as a deerhound would between two deer. Therefore, if I was mute when I was pulled equally in two directions by my puzzlement, I deserve no blame or credit because I couldn't help it.[1]

I held my tongue, but my powerful urge and my questions were painted on my face more vividly than if I had spoken them. And Beatrice played the part that Daniel had played when he calmed Nebuchadnezzar's wrath that had made him tyrannically cruel.[2]

She said, "I see how two different desires are pulling you so that your urgency is in a tangle and can't get out of your throat.[3] You argue, 'If my commitment to goodness persists,

---

[1] Philosophers used to theorize that if we were motivated by two equally compelling but mutually exclusive options, we would be paralyzed by the impossibility of choosing between them. In this case, Dante had two urgent questions for Beatrice but could not decide which to ask first.

[2] According to Daniel 2, Daniel miraculously described the forgotten dream that was obsessing Nebuchadnezzar and correctly interpreted it as well. Similarly, Beatrice knew the questions that were on Dante's mind as well as their solutions.

[3] In Canto 2, lines 49-148, Beatrice delivered a learned discourse about the spots on the moon. Here she launches into a discourse on the influence of the stars and free will (Canto 4, lines 16-142). In Canto 5, lines 1-84, she will deliver a discourse about breaking vows. In *Dante's Christian Astrology* Richard Kay notes, "The cumulative mass of these lectures is imposing; not counting the 39 preliminary verses, the Lunar discourses proper run to some 309 lines."

why should someone else's violence deprive me of due credit?'
Your other perplexity is caused by souls appearing to return to
the stars as Plato taught. These are the questions that weigh
equally on your mind; and therefore I will deal with the
potentially poison one first.[4]

"Neither the most in-Godded of the Seraphim,[5] nor Moses,
nor Samuel, nor either John you choose, nor even Mary is
lodged in any other heaven than the spirits you just saw; nor
are any of them allotted more or fewer years of blessedness
there. But all add to the beauty of the highest heaven and share
one sweet life; the only difference is how much of the Eternal
Breath they feel.[6]

"These spirits have appeared to you here not because this
sphere is their assigned abode, but to show that they are lowest
of the heavenly host. This form of communication is necessary
to the human condition because your mind must be furnished
with sense impressions before it can conceptualize.

"That is why the Bible accommodates itself to human needs,
attributing hands and feet to God to symbolize truths. And the
church attributes human faces to Gabriel and Michael and the
one who healed Tobit.[7]

"What Plato's *Timaeus* said about human souls is not like
that, because he seems to mean it literally. He says that at death
the soul returns to its own star because it was exiled from its star
while nature used it to make a human being. But it's possible
that Plato's real meaning is different from his apparent
meaning and has significance that shouldn't be disparaged.[8] If

---

[4] Plato's doctrine (as understood by Dante) is poisonous because it
attributes so much to the influence of the stars that it eliminates the role
of free will and human responsibility. Greek was in eclipse in Dante's
day, and so he had not read Plato for himself.

[5] Like Shakespeare, Dante invented a variety of new words — close
to 100. One of them means to in-God oneself.

[6] All the spirits in the Empyrean feel God's love fully, according to
their individual capacities.

[7] To portray spiritual realities about God and angels, the Bible and
church art use anthropological images. According to the Apocrypha, it
was the angel Raphael who healed the eyes of Tobit.

[8] Aristotle took Plato literally and refuted him, but Thomas Aquinas

he means that appropriate honor or blame returns to the stars because of their influence, his bow may have hit on some truth. This misunderstood idea used to misdirect almost the whole world, so that it rushed off to give the planets names like Jove and Mercury and Mars.[9]

"The other puzzle that troubles you is less poisonous, because its malice wouldn't lead you elsewhere and away from me.[10] The fact that heavenly justice looks unjust to mortal eyes is a faith problem, not harmful heresy. But since your intellect is strong enough to reach and penetrate this truth, I will satisfy you according to your desire. If violent coercion means that the one who suffers it does nothing to cooperate with it, then these souls can't claim violent coercion as their excuse; for if a person's will holds fast it cannot be crushed, but persists like the nature of fire in spite of a thousand strong gusts.

"If the will bends either greatly or slightly, it is capitulating to force; and that is what these spirits did, since they could have returned to their sacred place. If their will had remained unbroken, like that which held Lawrence on the grill and made Mucius ruthless to his own right hand, as soon as they were free to go it would have thrust them back onto the path from which they were diverted; but such firm will is all too rare.[11] Now if

---

taught that Plato was presenting his wisdom in figures of speech and analogies. Seven hundred years after Dante, scholars still disagree about whether Plato meant to be taken literally or not.

[9] Beatrice means that the Hebrews alone avoided astrological idolatry. Jove is the alternative name for the pagan god Jupiter.

[10] It is important to remember that in Heaven Beatrice is still a very real human person, but she also serves as a symbol for heavenly wisdom.

[11] As usual, Dante gives a sacred example and a secular example. Because of his refusal to reveal the location of the church treasury, St. Lawrence was grilled alive in Rome in 258 A.D. by the emperor Valerian. He allegedly mocked the emperor by advising his executioners to turn him over midway to roast him evenly. Mucius (Caius Mucius Scaevola) was a defender of Rome who was captured when he tried to assassinate an attacker named Porsena. When Porsena condemned him to be burnt alive, Mucius thrust his right hand into a small flame and held it there to demonstrate the strong willpower of

you have gleaned the meaning of my words as you should, the doubts which would have kept on troubling you are rendered void.[12]

"But now across your path you see another obstacle, through which it would be too exhausting for you to make your way alone. I have taught you that it is certain that no blessed soul may lie, because it lives forever next to the Primal Truth; and then you heard from Piccarda that Constance's devotion to the veil remained inviolate, so that she seems to contradict me.

"Many times now, my brother, it has come to pass that to escape danger people have regretfully done wrong things; so it was that Alcmaeon, moved by his father's prayer killed his own mother and—in order to be a good son to his father—was evil.[13] At that point, I want you to realize that outside force mixes with one's will, and there is no excuse for what they do together. A person's absolute will does not consent to evil, but it relents according to how much it fears that resistance will result in something worse. Thus when Piccarda spoke she referred to the absolute will, and I referred to the mixed will; so we were both telling the truth."[14]

Such was the rippling of the sacred stream that poured from the fountain that flows with all truth; and being such, it set at peace both of my longings.[15] "O beloved of the First Lover, divine one," I said, "whose speech flows over me and warms me so that it makes me more and more alive, my love is not

---

the Romans. Porsena was so impressed that he pardoned Mucius and ended his attack.

[12] Piccarda and Constance submitted to their abductors rather than fleeing back to their convents at the first opportunity. Dante may also be implying that they could have resisted to the point of martyrdom and death if necessary.

[13] Alcmaeon fulfilled his dying father's request for vengeance. Thus Alcmaeon chose what seemed to him the lesser of two evils. His story appeared previously in Canto 12 of *Purgatory*.

[14] Piccarda spoke of Constance's "absolute will," the will to fulfill her monastic vows; and Beatrice spoke of Constance's "relative will" or "contingent will," the will to yield to outside force.

[15] The holy stream is Beatrice's explanation, which flows from the fountain of God, the First Lover.

deep enough to be able to match your favors with favors in return; but may He who sees it and has the power do it for me.

"Now I see that our intellect can never be satisfied unless the Truth shines on it beyond which there is no more truth. There our intellect can rest as safely as an animal that has finally reached its den. And it will reach it; otherwise our longing would be in vain. That is why our questions spring like tendrils from the root of truth; it is what impells us toward the summit, from one pinnacle to the next.[16]

"This invites me and gives me confidence, Lady, to reverently ask you about another truth that is obscure to me. I would like to know if one can ever compensate for broken vows with other good deeds, to somehow balance the account."

Beatrice looked at me with eyes so divine, so full of sparks of love, that I was stunned and had to turn away. All I could do was stand there with my eyes downcast.

---

[16] Barbara Reynolds explains in her notes for Canto 4, "The desire of the mind for knowledge and understanding is itself a natural image of the desire of the soul to see God; in another sense the two desires may be seen to be identical, since the mind can be satisfied only by the ultimate Truth, which is God. Throughout *Paradise*, Dante's advancement in understanding is a symbol and a measure of his progress towards his ultimate vision in the last canto."

CANTO FIVE

The Second Heaven: Mercury

"If in the warmth of love I blaze brighter than anything visible on earth, and so completely stun your eyes, don't marvel; for this is the result of enhanced vision, which, as it comprehends goodness, moves closer, step by step, to that goodness.[1]

"I see clearly that the eternal light is already shining in your mind; once this light is seen, it kindles the only everlasting love.[2] And if any lesser thing captures your love, it is only a stray splinter of this very light.

"You want to know whether a person can ever compensate for a broken vow to God with adequate good deeds to clear the soul of guilty debt." So Beatrice began this canto, and as one who does not interrupt her speech she continued her holy discourse. "The greatest, most generous gift that God made at creation, the most characteristic and the most costly to Him, was the free will He has bestowed upon all intelligent creatures and those alone.[3]

---

[1] Beatrice comprehends God's love and blazes with that love. As Dante is increasingly enlightened (as he sees more truth), he too moves closer to God. In *The Ladder of Vision*, Irma Brandeis points out that when Dante was a child, encountering Beatrice was his "first great *eye-opener*" because it snatched him out of preoccupation with himself. In *Paradise* "...Beatrice leads him from sphere to sphere of insight. With every apparent brightening we know that some further film of the human limitation has been lifted from his eyes."

[2] In *A History of Heaven*, Jeffrey Burton Russell says, "In the beatific vision of God, the person's 'seeing' is his or her complete understanding and love of Christ.... In the heavenly union complete love and complete knowledge are one and the same."

[3] Angels and humans are the intelligent (fully conscious) creatures Dante refers to. In *Etterno Spiro* Sheila Ralphs observes, "Free will was God's greatest gift to man, for by it He gave the creature to itself."

"The great value of a holy vow should be clear to you if you think about it. If the vow is made as a pact that you and God freely agreed to, you have used this treasure I speak of to sacrifice itself. What can be given then as restoration? If you were to use the gift you took back, you would be doing good deeds with stolen goods.

"You are now clear about the main point; but since the church grants dispensations, a fact that seems to contradict the truth I just explained, it behooves you to keep sitting at the table, because you need further help to digest the tough food you have taken in. Open your mind to take in what I explain, and keep it there; for to have understanding without retention is not knowledge.

"The essence of making a sacrifice consists of two things: first, the matter to be sacrificed, and then the act itself. The latter obligation can never be satisfied except by being fulfilled; and that is what my explanation was about. That is why it was essential for the Hebrews to always offer sacrifice, although the offerings could vary, as you no doubt realize.

"The other part, which I referred to as the matter to be sacrificed, may actually be such that there is nothing wrong with replacing it with something else. But let no one independently decide to switch the load upon his shoulder without the turning of both the white and yellow keys.[4] And it would be useless for a man to contemplate changing his vow unless the replacement is one and a half times the value of the original item that was to have been sacrificed. Therefore, if something is of such great value that it outweighs everything else, it can never be satisfactorily replaced by anything else.

"Mortals should never make a vow lightly. Be true to your vow; but in doing so don't have tunnel vision, as Jephthah did in sacrificing the first one he met. He would have done better to say 'I vowed wrong' than to keep such a vow.[5] For similar folly

---

[4] The silver key represents a qualified priest's informed judgment and approval of the substitution, and the gold key represents the priest's actual authorization of the substitution.

[5] See Judges 11:29-40. Jephthah was the Hebrew leader who promised God that if he won the war against the Ammonites he would

you may follow the great Greek chieftain's story that caused
Iphigenia to weep because her face was fair, and has made both
the foolish and the wise weep when they heard about her.[6]

"Christians, be more firm and steady than that, not like a
feather blown about by every wind; and don't think that just
any water can wash you clean.[7] You have the Old and the New
Testament and the shepherd of the Church to guide you; let this
suffice for your salvation. If evil greed tells you something else,
be men, not senseless sheep; otherwise any Jew in your locale
will scoff at you.[8] And don't be like the silly, capricious lamb
who wanders away from his mother's milk, fighting with
himself as he frolics."

Thus Beatrice spoke to me, as I write it down; then she
turned her eyes longingly to that part of the sky where the
world is most alive with light.[9] Her silence and her transformed
appearance imposed silence on my eager mind, which already
had new questions ready.[10] And like an arrow that hits the
target before the bowstring is still, so we soared to the second
kingdom. There I saw my Lady so joyful to enter the light of
this Heaven that the planet itself became brighter because of
her presence. And if the planet was changed and laughed,

---

sacrifice as a burnt offering whatever came out of his home to greet him
first when he returned. To his horror, his only daughter came out first.

[6] According to legend, Agamemnon vowed that he would sacrifice
the loveliest creature born that year; but his beautiful daughter
Iphigenia was born, and so he ignored his vow. Years later, when
misfortune struck the Greeks, other leaders attributed it to the unkempt
vow and pressured Agamemnon into sacrificing his daughter.

[7] Beatrice is warning Christians to use good judgment in making
vows and in seeking release from vows and other obligations.

[8] Beatrice is warning Christians not to be misled by unscrupulous
people who sell indulgences and claim to release their customers from
vows. Jews took vows seriously and would have contempt for such
behavior.

[9] Given the date, this would probably have been in the eastern sky at
the point where the four great circles coincide at the vernal equinox.

[10] At this point Beatrice has finished her lunar discourses, and with
Dante's increased understanding the two are ready to shoot to the
second realm of Heaven.

what else could I do, since I am by my very nature prone to every sort of change!

As fish in a still, clear pool will gather around anything that drops into the water to find out if it is food for them to eat, so I saw more than a thousand splendors draw toward us, and each one was saying, "Look! Here is one who will increase our loves."[11] As each soul approached us, the bright radiance that it spread revealed the joyousness that filled it.

Think, Reader, if this account I am beginning were to halt abruptly, how anguished you would be—famished to know more. That in itself will show you how much I longed to hear all about these souls as soon as I saw them.

"You born for blessing, who by God's grace are allowed to see the Thrones of eternal triumph before you have finished with the battles of mortal life, we are kindled by the light that shines through all of Heaven; therefore, if you want light from us, help yourself to as much as you want."

That is what one of those devout spirits said to me; and Beatrice added, "Speak, speak confidently; and trust them as you would trust gods."

"I see how you nestle in your own light, and that you beam it through your eyes, because they flash when you smile;[12] but, Worthy Soul, I don't know who you are or why you are located in this sphere, which is concealed from mortals by another's rays."[13]

This is what I said, turned toward the light that had just spoken to me. At that it gleamed far more brilliantly than before. As the sun hides itself from our eyes by excessive light once heat has eaten away the sheltering cloud cover, so by

---

[11] Dante will increase their loves by his presence and their service to him.

[12] In the Moon Dante could see very faint faces. Here he briefly sees the expression in this spirit's eyes. At each level of Heaven the saints will reflect more of God's light, and until Canto 30 Dante's eyes will not be strong enough to penetrate their halos of Godlight.

[13] This is the sphere of Mercury, a planet so near the sun that it is seldom visible from Earth.

excess of joy the sacred soul hid himself in his own radiance. Thus concealed, he answered me as the next canto will relate in song.

CANTO SIX

The Roman Eagle

"For more than two hundred years after Constantine returned the eagle (contrary to the star track it followed when the ancient one married Lavinia), this bird of God dwelt on Europe's rim near the mountains from which it first arose; and there it governed the world beneath the shadow of its sacred wings and passed from hand to hand until by a succession of changes it came to my hand.[1]

"Caesar I was, and am Justinian—who, propelled by the primal love that I can feel now, eliminated waste and inefficiency from the body of Roman law.[2] Before I undertook this work, I held that there was one nature in Christ and no

---

[1] The eagle is the symbol of the Roman Empire, which Dante held sacred because it fostered the early spread of Christianity. Constantine the Great, first Christian emperor, ruled from 306 to 337 A.D.; he is the one who moved the seat of government eastward from Rome to Byzantium (which became Constantinople). Constantinople is in the general region of the site of ancient Troy, the home that—according to Virgil's *Aeneid*—Aeneas left behind shortly after 1200 B.C. when he ventured to Italy, married Lavinia, and founded the kingdom that became the Roman Empire. Thus Aeneas followed the sun and stars westward, but 1500 years later Constantine moved his government eastward. Dante believed that moving the government away from Rome led to the disastrous wealth and corruption of the church hierarchy in Rome.

[2] Justinian the Great was Emperor of the Roman Empire from 527 to 565 A.D., and he moved the Imperial government back to Italy—to Ravenna. (On earth his title was Caesar, but in Heaven earthly titles and rank are left behind.) Justinian (a name related to justice) served God's purpose by organizing Roman law and thus serving the cause of world justice. Dante lived in Ravenna when he wrote *Paradise*, and he was no doubt well acquainted with the famous 800-year-old mosaics of Justinian and his wife Theodora there in the Church of San Vitale. (They are now 1500 years old.)

more, and with that faith I was content. But the blessed Agapetus, who was principal pastor, led me with his teaching to the purely true faith.[3] I believed him, and now I see the content of his faith as clearly as you see how a contradiction is both false and true.[4]

"As soon as I fell in step with the Church, in His grace God was pleased to inspire me with my high task, and I gave myself completely to it. To my Belisarius I entrusted my military affairs; heaven's right hand so favored him, it was a signal I should retire from military affairs.[5]

"Now you have my answer to your first question,[6] but its nature forces me to go on to some supplementary information so you can see how much right people have to attack the sacred emblem, whether they seize it for themselves or oppose it.[7]

"Behold what great valor has made the eagle worthy of reverence, beginning with the hour when Pallas died to give it sovereignty.[8] For over three centuries it dwelt in Alba, until the end, when three fought against three contending for that ensign.[9]

---

[3] Agapetus was the pope from 533 to 536 A.D. He convinced Justinian that Christ was fully human as well as fully divine.

[4] It seems obvious that if a statement contradicts itself, both parts cannot be true. The statement that Christ is fully human and fully divine sounds like that, but Justinian has faith that this doctrine is in fact contradictory. He is referring to the nature of apparent paradox.

[5] Belisarius was an outstanding general, and his victory over the Goths is what enabled Justinian to rule from Ravenna. It is thought that Belisarius is the figure next to Justinian in the mosaic in the Church of San Vitale.

[6] At the end of Canto 5 Dante had said, "Worthy Soul, I don't know who you are or why you are located in this sphere."

[7] This is Justinian's ironic preface to his condemnation of both the Ghibellines, who had taken the eagle symbol for their own banner, and the Guelphs, who opposed it.

[8] Justinian will review the costly history of the Roman Empire, and he begins with Pallas, who died while fighting for the newcomer Aeneas (according to Virgil).

[9] The kingdom of Aeneas was founded at Lavinium and promptly transferred to Alba Longa, where it remained for over three centuries.

"And you also know what actions it took between the time of the Sabine women's woe and Lucretia's woe, how under seven kings it conquered its neighbors.[10]

"You know what it accomplished, carried by the chosen Romans against the force of Brennus, Pyrrhus and other princes and governments; from which Torquatus and Quintius (named for his curly hair), the Decii and the Fabii, all garnered fame that I rejoice in preserving.[11]

"It cast down the pride of the Arabs who followed Hannibal across the Alpine rocks from which the Po glides down.[12] Under it, Scipio and Pompey triumphed at any early age, and it was bitter for the hill below which you were born.[13]

"Then as the time approached when all Heaven meant to bring the world a heavenly serenity, Caesar, with Rome's consent, took it in hand;[14] and what it wrought from the Var to

---

Before 700 B.C. Alba was absorbed into Rome when three Alban champions were defeated by Romans. According to tradition, both sides were descended from Trojans led by Aeneas.

[10] An Alban outcast named Romulus had founded a camp of outlaws on the Palatine (one of Rome's seven hills), and he became the first king of Rome. To obtain wives, he had his followers seize and rape Sabine women. Under Romulus and his six successors, the Roman kingdom thrived until Sextus, son of the seventh king, cruelly raped a virtuous woman named Lucretia. This so angered the public that in 510 B.C. the monarchy was destroyed. Then the Roman Republic began.

[11] Dante summarizes about 500 eventful years of the Roman Republic in a few lines commemorating major heroes and victories. During this period Rome successfully repelled invasions and extended its dominion.

[12] The greatest of all the Fabii family, Quintius Fabius Cincinnatus, saved Rome from Hannibal, who crossed the Alps and successfully invaded Italy in 218 B.C. (At one time all North Africans were called Arabs; Hannibal and his "Arabs" were Carthaginians.) In 218 B.C. Scipio Africanus the Elder, then a boy of seventeen, won fame by saving his father's life in battle. Years later Scipio forced Hannibal to withdraw from Italy.

[13] Fiesole was on the hill above Florence, the city where Dante was born; Fiesole was defeated and brought into the Roman Republic.

[14] About 500 years after the eagle came to Justinian's hand, it came to Caius Julius Caesar's hand. His last name became the official title for

the Rhine is also known by Isère and Arar, and known by the Seine and every valley fed by the Rhone.[15]

"What it did then, when it took off from Ravenna and leaped the Rubicon, was such a flight that neither tongue nor pen can describe it. It wheeled its army toward Spain, then toward Durazzo, and struck Pharsalia so hard that even the warm Nile felt the pain.[16]

"It saw Antandros and the Simois again, where it had come from, and saw the spot where Hector lies buried; and then— alas for Ptolemy—ruffled itself again. Next it swooped like a thunderbolt on Juba, then wheeled toward the west, where it heard Pompey's trumpet.[17]

"Brutus and Cassius howl in hell because of what it accomplished with the next one who carried it, and it made Modena and Perugia grieve. The wretched soul of Cleopatra is still crying; she fled from it and suffered sudden black death from the bite of an asp.[18] With him it went to the shore of the

---

Roman emperors, and it evolved into the German word *kaiser* and the Russian word *czar*.

[15] Justinian refers to Caesar's campaign in Gaul (58-50 B.C.) by naming the principal rivers there.

[16] In 49 B.C., when Caesar rebelliously crossed the Rubicon between Ravenna and Rimini, he was launching a civil war against Pompey, who had enjoyed a great military triumph 32 years earlier at age 24. Caesar defeated Pompey at Pharsalia in Thessaly (an area in northern Greece). Pompey escaped to Egypt, where he was murdered by Ptolemy; thus "even the warm Nile felt the pain."

[17] The eagle returned with Julius Caesar to the region of Troy where it had begun when Aeneas set sail from Antandros. Caesar seized Egypt from Ptolemy and made Cleopatra queen. Then he conquered Juba, the king of Numidia who was sheltering his opponents, and in 45 B.C. returned to Spain, where Pompey's sons had raised an army.

[18] After Brutus and Cassius assassinated Julius Caesar on March 15, 44 B.C., his nephew Augustus took the eagle. He defeated Mark Antony at Modena in 43 B.C., and in 42 B.C. he defeated Brutus and Cassius at Philippi in Macedonia. (Paul wrote his letter to the young church in Philippi just one century later.) In 41 B.C. Augustus killed Antony's brother at Perugia. Ten years later, he finally defeated Marc Antony, who committed suicide; then Antony's lover Cleopatra killed herself by

Red Sea; with him it made such world peace that Janus saw his
temple door locked shut.[19]

"But everything the ensign I speak of had done before, and
everything it would still do throughout its dominion, all shrinks
and fades if it is seen with a clear eye and a pure heart, when
compared to what it did in the hand of the third Caesar.[20] The
Living Justice that inspires me granted to that very hand the
glory of avenging His just wrath.[21]

"Now marvel at the double thing I tell you: Not much later,
under Titus, the vengeance for the ancient sin was itself
avenged.[22]

"And when the Lombard fang bit into the Holy Church,
victorious Charlemagne defended her under its wings.[23]

---

holding a poisonous snake to her breast.

[19] The god Janus was presumed to be on the battlefield with Roman
soldiers whenever they were fighting, and so his temple doors were
almost always open. In the cessation of war under Augustus, those
doors were kept shut.

[20] This statement begins in line 82 of Canto 6, and for five stanzas
Justinian reflects on the pivotal role the Roman Empire played in the
beginning of Christianity.

[21] In the peace that prevailed under Tiberius, the third Caesar, Christ
was crucified, thus (according to Allen Mandelbaum) "avenging
[God's] own wrath for Adam's original sin." His motive was the
redemption of mankind. All the history of Roman accomplishments
fades into insignificance compared to this event.

[22] In response to a Jewish uprising about forty years after the
crucifixion of Christ, Titus, the fourth Caesar, devastated Jerusalem and
destroyed the irreplaceable holy temple built by Solomon almost a
thousand years earlier. Although the Romans did this as punishment of
the Jews for current insurrection, the Jews were thus punished for
choosing to crucify Christ, which was itself divine vengeance for
Adam's sin. In a footnote John Ciardi comments, "If God decreed the
Crucifixion, had the Jews any choice? Are they more guilty than Pilate
who simply washed his hands and let his soldiers drive the nails?
What is free will in confrontation with a preordained act of God's
will? Such questions must be referred to a quality of revelation
unknown to footnotes."

[23] In 774 A.D. Charlemagne, founder of the Holy Roman Empire,
overthrew the Lombard King Desiderius when he invaded territory

"Now you may judge those I recently accused, as to whether their sins are responsible for your own misfortunes.[24] One of them wants to replace the traditional emblem with the golden lilies emblem, and the other misappropriates the traditional emblem for his own ends; so it is hard to see which abuses it more. The Ghibellines should pursue their ends under some other banner, for those who divorce this banner from justice follow it wrongly. And the new Charles had better not attack it with his Guelphs; he should fear its talons, which have ripped the hide from fiercer lions. Children have often suffered because of the sins of their fathers, and he should not presume that God will accept his lilies as the emblem of His might.[25]

"This little planet is adorned with good souls who exerted themselves admirably so that honor and fame might come their way,[26] and when desire is thus somewhat bent, the rays of love are bound to ascend less powerfully. But the appropriateness of our rewards to our merit is part of our joy, because we see that they match perfectly. Thus the Living Justice so sweetens our will that it may never be twisted to anything wrong. Just as on earth the variety of voices creates sweet harmony, so in Heaven

---

belonging to the Roman Church. By including Charlemagne here, Justinian indicates that the Holy Roman Empire was a *bona fide* continuation of the ancient Roman Empire.

[24] At line 97 Justinian has completed five stanzas about the role of the Roman eagle in Christian history and launches into five stanzas about the warring Guelph and Ghibeline parties, which had cruelly wronged Dante.

[25] Dante expresses contempt for Charles II of Anjou, who was king of Naples from 1285 to 1313 and leader of the Guelph party. Charles II was loyal to the royal emblem of France rather than the Roman eagle. Justinian warns that such audacity is apt to result in some kind of retribution on his descendants.

[26] At line 112 Justinian has completed five stanzas about the Guelphs and Ghibelines and launches into five stanzas about the nature of the Second Heaven. The planet Mercury is the smallest of all, and it is the level of good souls (like himself) whose virtuous lives were more motivated by personal ambition and desire for public approval than by selfless love of good.

the variety of our levels creates sweet harmony among these spheres.[27]

"Here within this same pearl the light of Romeo shines, whose good and beautiful service was so badly rewarded.[28] (The Provençals who schemed against him do not have the last laugh, because anyone who takes offense at someone else's good work treads a dangerous road.) Raymond Berengar had four daughters, and each one became a queen; this was accomplished for him by Romeo, a humble immigrant. Then lying accusations prompted him to demand accounting from this just man, who had given him twelve for every ten. So poor old Romeo went away; and if the world could know the heart within him as he begged for his daily survival, crust by crust — as much as it praises him, it would praise him even more."[29]

---

[27] In the sphere of the moon passive women who had not stayed in their religious communities rejoice eternally in the ultimate religious community. Similarly, in the sphere of Mercury active men who were eager for honor rejoice fully in the attainments of others. They have been freed from the pangs of personal ambition and competition, enabling them to rejoice fully in the perfection of things as they are.

[28] At line 127 Justinian has completed five stanzas about the Second Heaven and launches into five stanzas about Romeo da Villanova (1170-1250).

[29] Romeo was a loyal and talented steward for the prosperous Raymond Berengar IV, ruler of Provençe from 1209 to 1245. Thanks to wise management, all four of Berenger's daughters made highly profitable marriages. (They married Louis IX of France; Louis' brother, Charles of Anjou; Henry III of England; and Henry's brother, Richard of Cornwall.) According to legend, envious barons of Provençe maliciously accused Romeo of cheating his employer, who then challenged Romeo to prove his innocence. Such lack of confidence in his demonstrated integrity was too much for Romeo to bear; and in spite of his employer's plea for him to stay, he chose to depart in poverty for parts unknown, as he had come. Although Romeo was a very good man, he is relegated to Mercury because he overvalued his earthly reputation. Dante probably identified with Romeo because Dante placed great stock in his reputation, was falsely accused of malfeasance, and became an unusual kind of wandering beggar.

Venus – Charles Martel
Gustave Doré. (Canto 8)

CANTO SEVEN

Just Vengeance

"Hosanna, Holy God of Hosts, You who light the blessed fires of these realms with Your shining."[1] Thus I saw that pure being sing, revolving to his own music with twin lights above him.[2] Then he and the rest of the dancers, like sparks that shoot away, quickly disappeared behind the veil of distance.[3]

Much perplexed, "Tell her. Tell her," I said to myself; "Tell the lady who can quench my thirst with drops of sweet liquid." But the awe that overwhelms me at the mere sound of *Be-* and *-ice*, drooped my head like that of a man who is napping. Beatrice didn't leave me in this condition long before casting on me the light of a smile that would make a person feel blessed even while being incinerated.

"According to my infallible insight, you are perplexed about how just vengeance could be justly avenged, and I will quickly relieve your mind; listen well, because my words will provide

---

[1] As Dante wrote it, Justinian's brief hymn of praise is composed of both Latin and Hebrew words, reflecting the combined Hebrew and Roman origin of Christianity.

[2] The twin lights suggest Justinian's dual role as Lawgiver and Emperor, in itself reflective of the distinct Hebrew and Roman contributions to Christianity. Emperor Justinian's dancing before Dante is perhaps meant to bring to mind the account of King David's festive dancing in 2 Samuel 6:14-22. (David's wife Michal accused him of making a fool of himself in public, but he replied that he fully intended to continue praising God that way.)

[3] On earth the spirits who are identified in the sphere of Mercury, Justinian and Romeo, were focused on justice and injustice. As an emperor, Justinian devoted himself to legislating official justice; as a humble employee Romeo expected justice concerning his reputation but did not receive it. Justinian has come to where earthly justice is eclipsed by divine justice, and Romeo has come to where his reputation is more than restored but no longer important to him.

you with a great truth. Because the man who was never born failed to accept any constraint on his free will, he doomed himself and all his descendants.[4] Thus the human race lay sick in that great mistake for many ages, until it pleased the Word of God, in an act of eternal love, to descend to earth and unite Himself with the human race so long estranged from its Creator.

"Now look at what comes next. Human nature as newly created was united to its Maker and was pure and good. But on its own it got itself exiled from Paradise because it strayed off from the way of truth, and thus from its own life. If one considers the nature of fallen humanity, the sting of punishment inflicted by the cross could not have been more justified. Yet no punishment was ever so outrageous if we look at the Person who endured it, who had taken on Himself the nature of fallen humanity.

"So it was that a single event was more than one event. God and the Jews both welcomed the same death. In response to it the earth shuddered and heaven opened.[5] It should no longer seem difficult to you that just punishment was afterwards punished by a just court.

"But now I see that your mind is caught in a tangle of thoughts from which it is urgently awaiting release. You are saying, 'Yes, I understand what I just heard; but I can't see why God chose to redeem us in this particular way.'

"Brother, that cause is hidden from the eyes of everyone whose mind has not yet matured in the heat of love. But since many people aim at this target and fail to comprehend it, I will explain why this method was best.

"Divine Goodness, which shuns all envy, burns within itself and shoots out sparks of eternal beauties. Everything derived directly from that Goodness is unending, because once God's

---

[4] The only man who was never born was Adam.

[5] Certain Jewish leaders brought about Christ's death because of their cruel hatred, but God brought about that same death because of His love for the human race. There was an ominous earthquake at the time of the crucifixion (see Matthew 27:51), but the crucifixion enabled Heaven to welcome the human race.

signature has been imprinted it cannot be removed. Whatever flows directly from God has free will, because it is not subject to the power of secondary things. The more closely anything resembles that Goodness, the more He is pleased; for the sacred fire that lights all creation burns most brightly in things most like Himself. The human creature was endowed with all these features, and if one of them fails he falls from his high estate.[6]

"Sin is the one thing that cancels man's free will and his resemblance to the Highest Good, so that the light in man is dimmed. Man's high estate can't be restored unless man fills the gap where sin has made a breach, with recompense for his sinful pleasure. When the seed of human nature became corrupt, humanity lost these honors as well as Paradise. They may not be recovered in any way, if you consider the matter carefully, except by one or the other of these two river crossings: either that God, in His mercy, forgives; or that man himself pays fully for his folly.

"Set your eyes on the depths of eternal counsel, and concentrate as much as you can on my explanation. Man lacked the power, given his limitations, to make full amends. He could never plunge so far down in obedient humility as he had once tried to soar up in disobedience. That is why man lacked the power to pay his debt for himself.

"Thus God needed to reinstate man into fullness of life in his own ways, either one or two of them.[7] But because the more an act demonstrates the goodness of the heart that chose it, the more gracious it is, the Divine Goodness that imprints the world chose to proceed in both ways to lift you up again. From last night clear back to the world's first day, there has never been and never will be such a lofty and magnificent process as God's two ways. It was more generous for God to give His very self to enable man to rise again than if He had merely granted

---

[6] God gladly shares His attributes with His creatures. Thus mankind was created with immortality and free will, bearing the image of God.

[7] The two possible ways for God to provide salvation to mankind were mercy (pardon) and justice (payment of the just penalty). God chose both.

pardon; and all other procedures would have fallen short of justice, unless the Son of God humbled Himself to become flesh.

"To fulfill all your wishes, I'll return now to explain a certain point so that you may see it clearly, as I do. You say, 'I see the water, I see the fire, the air, the earth; and all their combinations atrophy and cannot last. Yet these things were God's creations, and if what was said is true they should be preserved from disintegration.'

"Brother, the angels and this pure realm where you are now may be said to be created exactly as they are in their entirety; but the elements that you named and all the things compounded from them have been formed by powers that were themselves created. The basic material in them and the formative influences of these stars that sweep around them were created directly. In contrast, the life of every animal and plant is derived from material compounds, aided by the light and movement of the sacred lamps.[8]

"But your life is breathed without intermediary by the Supreme Good, who makes it enamored of Himself so that it always longs for Him. From that you may infer your resurrection, if you remember how human flesh was made when both the first parents were created."[9]

---

[8] The natural universe is subject to change and eventual dissolution because it is engendered by mutable elements, forces, and processes. Only spiritual realities are immortal. The stars are spiritual realities because they are manifestations of angels.

[9] Beatrice has recently assured Dante, "Everything derived directly from that Goodness is unending." Man has always been breathed into life by God, which means that man is immortal.

CANTO EIGHT

The Third Heaven: Venus

When it was still imperiled, the human world used to believe that the fair Cyprian beamed down rays of love-delirium as she whirled in the third epicycle.[1] In their error, then, those ancient people not only honored her with sacrifices and votive chants, but also honored Dione and Cupid, her mother and her son, and told how Cupid had sat on Dido's lap.[2] That is why they gave the star that gazes adoringly at the sun (first at the back of his neck, then at his brow)[3] the name of the one with whom I just began this canto.

I had no sense of ascending, but I was sure I had arrived when I saw my Lady grow more beautiful. And just as we can see a spark inside a flame (or hear a particular voice in a duet if one voice holds steady and the other goes up and down), so in that light I saw other gleams circling at different speeds, according, I suppose, to the magnitude of their knowledge. Winds from cold clouds. visible or invisible, have never swooped down fast enough that they would not seem encumbered and slow to anyone who had seen those divine lights coming toward us, ceasing their circular dance that had begun among the holy seraphim.[4] And amid those who appeared in front, such a

---

[1] Before Christ, pagans believed that the goddess Venus could drive people mad with love. According to legend, Venus had emerged fully formed from the sea near Cyprus (as depicted in Sandro Botticelli's famous painting "The Birth of Venus"). According to ancient and medieval astronomers, each planet had a small extra rotation that accounted for certain minor variations, and they called this rotation the epicycle.

[2] According to Virgil, Dido's obsessive suicidal love for Aeneus was caused by Cupid's spell.

[3] Venus is both the evening star (following the sun when he goes down) and the morning star (preceding the sun when he rises).

[4] These saints who danced and whirled in the Sphere of Venus shot

"Hosanna" rang that since then I have never been free from longing to hear it again.

Then one drew closer to us and began alone, "We are all ready for you to receive joy from us when you please. We revolve in one circle and in one circling and in one thirst with those celestial Principalities[5] whom you once addressed from the earth — '*You who by understanding move the third heaven.*'[6] We are so full of love that in order to please you a pause will be just as blissful as that for us."[7]

After I had reverently raised my eyes to my Lady and she had assured them of her approval, I turned them back to the light that had just offered me so much. "Tell me who you are" I said, with my voice full of affection. How it grew in size and brightness then, because of the new joy that was added to its joy when I spoke!

Thus changed, he said to me "The world below had me there only briefly; if it had been longer, much evil yet to come would not have happened. The joy that enfolds me conceals me from you by shining around me, and hides me like a silkworm wrapped in its cocoon.[8] You loved me greatly, and with good

---

toward Dante like lightning. (The first eight spheres received their energy from the Seraphim of the ninth sphere.) According to Barbara Reynolds, in an unpublished letter to Charles Williams Dorothy Sayers referred to "the ecstatic flight from circle to circle of the mystic dance which is the joy and freedom of the spirit in the willed surrender of its own self-will."

[5] The saints and angels (Principalities) of the Third Heaven spin together in their degree of love for God.

[6] The soul quotes to Dante from his own *Convivio* (meaning *The Banquet* and sometimes called *Convito*), in which he had appealed to the angels that move Venus in the sky. Thus Dante the earthly poet writes that a blissful soul in Paradise quotes to Dante the spiritual traveler a phrase from Dante the earthly poet.

[7] Much of Cantos 8 and 9 is about the responsible kind of nonerotic social love that promotes the welfare of other people. In contrast, much of *Inferno* is devoted to condemning sins like fraud that violate this kind of responsible social love.

[8] It has been said that a silkworm in its cocoon resembles pictures of souls swathed in the reflected light of God as depicted in early Italian

reason; for if I had stayed below longer I would have showed you more of my love[9] than just the leaves alone.[10]

"That left bank that is bathed by the Rhone after it has mingled with the Sorgue waited for me to become its lord; so did the horn of Italy with its towns of Bari, Gaeta, and Catona, south of where the Tronto and the Verde pour into the sea.[11] Upon my brow already glowed the crown of the land watered by the Danube after it has left its German banks.[12] And lovely Sicily, overcast with sulphur (not from Typheus) between Pachynus and Pelorus, over the gulf lashed by the East Wind, would still have expected to have kings descended from Charles and Rudolf through me — if misrule, which always stabs the heart of oppressed people, had not caused Palermo to shout 'Die! die!'[13]

"And if my brother could have foreseen it soon enough, he would have shunned the greedy poor of Catalonia who were

---

art.

[9] This soul is the Charles Martel (not the most famous Charles Martel) who visited Florence for three weeks in 1294, when he evidently met Dante, became his friend, and promised to become his benefactor. According to one tradition, he intended to give Dante a high post on his personal staff. According to Richard Kay, Dante recognized the social value of their kind of nonerotic love, and "the second half of *Inferno* is dedicated to the various frauds that 'break the bond that nature makes' (*Inf.* 11.56). This socio-political form of love accordingly has its place in the cantos of Venus."

[10] Unfortunately, Charles Martel died the year after he met Dante, when he was only 24 years old. Therefore his promise was like green leaves to Dante, and through no fault of theirs the promised fruit never grew.

[11] As the firstborn son of Charles II, Charles Martel was in line to become King of Provence and King of Naples (southern Italy).

[12] Thanks to his mother, Charles Martel was theoretically the King of Hungary, but in fact a cousin had seized the throne. In 1310 a son of Charles Martel would ascend to that throne.

[13] Sicily (partly overcast by volcanic emissions, not by smoke from a mythological underground giant) would have been ruled by Charles Martel's father and father-in-law and then Charles Martel, if his grandfather Charles I of Anjou had not been overthrown in the Easter Day massacre in 1282.

apt to cause him harm. Surely he or another needs to take action, or else his ship, which is already loaded down, might take on a heavier load. His nature—tightfisted offspring of a generous father—needed officials who were not devoted to filling their money chests."[14]

"Sir, I believe that there where every good begins and ends you see as I do the great joy that your speech pours into me; and I rejoice that you see it while looking at God. As you have gladdened me, now enlighten me; for your words have made me wonder how sweet seed can produce bitter fruit."

I said that to him, and he answered, "If I can show you a certain truth, then you will have the answer before your eyes just as you have it now behind your back. The Good that rotates and nurtures all the realms through which you are climbing makes providence a powerful force in the heavenly bodies of these great realms;[15] and the Perfect Mind that provides for the diverse natures of creatures also wills their welfare.

"Therefore, whatever this bow shoots lands according to providence, just like an arrow aimed at its target. If this were not so, the realm you are passing through would not create works of art, but wreckage.[16] And that cannot be unless the Minds that move these stars are defective, and the First Mind—which failed to make them perfect—is defective also.[17] Do you want me to explain this truth any further?"

I answered, "No, for I see that it is impossible for nature, in any way, to fall short of whatever should be."[18]

---

[14] Charles Martel's brother Robert became King of Sicily in 1309. According to this account, he brought with him greedy officials from Spain who robbed the impoverished populace of Sicily.

[15] The light of the Empyrean moves and directs all the spheres below it, and in turn the heavenly bodies in those spheres influence the nature of things on earth.

[16] If God did not direct planetary influence, it would be destructive rather than beneficial.

[17] If God's angels (Minds) are not good, then God (the First Mind), who created them, is not good.

[18] Dante is quoting this particular idea from his authority, Aristotle. In Dante's era, philosophy was the most authoritative academic discipline, just as natural science is today. If Dante were writing

At that he added, "Now consider, would a man on earth be worse off if he were not a citizen?"[19]

"Yes!" I replied, "On this I need no explanation."

"And is that possible, unless on earth men function in a variety of roles, with a variety of skills?[20] No, not if what your authority wrote for you is true."[21]

Step by step, he had arrived at this point. Then he concluded, "That is why there must be a variety of abilities; that is why one person is born a Solon and one a Xerxes, one a Melchizedek and one the man who lost his son by learning to fly.[22] The circling of the cosmos imprints patterns on the soft wax of new human beings without regard for their families of origin. That is how it happened that even in the womb Esau differed from Jacob, and Quirinus came from such a nondescript

---

Paradise in the twentieth century, he would use contemporary astronomy as his model and refer to modern scientific conceptions such as the theory of relativity and chaos theory.

[19] As used here, *citizen* means a member of a civilized society.

[20] Humans are endowed with a diversification of aptitudes that make civilized society possible.

[21] Charles Martel reminds Dante that Aristotle, whom Dante has just quoted, taught that man is a social animal. (Everyone agrees with that, although today many reject Aristotle's claim that God and nature must be beneficent.) Richard Kay points out that Aristotle went on to say that mutual good will is also necessary in civilized society. "In a society that lived in accordance with nature, each person would be motivated by love of his fellow citizens to do for them what he was best fitted by nature to do, and conversely those who are not so benevolent will ignore their natural duties and disrupt society." Thus the nonerotic love that pervades the Heaven of Venus "makes that heaven the appropriate place for Dante to treat the theme of duty to fellow men."

[22] Solon (a famous Athenian lawgiver) represents legislators. Xerxes (a famous Persian king) represents military leaders. Melchizedek (a famous Old Testament priest) represents spiritual leaders. The man who learned to fly (Daedelus, a famous mythological inventor) represents artisans, including mechanics and engineers. (Daedelus is best known for the fatal accident of his son Icarus, who fell when the two were escaping Crete on wings made by Daedelus. See Peter Bruegel's "Fall of Icarus," painted two centuries after Dante.)

human father that people claimed he was a son of Mars.[23] A son's nature would always be like his father's, if providence did not interfere.[24]

"Now what was behind you is in front of you. But to show you how much you delight me, I will also wrap a corollary around you.[25] If human nature finds itself in inappropriate circumstances, it will do as poorly as any other seed planted in the wrong place. If the world below would pay attention to the foundation laid by nature and build on that, it would have better men; but you wrench into a religious order a man born to strap on a sword, and you make a king of a man who should be writing sermons.[26] That is why you run clear off the road."

---

[23] Jacob and Essau were the contrasting twin sons of Isaac and Rebeccah (see Genesis 25). Quirinus, better known as Romulus, was the first king of Rome. He was of such humble, unknown parentage that his followers pretended he was a son of the god Mars.

[24] Today's knowledge about genetics and DNA would have solved part of the mystery about inborn characteristics that used to intrigue philosophers and theologians. In Dante's day the most educated still believed that human traits came from the father, not from both father and mother, and that they were transmitted in the semen itself, not in a great variety of competing sperm. But the theorizers correctly discerned that both inheritance and environment were involved.

[25] Charles Martel is apparently relegated to the realm of Venus because of the friendship love he had for Dante and his failure to promptly express it on earth financially as he had intended. In Heaven he is radiant with joy because he is able to express his love for Dante with a gift of precious knowledge. If in fact Charles, like other residents of Venus, had a noteworthy erotic love life, Dante tactfully avoids mentioning that characteristic directly.

[26] One of Charles Martel's brothers was made Bishop of Toulouse, and one was made King of Naples. Unfortunately, they were well suited for each other's positions, not those assigned to them.

CANTO NINE

A Ruby Struck by the Sun

Fair Clemence, after your Charles had enlightened me he told me how his offspring would be cheated.[1] But he added, "Hold your peace and let the years roll by." All I am free to say is that the wrongs you are going to suffer will be appropriately redressed.

That holy light had already turned his living spirit toward the Sun that fills him, the Goodness that fulfills everything. Ah, deluded souls! Ah, godless creatures who twist your hearts away from Good and set your sight on emptiness!

Then another of those splendors came toward me and showed its desire to please me by brightening outwardly. Beatrice's eyes, which were still fixed on me, assured me of her precious permission.

"Blessed spirit, pray quickly satisfy my hope," I said, "and show that you can mirror what I think."

At that, this unidentified light that had been singing from the depths of its heart began to speak like someone delighted to be kind. "In the region of the depraved Italian land between Rialto and the springs of the Brenta and the Piaver, a hill of modest height arises, and from there a firebrand descended, devastating the countryside.[2]

---

[1] Clemence was the name of the mother, the wife, and the daughter of Charles Martel, and Dante is probably addressing the wife. According to Dante, their son Charles Robert was cheated out of the throne of Naples by his uncle, Charles of Anjou.

[2] The hill of Romano is between Venice (Rialto) and the Alps. The tyrant Ezzelino da Romano (1194-1259) swept down from there. According to legend, his mother dreamed she would give birth to a flaming torch that would destroy the area.

"I sprang from the very same root. I was called Cunizza, and I shine here because the light of this star overcame me.[3] But I don't regret what relegated me to this sphere; I rejoice in it, although that would no doubt be hard for earthly people to understand.[4]

"This precious jewel next to me, brightening our sphere, is still famous and will remain so until the current centennial has been repeated five more times. You can see by that whether a man should aspire to excellence and thus extend his life on earth.[5]

"The present rabble between Tagliamento and Adige doesn't consider that; and although scourged, it does not repent. But it will soon come to pass that because the people are so stubbornly set against duty,[6] Padua will stain the marsh water

---

[3] In his youth Dante and this soul had good mutual friends and may have met. Cunizza da Romano (1198-1279), the sister of Ezzelino, was famous for her amorous life and was popular anyway. After an arranged marriage to the Lord of Ravenna, she was abducted by the troubadour Sordello (the "gentle soul" who escorted Virgil and Dante to the Valley of Flowers in *Purgatory*). After several years with Sordello, she eloped with Enrico da Bovio, with whom she lived and traveled in high style. After the deaths of Enrico and her first husband, she married two or three times more, once when she was about sixty. According to a commentary written barely fifty years after her death, she was a kind and generous woman, but overly generous with her romantic love. In her old age, she generously freed the slaves who had belonged to her father and her brother.

[4] By placing Cunniza in heaven, Dante is emphasizing the biblical truth that it is ultimate response to God, not circumspect living, that determines eternal destinies. Cunniza's satisfaction with her lot illustrates the fact that in heaven the redeemed have no guilts and no regrets. In *Letters to Malcolm*, C.S. Lewis said, "There is no morality in Heaven. The angels never knew (from within) the meaning of the word *ought*, and the blessed dead have long since gladly forgotten it. That is why Dante's Heaven is so right, and Milton's, with its military discipline, so silly."

[5] Cunizza means that because of his virtuous life this soul has extended his influence on earth for centuries (figuratively, until 1800).

[6] Cunizza condemns these citizens for ignoring their duty to conform to the dictates of socio-political love.

that has washed Vicenza.[7] And where the Sile meets the Cagnano, a net is being set to catch a certain ruler who is holding his head high.[8] A wail shall yet arise in Feltro for the sin of its wicked pastor, a sin so foul that no one has ever entered Malta for the like.[9] What a large vat is needed to hold Ferrara's blood, and how this "courteous" priest wearies himself weighing it ounce by ounce to prove himself a good party member.[10] Such gifts suit well that country's way of life.

"There are Mirrors above (you call them Thrones) where God's judgment shines on us so that we know the things we decided to tell you."[11] Here she fell silent and apparently shifted her attention, returning to her circular dance.

The other joy, pointed out already as something precious, shone in my sight like a fine ruby struck by the sun. Up there brightness is caused by joy, just as on earth a smile is caused by joy; and down below, darkness is caused by grief.

"Blessed spirit, God sees everything, and your mind merges with His," I said, "so that no wish is hidden from you. So why

---

[7] Cunizza is probably predicting the bloody 1314 defeat at Vicenza of the Paduans who were disloyal to the rule of the Empire.

[8] In 1312 the arrogant Lord of Treviso was stabbed to death while playing chess. According to Henry Wadsworth Longfellow's notes, this was the revenge of one of the husbands whose wives were used sexually by him.

[9] In 1314 Bishop Novello of Feltre pretended to shelter a group of 30 political refugees from Ferrara and betrayed them to their chief enemy, who beheaded them all. No priest condemned to the famous ecclesiastical prison at Malta had committed such a rank crime. (In *Inferno* the betrayal of guests was revealed to be such an abomination that the souls of traitorous hosts sometimes fell into the iciest depths of hell while their bodies were still alive on earth, playing host to devils. See the end of Canto 33 in *Inferno*.) According to Longfellow, this bishop was eventually beaten to death by bags of sand.

[10] Richard Kay points out that one of the astrological attributes of the planet Venus was an affinity for jewelry. The wicked priest dealt with precious human blood for his own profit, as a jeweler deals with precious materials.

[11] Dante calls angels "Mirrors" because they mirror God's light. The angels called "Thrones" reside in the ninth or Crystalline Heaven.

does your voice—which constantly pleasures Heaven along with the singing of those holy Flames that enfold themselves in six wings[12]—not grant my wish? I would not have waited until now to grant *your* wish, if I could know your mind as you know mine."

"The greatest basin into which sea water extends from the ocean girdling the earth," he began, "between its opposite shores reaches so far east against the sun that it turns what was its horizon into its meridian.[13] I dwelt on the shore of this basin midway between the Ebro and the Macra, which in its short course separates the Genoese people from the Tuscan people. Bougiah and the place I spring from, which once made the harbor warmer with its blood, are almost the same for sunset and for sunrise.[14]

"Those who knew about me called me Folco, and this sphere is now imprinted by me as I was imprinted by it.[15] Belus's daughter, who wronged both Sichaeus and Creusa, did not burn more than I did before time tampered with my hair; nor did the Rhodopeian maiden who was disappointed by

---

[12] See Isaiah 6:2.

[13] This basin is the Mediterranean Sea, which extends eastward from the Atlantic Ocean. Geographers in Dante's day mistakenly thought that the ends of the Mediterranean were a quarter of the way around the earth from each other, which would mean that when it was noon in Gibraltar it was sundown in Jerusalem. Later geographers discovered that the Mediterranean actually stretches more like an eighth of the way around the earth.

[14] The speaker is from Marseilles, a naval city on the same meridian as the North African city of Bougie, and Marseilles was defeated by Caesar in 49 B.C. This soul has given one clue after another in order to gradually reveal his birthplace by means of skillful rhetoric like that which made him famous.

[15] In his youth Folco was an eloquent troubadour who was always bewailing his hopeless infatuations with various women. In later years Folco was sobered by deaths of people he cared about, and became a Cistercian monk. As bishop of Toulouse (1205-1231) he took a leading part in the Catholic church's slaughter of Christians called Albigensians, but Dante does not refer to that rash and tragic behavior directly.

Demophoön; and neither did Alcides when he took Iole into his heart.[16]

"But here we don't repent; here we smile—not at the sin, which no longer comes to mind, but at the power that puts it all in order and fully provides. Here we are focused on the artistry that beautifies its creation, and we discern the goodness that receives the world below into the world above.[17]

"But for you to carry away full satisfaction for all your hungering questions born in this sphere, I must continue. You want to know who is within the light that sparkles by me like sunlight in pure water. Know, then, that in it Rahab has peace; know that by joining our order, she became our highest-ranking member.[18] To this heaven, touched by the tip of the

---

[16] Passionate love for Aeneas caused Dido, Queen of Carthage, to kill herself when he deserted her. (By loving him she had broken her vow to her dead husband Sichaeus and had wronged Aeneas's dead wife Creusa.) Passionate love for Demophoön caused Phyllis, princess of Thrace (where Mount Rhodope is located), to hang herself on an almond tree when he did not arrive for their wedding. Passionate love for Iole caused Hercules (Alcides) to kill Iole's husband and take her, which led his wife, Deianera, to give him a poison shirt because she was tricked into thinking it was a love charm. In each of these cases, a person who loved passionately committed rash and tragic acts.

[17] In my opinion, Dante wrote this canto with Romans 8:28-29 in mind, "And we know that all things work together for good to them that love God, to them who are called according to his purpose. For whom he did foreknow, he also did predestinate to be conformed to the image of his Son, that he might be the firstborn among many brethren. Moreover, whom he did predestinate, them he also justified; and whom he justified, them he also glorified."

[18] Rahab is the greatest saint in the Heaven of Venus. She began as a Canaanite prostitute, but in approximately 1250 B.C. she bravely hid spies that Joshua had sent into Jericho and helped them escape with their lives. When the Hebrews conquered Jericho, her relatives gathered in her house, and she hung a scarlet thread (a signal given to her by the spies) in her window; thus the lives of her family were spared. I am personally convinced that Rahab's signal to the invaders symbolized the blood on the doorpost that had miraculously saved the Hebrews from death at the occasion of the first Passover; and that to Dante it symbolized Christ's saving blood. Dante commentators refer readers

shadow cast by your world,[19] she was lifted up in Christ's triumph before anyone else.[20]

"And it was fitting for her to be a palm here of the lofty victory which was achieved with two palms,[21] because she

---

to the account in Joshua 2-6, but leave out the salvific red thread and its Christian meaning. Furthermore, they leave out the crucial fact that as a married woman Rahab actually became an ancestor of Christ. Both St. Paul (who stressed the importance of faith in God) and St. James (who stressed the importance of good works) praised Rahab in the New Testament. See Hebrews 11:31 and James 3:25.

[19] Venus was allegedly touched by the end of a cone-shaped shadow cast by the earth over the moon and Mercury. For Dante, that astronomical myth symbolized the fact that spirits relegated to those three heavenly spheres were dimmed somewhat by their particular earthly shortcomings.

[20] When Christ visited Hell immediately after the crucifixion and rescued many souls, he freed Rahab. Thus, she was the first soul who took her place in this sphere of Heaven.

[21] This single sentence is an ingenious and profoundly meaningful knot of wordplay and ideas touched on far too superficially by the commentators I have consulted. In Dante's youth countless brave and devout pilgrims spent months trekking to the Holy Land; they were called palmers because they usually brought home palm fronds as trophies from the long, arduous trip. Rahab serves as a "palm" in the Third Heaven, a trophy of Christ's journey to Hell and back. Thus Dante the writer has Folco begin this sentence by likening the crucified Christ to a palmer who has journeyed to the "unholy land" of Hell and back. Next he audaciously switches definitions and attributes Christ's victory over the kingdom of sin and death to Christ's two nail-pierced palms. (As Longfellow points out, Jesus set a precedent for religious puns when he said of Peter, whose name was Greek for *stone*, "On this rock I will build my church.") Folco claims that Rahab was an especially appropriate trophy of Christ's pilgrimage because of her role in Joshua's victory over the kingdom of Canaan. In my opinion the little-known key to this claim is the fact that the name Jesus is a Greek version of the Hebrew name Joshua, which means "Yahweh [God] is salvation." Dante the poet, speaking through Folco, is accomplishing a remarkable literary sleight of hand by juggling the identities and victories of the two Joshuas in the receptive reader's mind while juggling the salvific Passover blood on the doorpost with Rahab's red thread and the bleeding hands of God on the cross. And at this point the

helped toward Joshua's first glorious victory in the Holy Land — which the popes no longer seem to recall.[22]

"Your city — planted by the first one who ever turned his back on his Creator, and whose envy caused all our lamentation — makes and distributes the damned flower that sets sheep and lambs astray, for it has turned the shepherd into a wolf.[23] That is why the gospel and teachings of the great church fathers are ignored and now only the decretals are studied, as their margins show.[24]

"Thus the attention of the pope and cardinals is narrowly foc-

---

sentence is not quite finished.

[22] When Dante was 26 years old, the Holy Land was lost to Christians when Acre was captured by Saracens in 1291. This was a great loss to the devout who longed to be palmers, but the popes were indifferent about it. Given the nature of this entire sentence, Folco seems to imply that the popes were as indifferent to the heritage from Christ's victory as they were to the heritage from Joshua's victory.

[23] Folco says that Florence was founded by Satan himself, and that the wealth of Florence (the lily on gold coins from Florence) has corrupted the church hierarchy. Folco's image of mercenary pastors as wolves recalls the wolf that blocked Dante's upward way in the first canto of *Inferno*. See also Christ's warning in Matthew 7:15 about false teachers who prey on His sheep like wolves.

[24] Immense wealth was available to church leaders who were absorbed in details of ecclesiastical law, just as great wealth is available to corporate lawyers today. Dante's opinion of those church leaders was similar to the opinion that responsible Christians have about certain notoriously greedy and hypocritical televangelists today. In any age, corrupt clergy fail to love their fellow citizens and fail to do their duty to them. One could see the leaders' obsession with church law visually if one looked at all the wear and tear and marks in the margins of important church law books.

used, and they never turn their thoughts to Nazareth, where Gabriel once spread his wings. But the Vatican and Rome's other burial sites of the brigades that followed Peter shall soon be freed from such adultery."[25]

---

[25] Although I haven't come across other Dante commentators who mention the theme of the conclusion of Canto 9, I think it is important. In Nazareth Gabriel informed a young virgin that she would miraculously bear a child and name him Jesus. Natural impregnation was accomplished by sexual intimacy, attributed mythologically to the influence of Venus. In contrast, Mary was supernaturally impregnated by the Holy Spirit, God's primal, perfect Love. (See the middle stanza of the verse above the Gateway to Hell in Canto 2 of *Inferno*.) In *Paradise* Dante repeatedly condemns inordinate earthly loves. Thus he has Folco close Canto 9 with a prophecy of the 1305 transfer of the Papacy from Rome to Avignon, and with the charge that church leaders who love money instead of God are adulterers.

CANTO TEN

The Fourth Heaven: the Sun

Gazing at His Son with the Love which the two of them breathe forth forever, the indescribable First Power[1] made everything that circles through mind or space so well orchestrated that whoever contemplates it all is bound to have a taste of Him.[2] Therefore, reader, look up with me high into the starry sky, to that part where one rotation crosses another;[3] and start to contemplate with yearning love the art of the Master, who loves it so much that He Himself never stops gazing at it.

See how the circle that carries the stars around branches off at a slant there, to satisfy the crying needs of the world. If that circle did not tilt, much of Heaven's power would be wasted and most of the life force on earth would be dead. And if its tilt were any more or any less, the cosmic order would be deficient in both the Northern and the Southern Hemisphere.[4]

---

[1] This section of *Paradise* begins with a prologue about the Trinity. God the Father (Power) and Christ the Son (Wisdom) breathe forth eternally the Holy Spirit (Love). The Father is indescribable, but the Son is light, and the Holy Spirit is heat.

[2] According to C. S. Lewis's essay "Imagination and Thought in the Middle Ages," in those days most intellectuals were essentially categorizers. "Characteristically, medieval man was not a dreamer nor a spiritual adventurer; he was an organizer, a codifier, a man of system. His ideal could be not unfairly summed up in the old housewifely maxim 'A place for everything, and everything in its (right) place.'" This explains Dante's great emphasis upon how God has arranged all the cosmos in an orderly way.

[3] Dante instructs his reader to consider the role of the sun. Dante devotes more space to the Heaven of the Sun than to any of the others. Twenty-four different individuals are introduced there, like the 24 hours of a day.

[4] The sun crosses our sky every day (as the earth revolves eastward) in a regular course from east to west. But every year (as the earth sways

Now, reader, stay on your bench and think about this foretaste, if you want to enjoy the coming feast before you lose your energy. I set the food before you; you must feed yourself. The subject matter I am supposed to be writing about demands all my attention again.

The chief executive of Nature, who imbues the world with the will of Heaven, provides our measurement of time with his light;[5] and in the conjunction I just referred to he was circling in those spirals where he rises earlier and earlier.[6] And I was there with him; but of my ascent I was no more aware than a man is aware of a thought before it has arrived. Beatrice is the one who leads me thus from good to better, so instantly that doing so takes no time at all.

How brilliant what revealed itself to me in the sun (which I had just entered) must be, distinguishable there not by its color but by its brightness! If I marshaled all my genius, my art, and

---

on its axis) that daily course slowly and steadily sways northward, then southward. If the sun circled at the equator all year, there would be no summer and no winter. And if the sun stayed any closer to the equator or strayed farther from the equator, the seasons would be too long or too short. The equinoxes (about March 21 and September 23) are the midpoints of the sun's northward and southward swings, when the sun's daily course coincides exactly with the equator. This annual pattern is essential for prolific earthly life as we know it.

[5] In the system of astronomy inherited from Ptolemy, the sun was considered the fourth and most obviously important "planet." As Barbara Reynolds observes, "Dante, like all writers on similar subjects, embellishes his tale with a multitude of astronomical and geographical details, so as to lend an air of conviction in his narrative. But this conventional picture is in no way necessary to his thought, or to the significance of his allegory. He could, for instance, have managed very well with a Copernican universe centered about the sun; in some ways it would have accommodated itself better to his ideas than the earth-centred universe he knew."

Because the sun is our chief natural means of measuring time, the chief theme of this canto is timekeeping. The main image is a circle set with twelve spirits; it is likened to a crown, a halo, a wreath of flowers and, finally, the face of a clock.

[6] Dante's pilgrimage takes place shortly after the spring equinox.

my experience, I could never describe it well enough to make it imaginable; but one can trust and long to see it. And if our imaginations fall short of such heights, it is no wonder; for there never was an eye that could see anything brighter than the sun. That is the brightness of the family of the High Father there, who are filled with bliss by His showing them how He breathes forth and creates.[7]

Beatrice began, "Give thanks, give thanks to the angels' Sun, who by his grace has lifted you to this material sun."[8]

Never was a mortal heart so disposed to worship and so keen to give itself to God with all its will, as I was in response to these words; and my love was so wholly committed to Him that it eclipsed Beatrice from my consciousness. Not at all displeased, she smiled so brightly in response that the splendor of her laughing eyes brought my mind back into multiple focus.[9]

Then I saw many supremely living lights encircling us like a crown—even sweeter to hear than they were brilliant to see![10] We sometimes see Latona's daughter sashed this way when the air is vaporous enough to hold the threads that compose her broad waistband.[11]

In the royal court of heaven from which I have returned, there are many gems so precious and beautiful that they cannot be taken out of that realm; and the song of these lights was one of them. Anyone who doesn't get wings to fly up there for

---

[7] As the physical sun blesses earth's children with light and heat, so the spiritual Sun (God) blesses spirits in the Empyrean with understanding and love. (See Cantos 30-33.)

[8] The angels' Sun is God.

[9] This is a foretaste of Canto 31, where Dante sees the splendor (reflected light) in the face of Beatrice for the last time and then prepares to look into the Light itself with single focus in Canto 33.

[10] Dante and Beatrice are surrounded by a circle of joyful spirits who sing together in an exquisite harmony that is beyond description. They turn out to be intellectuals (types sometimes prone to joylessness, professional jealousy and grudges).

[11] Latona's daughter is the moon (Latona's son Apollo is the sun), which sometimes appears to have a misty halo.

himself will have to wait to hear about it from the voice of a voiceless messenger.[12]

After the blazing suns singing this way had circled us three times like stars circling close to the poles, they seemed like dancing women who pause quietly while listening for new strains of music in order to resume their dancing.

From one of them I heard some words begin: "Since the Ray of Grace shining in you (from which True Love is kindled, then grows and multiplies in you by loving)[13] has guided you up the stairway — which, except to re-ascend, no one ever descends — anyone who would refuse you his flask of wine to quench your thirst would be no more free than water that cannot flow toward the sea.[14]

"You want to know what kinds of flowers are woven into this garland that lovingly encircles the beautiful woman who strengthens you for Heaven.[15] I was one of the lambs of the sacred flock led by Dominic on the path where they fatten well if they don't stray away.[16] The one closest to me on my right

---

[12] Because no one can possibly describe this music, one would wait in vain to hear it described.

[13] In my opinion, the Ray of Grace is the Son, and True Love is the Holy Spirit. Like lightning that can set a forest on fire or a light beam from a magnifying glass that can set paper on fire (and like the tongues of flame at Pentecost that set the world on fire), understanding bestowed by grace has lit Dante's ascent through Paradise.

[14] The voice assures Dante that he will never be permanently exiled from heaven (as he was from Florence). Furthermore, he is loved so much that others in heaven are eager to give him whatever he wants. This good news is announced by Thomas Aquinas, who was in fact Dante's chief mentor. Thomas's speech continues for 287 lines, more than Dante allotted to anyone else except himself, Virgil, Beatrice, and his ancestor Cacciaguida.

[15] Thomas may be alluding to Ecclesiasticus 1:18, "Wisdom's garland is the fear of the Lord, flowering with peace and health."

[16] Richard Kay points out that most of Canto 11 will be a commentary on this one sentence. The ram and sheep imagery in the sphere of the Sun is astrologically fitting because the sun is exalted in the sign of the ram (Aries), which begins at the spring equinox -- when Dante journeys to Heaven.

here was my brother and teacher, Albert of Cologne.[17] I was Thomas of Aquino.[18]

"If you want to know who all the rest are, move your eyes around this blessed wreath along with my words. The next flame flares from the smile of Gratian, whose service to both courts pleased Paradise.[19] The next one who adorns our choir was good Peter — who, like the poor widow, gave all he had to the Holy Church.[20]

"The fifth and loveliest light among us breathes out such love that all the world below thirsts for news about him; the lofty mind in this light was granted such wisdom that, if truth be true, no one else ever rose to such deep wisdom.[21]

---

[17] Albertus Magnus (1193-1280 A.D.) was a prolific Dominican theologian who taught in Cologne and Paris and was instrumental in promoting the teachings of the Greek philosopher Aristotle (384-322 B.C.) among late medieval thinkers.

[18] Thomas Aquinas (1225-1274 A.D.) was a Dominican theologian who studied under Albertus Magnus and embraced the teachings of Aristotle. Aquinas harmonized Christianity with the great heritage of classical learning that had been rediscovered by European scholars at that time. The most influential book by Aquinas was *Summa Theologica*, in which he systematized Christian theology; it is still a basic part of Roman Catholic doctrine. The lives of Albertus Magnus and Thomas Aquinas overlapped Dante's, and so their teaching was still new when Dante embraced it. See Dorothy Sayers' 1946 essay "The Divine Poet and the Angelic Doctor" in *Further Papers on Dante* (London: Methuen, 1957).

[19] Gratian was a scholar who harmonized civil and church law over a century before Dante. Dante is repeating what Aquinas wrote about him.

[20] Peter Lombard was a contemporary of Gratian who was commended by Aquinas. He harmonized the writings of the early church fathers with the Bible and likened himself to the poor widow in Luke 11:1-4, who had little to give to God but gave it all.

[21] King Solomon, son of King David, ruled Israel circa 950 B.C. (See 2 Samuel, 1 Kings, and 1 and 2 Chronicles.) Because of his sins, his eternal destiny was a matter of grave doubt in Dante's era; but Dante believed he was saved. Solomon was taken to be the author of the famous Old Testament love poem Song of Solomon, as well as Proverbs, Ecclesiastes, and the apocryphal Book of Wisdom. According

Next, look at the light of the slender candle that in its life below saw deepest into the nature of angels and their ministry.[22] In the next little light that defender of the Christian era whose book was useful to Augustine is laughing.[23]

Now if your mind's eye is following my praises from light to light you are already eager for the eighth. Because he saw the Total Good, the sainted soul that exposed the world's deceit to those who would heed rejoices there. The body from which it was driven lies below Cieldauro, and he came from martyrdom and exile to this peace.[24]

---

to 1 Kings 3:5-13, no one would ever match Solomon's God-given wisdom.

One of the 24 elders in the pageant in Canto 29 of *Purgatory* represented the books of Solomon, and in Canto 30 he sang out the words "Come, bride of Lebanon" from Song of Solomon 4:8. Some commentators express puzzlement about Solomon's inclusion in this circle of Christians, and Barbara Reynolds suggests that Solomon is here because of his famous ability to judge truth and error. In my opinion, it was highly significant to Dante that Solomon wrote about both wisdom and love. Solomon is introduced here by Thomas, and in my opinion Dante was no doubt aware of the fact that on Thomas's deathbed (in G. K. Chesterton's words) "he asked to have The Song of Solomon read to him from beginning to end." Furthermore, Solomon's erotic portrayal of spiritual love in Song of Solomon is echoed by Dante in the conclusion of this canto.

[22] In the Middle Ages a book titled *On the Celestial Hierarchy* was attributed to the Athenian named Dionysius whose conversion by St. Paul is recorded in Acts 17:34. Because *Celestial Hierarchy* is no longer considered to be that old, the sixth light is in fact an anonymous author.

[23] This may be the fifth century Spanish priest named Paulus Orosius, whose book *Historiarum adversus Paganos* disputed the theory that Christianity had ruined the Roman Empire. This book correlated well with St. Augustine's *City of God*.

[24] Boethius (circa 475–525 A.D.) was a Roman philosopher and statesman who had studied in Greece. He held a high post under Theodoric, king of the Ostrogoths and ruler of Italy, until he was falsely accused of plotting against Theodoric. While imprisoned he wrote his most celebrated work, *On the Consolation of Philosophy*; and then he was executed. His writing was cherished by Dante and other Christian thinkers in the Middle Ages, and it is still cherished by some Chris-

See next the flaming breath of Isidore,[25] of Bede,[26] and of Richard, whose speculation was beyond that of a mere mortal.[27] The one from whom your eyes return to me is the light of a spirit in whose weighty thoughts death seemed to come too slowly; it is the eternal light of Siger, whose lectures at Straw Street set forth truths that caused him to be hated."[28]

Then like a clock calling us when God's Bride rises to sing her morning song to her Groom to encourage His love—in which the clock parts pulling and pushing each other, "Ting-ting," resound with sweet chimes that swell the willing one with love—that is how I beheld the glorious circle revolve and

---

tians. Boethius is buried in St. Peter's Church in Cieldauro, and Aquinas plays with that place name, which means *golden ceiling.*

[25] Archbishop Isidore of Seville (circa 560–636) wrote a highly influential encyclopedia and other books.

[26] The Venerable Bede (circa 673-735) was an Anglo-Saxon monk and scholar who is considered the father of English history because of his *Ecclesiastical History of England.*

[27] Richard of St. Victor, who was probably from Scotland and died circa 1173, studied in Paris along with Peter Lombard and became prior of a monastery in Paris. He is remembered as a mystic as well as a theologian. He dedicated some of his writings to his friend Bernard of Clairvaux, who becomes Dante's guide in Canto 31 of *Paradise.*

[28] Siger of Brabant (circa 1225-1283) was a professor of philosophy at the University of Paris. His interpretation of Aristotle was hotly opposed by many church authorities and academics, including Aquinas—which makes their closeness in Paradise highly significant. (C.S. Lewis might have had these two in mind when he wrote the last paragraph of "The Weight of Glory.") Siger was persecuted as a heretic, and in vain he fled to Rome for protection. He was supposedly stabbed to death by a mentally ill secretary, but the murder might have been arranged for political reasons.

In Dante's day the University of Paris was located on Straw Street, which was originally a hay and straw market. Many people believe that at some point during his exile Dante himself lectured there, and so the name has reportedly been changed to Dante Street.

link voice to voice in such harmony and sweetness that it can only be known where joy begets joy eternally.[29]

---

[29] Although I saw no analysis of it in several commentaries I consulted, I was struck by this surprisingly erotic multiple metaphor that combines an echo of the imagery of carnal love in the Song of Solomon (tenth century B.C.) and the imagery of the newly invented mechanical clock (thirteenth century A.D.) with the imagery of Christians attending a traditional morning prayer service—all to describe allegorically the relationship of the Church to Christ, in order to describe the state of being of twelve specific spirits in Paradise who are in turn Dante's allegorical illustration of truth about ultimate love. This rather playful exhibition of Dante's intellectual complexity at the conclusion of a passage about a dozen intellectuals who had ascended from intellectual complexities to ecstatic love is presumably intentional on his part.

CANTO ELEVEN

Remembering Francis

O blind ambition of mortals, how worthless are the strategies that cause your wings to fly downward to the mundane!

One person was pursuing law, another medicine, another the priesthood. One was pursuing success through forcefulness or clever persuasion, another business, and another politics. One was exhausting himself in the pleasures of the flesh, and another was abandoning himself to idleness.[1] And meanwhile, delivered from all these things, I was being received into glory with Beatrice high in Heaven.

When each of the spirits had returned to the point in the circle where he was before, he stopped and waited there, like a candle in its stand.[2]

And from within the smiling light that spoke to me before—now shining even more radiantly—I heard: "Just as I glow with the Eternal Light I am gazing at, so I also understand your thoughts and why you think them. You are perplexed and want me to explain, in clear, direct words, at your level of understanding, what I meant when I told you 'where they fatten well' and 'no one else ever rose.' And here we need to make a precise distinction.

"The Providence that rules the world (with wisdom so deep that any creature that tried to plumb it would be bound to fail) ordained two princes, one on this side and one on that, to be guides for the bride of Him who, crying loudly, wed her with

---

[1] However one translates these specific human pursuits (some of the words have more than one meaning), they represent options in Dante's life and in the lives of many of his readers.

[2] The spirits shine in a ring that resembles a chandelier or circle of votive lights.

His blessed blood—so that she could go on to her delight with increased self-certainty and faithfulness to Him.[3]

"One was like the Seraphim in his love, and on earth the other was like the shining splendor of the Cherubim, because of his wisdom.[4]

"I will tell about only one of them; but whichever one a person praises, he praises both, in that their works served the same purpose.[5]

"From a high mountain peak there hangs a fertile slope between Tupino and the stream that descends from the hill chosen by the blessed Ubaldo, and from that peak Perugia receives both cold and heat through Porta Sole; behind it Gualdo and Nocera weep about their heavy yoke.[6] On this slope, where the steepness of the mountainside is most broken, a sun was born into the world,—like an extraordinary sunrise over the Ganges. Therefore one who speaks of that place should not say merely 'Ascesi,' but 'the Orient,' if he wants to identify it adequately.[7]

---

[3] The church universal (made up of all Christians) is the bride of Christ; He wed her when He died on the cross. To help her to prosper spiritually until Christ comes for her, God sent two guides: Francis (1182-1226) and Dominic (1170-1221), founders of the Franciscan and Dominican orders.

[4] The angels called Seraphim burn with love, and the angels called Cherubim represent knowledge.

[5] In Heaven all competition between the Franciscans and Dominicans has disappeared. Therefore Thomas, a Dominican, praises Francis rather than Dominic.

[6] Mt. Subasio is the high point in this passage of geographical poetry. The Chiascio is a stream that descends from the hill where Bishop Ubaldo hoped to retire to his hermitage. Perugia is a city occasionally buffeted by icy winds from Mt. Subasio and heated by sunlight reflected from the mountainside. Porta Sole is the gate in Perugia through which the severe heat and cold enter. Gualdo and Nocera are towns on the other side of the mountain; opinions vary about whether this passage refers to their political oppression or their darker and colder location. Thomas is eloquently drawing Dante's attention to the region of Assisi.

[7] St. Francis of Assisi was linked to the sun ever since Bonaventura

"He was not yet far from his rising before his great power had begun to benefit the earth; for in his youth he went into battle against his father for the sake of the lady for whom, like death, no one gladly opens the door. He married her in the spiritual courtroom, in his father's presence; and from that day forward he loved her more and more.[8] Bereft of her first husband, for more than a thousand years and a century she was despised, obscure, and without another suitor. Somehow it had made no difference that when a certain man's voice terrified the entire world, she was unterrified along with Amyclas; and somehow it had made no difference that she was so loyal and brave that when Mary stayed below, she mounted the cross with Christ.[9]

"But, lest I proceed too obscurely, understand now in plain speech that Francis and Poverty are these two lovers.[10] Their harmony and joyous looks, their love and wonder and tender glances, inspire such sacred thoughts that the venerable

---

linked him to Revelation 7:2: "And I saw another angel ascending from the east, having the seal of the living God." Thomas may be echoing the old belief that the sun was more brilliant in India (the East). The old form of the name Assisi was "Ascesi," the same as the verb "I ascended." As John Ciardi points out, this wordplay is untranslatable; but Thomas is contrasting the claim "I have risen" with sunrise.

[8] St. Francis was about twentty-four years old in 1206 when he embraced a life of poverty (Lady Poverty). His prosperous father, a wool merchant, took him to the episcopal court to try to stop him from giving away his inheritance; and there he willingly stripped himself of all he had. His example inspired others, and his ministry began. Almost 800 years later he is venerated by many non-Christians for loving and rejoicing in all God's creatures.

[9] Jesus Christ was the first husband of Lady Poverty. According to Lucan, an impoverished fisherman named Amyclas was indifferent when Caesar awakened him and demanded some service. As one modern song has expressed such detachment, "Freedom's just another name for nothing left to lose." Paradoxically, people tend to be possessed by their possessions; and the very security offered by possessions often creates insecurity.

[10] Although Thomas promises to use plain speech, he continues allegorically.

Bernard was the first to cast off his sandals and run after that great peace.[11] And as he ran he felt that he was moving too slowly.

"O wealth undreamed![12] O fruitful good! Egidius bares his feet and Sylvester bares his feet, following him because his bride delights them so. From then on this father and leader continued with his lady and his family that was already tying on the humble cord.[13]

"Neither being the son of Pietro Bernadone nor being the object of public scorn ever seemed to humiliate him. With regal bearing he revealed his strict rules to Innocent and received the first papal approval of his order.[14] As more joined him in poverty, then the work of this chief shepherd—whose marvelous life is better sung in heaven's glory—was crowned also by Honorius, as inspired by the Eternal Spirit.[15] Then in his zest for self-sacrifice he went into the proud presence of the Sultan to preach about Christ and his earthly brotherhood; but because he found those people unripe for conversion, he returned to harvest more fruit in the Italian garden rather than to stay on in vain.[16] At last, on the rocky crags between the

---

[11] Bernard was a wealthy businessman who sold all he had and gave it to the poor in order to follow Francis.

[12] Voluntary poverty is wealth in disguise, not often recognized as wealth.

[13] Egidius and Sylvester were two of the earliest followers of Francis. In those days impoverished people tied cheap ropes around their waists to hold their clothes in place, and this practical necessity was eventually transformed into the symbol of the Franciscan order.

[14] In 1210 Innocent III granted provisional approval to the Franciscan order.

[15] Thomas means that Francis is better celebrated in Heaven than on earth, or else that he is better celebrated in the Empyrian than in the Heaven of the Sun. In 1223 Honorius granted full papal approval to the Franciscan order.

[16] Thomas is referring to one of Francis's missionary journeys. Geoffrey Nuttall points out that in *The Divine Comedy* Dante rhymes *superbo*, "proud," with *acerbo*, "unripe," eight times.

Tiber and the Arno he was imprinted with his final insignia from Christ, and he bore it on his body for two years.[17]

"When it pleased the One who had ordained him for this goodness to draw him upward to his reward which he had earned by lowering himself, he commended his cherished lady to his brothers, his rightful heirs, and directed them to love her faithfully. Then from her bosom his glorious soul was ready to go away to its own kingdom, and for its corpse desired no other coffin.[18]

"Think now what kind of man was a worthy fellow helmsman to guide Peter's ship through deep seas on the right course! And such was our founder; therefore, as you can see, whoever follows his instructions is laden with precious cargo. But his flock has grown so greedy for new foods that they are bound to stray through dangerous countryside; and the more his sheep wander away from him, the less milk they return with. Indeed, some of them fear harm and stay close to their shepherd, but these are so few that not much cloth would be needed for all their hooded robes.[19]

"Now unless my words have been unclear, and if you have listened carefully and remember what I have said, your wish must be half fulfilled;[20] for you will see the kind of tree that is splintering, and you will see the rebuke that is intended by my words 'where they fatten well if they don't stray away.'"

---

[17] On Mt. Alvernia in 1224 Francis reportedly had a vision of Christ and received the stigmata (a miraculous appearance of Christ's wounds on his body).

[18] According to biographical accounts, when Francis was dying he told his followers to strip his body, lay it on the bare earth, and pour ashes on it. Thus as his soul ascended to eternal riches, his body remained committed to poverty.

[19] After praising Francis and his monastic order, Thomas now focuses on Dominic, founder of his own order, and rebukes his fellow Dominicans. This exemplifies the magnanimity and love that abounds in Paradise, where earthly rivalries no longer exist.

[20] Dante wished to know what Thomas meant by "where they fatten well" and "no one else ever rose." Thomas has explained the first, but not the second.

The Sun – Glorified Souls
Gustave Doré (Canto 12)

CANTO TWELVE

The Double Rainbow

As soon as the blessed flame had spoken its final words, the sacred millstone began to revolve again; and it had not yet completed a full revolution when a second one ringed it round, matching its motion with motion and its song with song.[1] The song of those sweet instruments [2]surpasses that of our Muses and Sirens as much as an original light surpasses its reflection.[3]

As it is when Juno sends forth her handmaiden (assuring people on earth that because of God's promise to Noah the world will never be drowned again) and two bows with the same colors arch together over the thin clouds, the outer one born from the inner one, like the voice of that wandering nymph whom love consumed as the sun consumes mist,[4] so those everlasting roses revolved around us in two garlands, and so the outer one responded to the inner.

As soon as the dance and jubilation—a festival of song and leaping lights, radiance upon radiance, gladness and benevolence—had stopped simultaneously, like a pair of eyes that have to blink at the same instant, then from the heart of one of the new lights there came a voice that drew me to itself like a

---

[1] Dante has likened the circle of twelve spirits to a rainbow, a wreath, a crown, a chandelier, and a clock. Now as the circle begins to move again he likens it to a revolving millstone. The first circle is promptly joined by a second circle of spirits.

[2] The second circle of spirits raises the total to be introduced in the sphere of the sun to twenty-four, the most in any sphere.

[3] Our most beautiful earthly poetry and music are only a reflection of this song.

[4] In classical mythology the rainbow (the nymph Iris, who wasted away because of her love for Narcissus) was the handmaiden of Juno; in the book of Genesis the rainbow was God's sign that He would never again destroy the world with a flood. An outer rainbow is fainter than an inner one, just as an echo is fainter than the original sound.

compass needle drawn to the North Star; and it began, "The love that makes me beautiful draws me to tell of the other leader, on whose account such fair words were said about my own.[5] Wherever one is spoken of, it is fitting for the other to be spoken of—so that just as they used to fight for the same cause, now they may shine in glory together. Christ's army, rearmed at such great cost, was lagging behind its emblem, timid and thin-ranked, when the Emperor who reigns forever decided to help His imperiled ranks (out of His grace, not the army's merit); then, as was said, He came to the aid of His bride with two champions whose deeds and words rallied the straggling squadron.[6]

"Not far from the crashing of the waves beyond which, because of his long course, the sun hides himself from everyone part of the time, in the land where the sweet west wind rises to open spring leaves that will deck all of Europe, fortunate Calahorra rests under the protection of the mighty shield where a lion submits and also rules.[7]

"There the ardent lover of the Christian faith was born, the holy athlete, kind to his own and ruthless to his opponents; and as soon as he was created, his mind was so full of surging power that when he was in his mother's womb he enabled her to prophesy.[8] He and the Christian faith brought gifts of holy

---

[5] The speaker is Bonaventure (1221-1274), who became leader of the Franciscans in 1257. He wants to praise St. Dominic, founder of the Dominicans.

[6] Christ paid the cost of His army on the cross, and the cross is its emblem.

[7] Bonaventure's poetic description of Dominic's birthplace echoes Thomas's introduction of Francis. Bonaventure links Dominic to the west wind, as Thomas linked Francis to the sun. The land is Spain, and geographers in Dante's day thought that the Atlantic Ocean extended around the world, which led Europeans to assume that there was no one to see the sun between sunset and sunrise as known in Europe. Dominic's birthplace, the village of Calahorra, thrived under the banner of Castile, which featured a lion under a castle and a lion over a castle. A love of details about the earth and human history flourishes among the spirits in Heaven.

[8] Legend has it that Dominic's mother dreamed about the future

power to each other when their marriage bond was pledged at the baptismal font; then the lady who spoke for him there saw in her sleep the marvelous fruit destined to issue from him and from his heirs.[9] And that he might be called what he was, a spirit from up here caused them to name him with the possessive form of the name of the One who owned him.[10]

"He was named Dominic; and I speak of him as one Christ selected to care for His garden.[11] He showed that he was a messenger and a close follower of Christ, for from the first he manifested the love that was Christ's prime admonition.[12] His nanny often found him wide awake, lying quietly on the floor as if to say, "It was for this I came." His father was truly Felix, and his mother was truly Giovanna—if the words mean what they say![13]

Dominican Order; a black and white dream dog symbolized these "hounds of the Lord" in their black and white habits. As Joseph Gallagher points out in *To Hell and Back with Dante*, "In their less inspiring moments, as inquisitors who violated their founder's belief in sharp arguments rather than sharp swords, they hounded heretics and supposed heretics mercilessly."

[9] Bonaventure describes Dominic's marriage to the faith, echoing the way Thomas described Francis's marriage to poverty. Legend has it that Dominic's godmother dreamed that he had a star on his forehead.

[10] "Dominic" meant "the Lord's."

[11] John Ciardi points out that in *Commedia* Dante avoided allowing any word to rhyme with the holy word *Cristo* (Christ). So at the ends of lines 71, 73, and 75 here he repeats the word *Cristo*. He will do that again in Cantos 14, 19, and 32.

[12] Many Dante commentators think this means that the first counsel of Christ was poverty (Matthew 19:21, "Go, sell what thou hast, and give to the poor"), and others think it refers to the first beatitude (Matthew 5:3). I have not found one commentator who suggests what I think Dante meant: Matthew 23 37-38, "Thou shalt love the Lord with all thy heart, and with all thy soul, and with all thy mind. This is the first and greatest commandment." This teaching is particularly appropriate for Dominic, because unlike Francis he was an intellectual. Francis typically ministered to lepers, and Dominic typically ministered to theology students. In addition to his devotion and charity, Dominic had immense zeal for education and correct doctrine.

[13] Felix, his father's name, means happiness. Giovanna, the feminine

"It was not for worldly gain—like the man from Ostia, and Taddeo[14]—but for love of true manna that in a short time he became such a great teacher that he began to tend the vineyard that soon fades if its keeper neglects it. And from the seat which used to be kinder to the virtuous poor (debased by its present occupant, through no fault of its own) he begged—not to return two or three for six, not for the fortune of the next vacancy, and not for the tithes belonging to God's poor[15]—but for permission to fight against the erring world[16] for that seed from which sprang these twenty-four plants that encircle you.[17] Then with education and enthusiasm working together, and apostolic sanction, he rushed forth like a flood spurting from a deep vein in a mountain; and he crashed most forcefully into the toughest thickets of heresy. From him many rivulets flowed which water the catholic orchard so that its saplings are greener.[18]

"If this was one wheel of the chariot in which the Holy Church defended herself successfully in doctrinal battles, the

---

form of John (in English Joan or Joanne), means full of grace. With a holy son like Dominic, the couple had appropriate names.

[14] Henry of Susa (circa 1200-1271), Cardinal Bishop of Ostia, was a successful authority on the Decretals. Taddeo d'Alderotto was a successful authority on medicine and philosophy, and Taddeo dei Pepoli specialized in canon law. These men, unlike Dominic, were not devoted to scripture and theology.

[15] Dante expresses through Bonaventure his contempt for Pope Boniface VIII, not for the office itself. Dominic did not, like many, ask for permission to skim part of the money intended for good works, nor for a choice position, nor for permission to use tithes for his own purposes.

[16] Dominic had to petition for years for permission to found the Dominican Order. Through preaching and teaching, he sought to combat heresies, particularly the Albigensian heresy centered in Provence, southern France. But church violence against the Albigensians prevailed, and they were exterminated. Although Dominicans took part in the Inquisition, that was years after Dominic's death.

[17] There are 24 spirits in the two circles around Dante. In his riot of mixed metaphors in *Paradise*, Dante has Bonaventure liken them to plants that grew from the good seed of right doctrine.

[18] This is the only use of the word catholic in *The Divine Comedy*.

excellence of the other one, described so kindly by Thomas before my coming, should be obvious. But that wheel's outer rim has not kept following its old track, and now there is mold where there used to be sediment.[19] His household, that used to follow in his footprints, has turned in the opposite direction, so its toe now lands on his heelprint; and we shall soon see the harvest of this bad farming, when the tares shall be cast out of the storehouse and weep. I readily admit that whoever searches through every page of our volume might yet find a page that reads 'I am still what I used to be.' But that won't be from Casale or Acquasparta, where some make our rule far too loose and others make it far too tight.[20]

"I am the light of Bonaventura of Bagnoregio;[21] in high office I always put left-hand matters second.[22] Illuminato and Augustine are here, who were among the first poor, barefoot brethren to put on the cord and befriend God. Hugh of St. Victor is here with them, [23] and Peter Mangiador[24] and Peter of

---

[19] Here Bonaventure switches from praising the Dominican Order to lamenting the faults of his own Franciscan Order. He likens those two orders to the two wheels on the chariot representing the church in the pageant near the end of *Purgatory*. As John Ciardi points out, the image of a two-wheeled war chariot changes to that of a two-wheeled grape cart; and because the Franciscan wheel has gone astray, the wine cask of the church has grown moldy.

[20] As soon as Francis died, his followers began to divide into two camps: one very lax and permissive, and the other extremely strict and severe. Bonaventura tried to promote a middle way between the two unhealthy extremes.

[21] The introductions begin with Bonaventure, who was born Giovanni de Fidanza. According to Joseph Gallagher, when he was a very sick child he was blessed by Francis and then recovered. Upon hearing the good news, Francis was thankful for the "buona ventura," good result.

[22] According to St. Thomas, left-hand matters are worldly concerns. See Proverbs 3:16, "… in her left hand are riches and honor."

[23] Hugh (circa 1097-1141) was a great theologian, teacher and writer at the Abbey of St. Victor near Paris. On earth he was the teacher of Peter Lombard and Richard of St. Victor, two of the shining spirits in the first circle.

Ispano who still gives light below in twelve booklets;[25] Nathan the prophet,[26] the metropolitan Chrysostom, [27]and Anselm,[28] and that Donatus who willingly set his hand to the first art; [29] Rabanus is here,[30]and at my side shines the Calabrian abbot Joachim, who was endowed with the spirit of prophecy.[31]

---

[24] Peter "the eater" (circa 1100-1179) was a devourer of books. He was chancellor of the University of Paris and canon of the monastery of St. Victor.

[25] Peter of Spain (circa 1226-1277) was the medical doctor of Pope Gregory X and was himself elected pope (Pope John XXI) in 1276. His "12 books" comprised one very popular analysis of logic. Ironically, he was from Portugal, not Spain; and he was killed by the collapse of a ceiling in the Vatican. He is the only contemporary pope that Dante locates in Paradise.

[26] Solomon was the only Old Testament character in the first circle, and Nathan is the only Old Testament character in the second circle. See 2 Samuel 12:1-15 for the story of Nathan's bold rebuke to King David (1000 B.C.) for causing the death of Uriah in order to seize his beautiful wife Bathsheba. Because of Nathan's wise words, David repented.

[27] John Chrysostom (circa 344–407), Archbishop of Constantinople, was called Golden Mouth for his fearless eloquence. He is placed next to Nathan because he daringly denounced the corruption of the court, and as a result he was exiled by Empress Eudoxia.

[28] St. Anselm (1033-1109), Archbishop of Canterbury, also opposed his ruler; as a result, he was forced into temporary exile. He was a theologian known as the second father of scholasticism,

[29] Donatus (fourth century) was the Roman author of a famous Latin grammar book.

[30] Rabanus Maurus (circa 766–856) was Archbishop of Mainz and compiled a 22-volume encyclopedia of the universe. He was one of the greatest scholars of his day.

[31] Joachim (circa 1130-1202) is placed next to Bonaventure because on earth Bonaventure opposed Joachim's teaching. Joachim was a Cistercian, not a Franciscan, but his teaching became very important to some extremist Franciscans. He originated the doctrine that there are three dispensations of human history: first, that of the Father; second, that of the Son; and third, that of the Holy Spirit. His belief that 1260 would be an apocalyptic year of some kind eventually proved false. In *To Hell and Back with Dante*, Joseph Gallagher points out that the mystery novel *The Name of the Rose* is about this aspect of Franciscan history.

"The glowing courtesy of Brother Thomas and his apt speech stirred me to corresponding speech, my praise of this great paladin, and stirred my companions along with me."[32]

---

[32] Bonaventure adds that it was Thomas's gracious praise of Francis that triggered his responsive praise of Dominic, this other renowned champion.

CANTO THIRTEEN

The Wisdom of Solomon

Whoever wants to grasp well what I saw next should cling to this image like a firm rock while I speak. Let him picture in his mind the fifteen stars here and there in the sky that kindle it with such brilliance they can pierce the mist; then let him picture the wan constellation that is on the breast of our sky night and day, so that it is never without its turning center. Finally, let him picture the bell-mouth of the horn that springs from the tip of the axle around which the Crystalline Heaven revolves.[1]

Imagine these stars forming two constellations in the sky, like those Minos' daughter created when the chill of death came upon her—the rays of one inside the other, turning so that one takes the lead and the other follows.[2] Then one will have only a shadowy idea of the constellation and the double dance circling the point where I stood; for the reality surpasses our imagination as far as the speed of the swiftest heaven surpasses the speed of the Chiana.[3]

They sing not in praise of Bacchus or Apollo, but of the three Persons in the divine nature; and that divine nature combined

---

[1] First, the reader is to imagine fifteen brilliant stars. Then he is to add the seven bright stars of the Big Dipper constellation, which never sets in the Northern Hemisphere. Then he is to add the two brightest stars of the Little Dipper constellation, which includes the North Star.

[2] These 24 stars arranged in a double circle (like those in the constellation with which Bacchus once commemorated a dying princess's flower wreath) would provide a feeble image of the dancing double circle of Christian scholars and thinkers at this level of Paradise.

[3] The Chiana was a slow, swampy river. The brilliance of the twenty-four dancers exceeds the brilliance of the twenty-four brightest stars in the sky as greatly as the speed of the whirling Crystalline Heaven exceeds the speed of the Chiana.

with human nature in one Person. When the song and dance were completed, the holy flames turned their attention to us, rejoicing as they passed from one task to the next.

Then the silence of the harmonious circle was broken by the light who had described the wondrous life of God's pauper. He said, "Since one sheaf is threshed and its seed has been garnered, now love bids me to thresh the other one.[4] You believe that the total light that human nature may receive was imparted by the Creator into these two: the chest from which the rib was drawn that formed the lovely cheek whose palate imposed a penalty on all the world, and the one which, pierced by the lance, paid the fine for all time, balancing the scales of justice.[5] And so you were puzzled when I claimed that the wisdom wrapped in the fifth flame has never been matched.

"Now open your eyes to my answer, and you will see that what you believe and what I say are both in the center of the target.[6] All that never dies and all that dies is nothing other than reflection of that Idea which our Father begets in Love; for that Living Light—that flows forth from its Source and does not depart from it, nor from the Love that unites the Trinity[7]—by

---

[4] Thomas answered Dante's first question and was echoed by Bonaventure. Now Thomas will answer Dante's second question.

[5] Adam and Jesus Christ were presumably the two men most directly (hence fully) infused with wisdom. According to Genesis, God created Eve from Adam's rib, and her sin of eating the forbidden fruit brought death into the world. Christ was pierced in the chest as He hung on the cross, and His crucifixion paid the penalty for human sin.

[6] At this point Thomas launches into a discourse about the nature of God and God's creation.

[7] The Idea and the Light, called the Logos (Word) in John 1:1, is Christ. (Heraclitus [circa 540-480 B.C.] had used the word Logos to mean Reason.) The Source of the Logos is God the Father. The Love that unites the Father and the Son is the Holy Spirit. Thus Thomas is teaching about the Trinity and creation. Although I have not seen a reference to Colossians 1:15-17 in commentaries on this passage, I believe Dante had it in mind when he attributed all of creation to Christ, the Light. There Paul taught that Christ is the image of the invisible God, the firstborn over all creation. "For by him all things were created, in heaven and on earth, visible and invisible, whether

grace sheds its rays as reflections through the nine levels of existence, remaining forever one.[8]

"Thus the Light descends through the moving heaven from act to act down to its weakest potencies, to the level where it produces ephemeral things; by these I mean things which develop from seeds or even without seeds.[9] The wax in these varies, and so do the stamps that give it shape; therefore, the perfection of the imprint of the divine Idea varies in quality. That is why trees of the same kind don't all bear equally good fruit, and why people are born with differing abilities.

"If the wax were perfectly ready and if heaven's power were at its fullest, the light of the stamp would show in its imprint; but nature always falls short of such perfection, like an artist who knows his craft but has a shaky hand. Yet if ardent Love Himself wields the original Ray of Light from the First Power directly, the insignia it imprints will be perfect.[10] Thus human clay was once imprinted perfectly; and thus the Virgin was impregnated. Therefore I affirm your belief that no human being ever matched those two persons.[11]

---

thrones or powers or rulers or authorities. All things were created by him and for him."

[8] According to the second century cosmography of Ptolemy, our cosmos was made up of nine nesting spheres with the earth as the innermost and the starry constellations in the eighth sphere. The ninth sphere was invisible. For theologians, the tenth sphere was the abode of God, beyond space, from which the cosmos emanates. Thus the nature of God filters down with decreasing potency through the nine levels of angels that vitalize these spheres.

[9] Life energy emanates from God by way of the Crystalline Heaven (the *primum mobile*). On earth God's nature is most fully manifest in mankind, less fully in the animal kingdom, and even less fully in plant life.

[10] If the triune God (Love, the Holy Spirit; the Ray of Light, the Son; and the First Power, the Father) creates something without intermediaries, the product is perfect.

[11] This seems to mean that the only times God created humans directly were when he created Adam and Jesus Christ. It is not clear how Eve fits in.

"If I failed to continue now, you would promptly ask how anyone else could rise beyond this standard. But in order to see what is not yet obvious to you, think about who this was and what his motive was when he was told to choose what he wanted most. I say this so you will realize that he was a king and chose the wisdom to rule well—not wisdom about the numbers and classes of angels, nor whether a logical possibility can produce a logical necessity, nor whether motion is possible without a cause, nor whether the diameter of a semicircle can be used as the base of a triangle without a right angle.[12]

"Therefore, the unequaled wisdom I was aiming my arrow at was wisdom to govern justly. And if you focus on my word 'rose,' you shall see that it applies only to the rise of kings; there are many of them, and few good ones.[13] Thus prepared, you accept my saying; it agrees with what you believe about the first father and about our Delight.

"And let this always be lead to weigh down your feet and make you move slowly, like a weary man, toward both 'yes' and 'no' where you can't see clearly. For whoever affirms or denies things indiscriminately is as low as any other fools; it often happens that hasty conclusions are wrong, and arrogance shackles one's intelligence. It is worse than useless for anyone to leave the shore to fish for truth if he doesn't know how, because he will return to shore worse off than before. Parmenides, Melissus, Bryson, and the many others who didn't know where they were, served as clear proofs of this to the world. So did Sabellius and Arius, and other fools who were like curved

---

[12] In 1 Kings 3, God came to King Solomon in a dream and told him to name what he wanted most. Solomon asked for a discerning heart, to enable him to govern well and to distinguish between right and wrong. God was pleased and answered that because Solomon had asked for the ability to administer justice rather than for something selfish, his request would be granted—and his wisdom forever unmatched. Thomas points out that this promise must be taken in context. Solomon's gift was practical wisdom, not answers to intellectual questions of the kind that intrigued medieval scholars.

[13] In Canto 10 Thomas claimed that the great mind in the fifth light had been granted such wisdom that "if truth be true, no one else ever rose to such deep wisdom."

swords that distort their reflections of the straight face of Scripture.[14]

"Men should not be overconfident in their judgments, like a farmer tallying his grain crop before it is ripe. I have seen a thornbush that was just a tough and prickly stem all winter, but it eventually bore a rose. And I have seen a ship sail straight and swift all the way across the sea, only to sink at the end of the trip as it entered its harbor.

"No John or Jane should think, if they see one person steal and another make donations, that they see the two as God does; for the thief may possibly rise, and the donor might fall."[15]

---

[14] Parmenides, Melissus and Bryson were Greek philosophers whose teachings were opposed by Aristotle and rejected. Sabellius and Arius were theologians whose ideas were also rejected.

[15] Thomas warns against the foolish presumption of judging the eternal fate of other people. In *Paradise* Dante rejects the opinion of theologians who figured that King Solomon could not be among the blessed in Heaven.

The Cross
Gustave Doré (Canto 14)

CANTO FOURTEEN

The Fifth Heaven: Mars

"From center to rim and then from rim to center—so water ripples in a round container, depending on whether it is struck from without or within."[1]

This image dropped suddenly into my mind when Thomas fell silent, because it resembled the relationship of his speech to that of Beatrice, who was pleased to say, "This man needs to trace another truth to its root, but he hasn't yet told you so with his voice or his thoughts. Tell him if the brilliance that blossoms around all of you now will continue to surround you forever or not; and if it will do so, how it can fail to hurt you when your bodies are made visible again."[2]

Just as it is when circling dancers spin and surge, lifting their voices and stepping more lightly with increased pleasure in their pleasure—so at her earnest supplication the sacred circlers showed increased joy in their revolving and their marvelous song. Whoever laments the fact that we must die and go to Heaven has not witnessed the refreshment of these eternal showers of light. The One and Two and Three who live and rule forever in Three and Two and One—contained in nothing but containing everything—was praised three times in song by each of these spirits, with melodious tribute to His utter excellence.[3]

---

[1] Thomas is on the rim of the inner circle of spirits, and Beatrice is at the center with Dante. Sound waves from Thomas's words ripple inward, and sound waves from Beatrice and Dante ripple outward.

[2] Dante wants to know how resurrected eyes will be able to endure such intense light.

[3] There is one God; Christ has two natures; and there are three Persons in the Trinity. God is encompassed in nothing, and He encompasses everything. Each of the twenty-four circling spirits praises God three times.

And I heard from the most splendid light of the inner circle a gentle voice that seemed to resemble the angel's voice to Mary, answering, "As long as the feast in Paradise exists, our love will clothe us in this shining garment. Its brightness is in proportion to our love, our love is in proportion to our vision, and our vision is in proportion to the unmerited favor we are granted.[4] When we are reclothed in our glorified and sanctified flesh, each of us will be more pleasing because more complete.

"Therefore the unearned light the Supreme Good gives us will increase—light that enables us to see Him; therefore our vision will increase, and our love that is kindled by our vision, and our light that radiates from our love. But as a burning coal outshines its flame so that its own form remains visible, so the radiance that robes us now will be exceeded by the appearance of the flesh that the earth is covering for so long; nor will such light overwhelm us, because our sense organs will be powerful enough for any pleasure."[5]

It seemed to me that the two choruses were so swift and eager to cry 'Amen' that it showed their desire for their human flesh; not only for themselves, perhaps, but for their mothers and fathers and others who were dear to them before they became these eternal flames.

And look! beyond the steady light there, a new light appears, like a brightening horizon. As it is at twilight, when new things begin to appear in the sky and seem real yet not quite real, so I began to see newly arrived entities encircling the other two circles. What sparkling of the Holy Spirit! It flared so suddenly and brilliantly that my eyes could not bear it![6]

---

[4] Solomon, credited with the Old Testament's book of wisdom (Proverbs) and the Old Testament's love song (Song of Solomon), explains that there is a chain reaction from grace to increased perception of reality, to increased love, to increased radiance.

[5] Solomon is the brightest in this circle of shining saints, and he explains that our resurrected bodies will be even more radiant than this present manifestation, but our eyes will be strong enough for all that light.

[6] Now there is a third, even more brilliant circle of light outside the other two. The three circles in the Heaven of the Sun are related to the

But Beatrice showed herself to me, smiling so beautifully that it must be left among those sights I can't remember. From this my eyes regained their power to look up, and I saw that I was transported with her alone to a higher realm of joy. This star's incandescent smile showed that I was lifted up there, because it seemed fierier than usual.[7] With all my heart, and in the language that is common to all, I thanked God for this new gift with an offering that was appropriate.[8] And before this burnt offering in my breast was consumed, I knew my prayer had been favorably accepted, because within two shafts of light such great splendors—ruby-red—appeared to me that I exclaimed: "O God! How You glorify them!"

As the Milky Way, adorned with minor and major stars, gleams whitely between the poles of the universe and intrigues astronomers—so it is that deep inside this sphere these two star-decked light shafts create the ancient sign in which two lines cross within a circle.[9] Here my memory outruns my skill, for I can't think of a worthy way to describe that cross, which radiates Christ. Whoever takes up his cross and follows Christ will forgive me for what I have to leave unsaid, when he himself sees Christ shining forth there.[10]

From arm to arm, from summit to base, moving lights sparkled brilliantly when they met and passed each other. Thus here on earth we see specks of material drifting—straight or zigzag, swift or slow, changing places, large or small—through

---

Father, the Son, and the Holy Spirit.

[7] Dante and Beatrice have ascended to the sphere of Mars, the red planet. The light of Mars intensifies because of Beatrice's presence.

[8] The language common to all men is that of the heart, which does not use words.

[9] A circle intersected symmetrically by a cross, representing the cross of Christ within a crown of thorns, was a well-known medieval symbol.

[10] In Matthew 16:24 Christ tells those who would be his followers to take up their crosses and follow Him. Dante never rhymes *Cristo* with any other word in his *Comedy*; here in lines 104, 106, and 108 he ends three lines with that holy name, rhyming it with itself. In Canto 19 he will do so again, again in lines 104, 106, and 108. And in Canto 32 he will do so again, in lines 83, 85, and 87.

beams of light that sometimes stripe the shade that men skillfully and artistically devise for their protection.[11]

And as a viol and harp, with all their well-tuned strings in harmony, chime sweetly for a person who can't identify the notes—so from the lights that I saw gathered on the cross a melody entranced me, although I could not identify the hymn. I could tell it was one of lofty praise, because I heard "rise" and "conquer," but I was like one who hears without comprehending.[12] And I was so enchanted that up until then nothing had ever captured me with such sweet chains.

This claim may seem too rash, as if I am overlooking the ecstasy of gazing into those lovely eyes where all my yearning finds rest. But anyone who considers the fact that the higher they are, the more these living insignias increase in beauty—and the fact that I had not yet looked into them here—should excuse me from my self-accusation; I accuse myself in order to excuse myself. Anyone may see that I am telling the truth and that I am not minimizing my holy joy here, because it becomes ever more intense as we rise.[13]

---

[11] Dust motes can sometimes be seen moving in a beam of light that spills through window shutters. The blessed spirits aloft in this cross made of light can be seen moving in it.

[12] Military victory is an especially appropriate analogy in the Heaven of Mars, the "martial" sphere.

[13] When Dante said of this music "I was so enchanted that up until then nothing had ever captured me with such sweet chains," he was not including the power of Beatrice's eyes to enchant him in Mars, because he had not yet had time to look at them there. But this music from the spirits in the cross was even more enchanting than Beatrice's eyes had been in the lower spheres.

CANTO FIFTEEN

Meeting an Ancestor

Benevolence—which is the essence of genuine love, just as selfishness is the essence of malice—imposed silence on that sweet lyre and stilled the sacred strings that the right hand of Heaven loosens and stretches.[1] How could such beings be deaf to righteous prayers, they who all fell silent and waited in place to hear my request? Whoever rejects this love in favor of love for things that perish deserves to bitterly regret that choice forever.

As a sudden light sometimes darts through a calm, clear night sky and catches the casual eye (like a falling star, except that where it started no star is missing, and it quickly disappears),[2] so from the right arm of the glowing cross constellation a star darted from its setting down to the cross's foot.[3] That gem did not leave its constellation—but sped to, then away from, the center;[4] and it glowed like flame behind a sheet of alabaster.[5] If our greatest muse is to be believed, with similar affection Anchises' soul rushed to greet his son in Elysium.[6]

---

[1] God's hand plays this metaphorical lyre by tuning or stroking and plucking it. (The cross was the lyre, and the sparkling spirits within it were the strings.)

[2] Educated people in Dante's day realized that a shooting or falling star is really a meteor, although they did not know what a meteor is made of.

[3] Dante is standing near the foot of the starry cross.

[4] The reader is now approaching the center of Dante's book *Paradise*, and the spirit that greets Dante here is so important to Dante that he takes up three cantos.

[5] The wealthy sometimes burned candles or torches behind thin sheets of alabaster, which is translucent and softens the light.

[6] Here Dante is intentionally reminding readers of Virgil, his father-figure. (In the *Aeneid* Virgil described how the soul of Anchises greeted his son Aeneas.) In *Inferno* and *Purgatory* Virgil repeatedly hinted to

"O blood of mine! O grace of God poured out beyond measure! To whom beside you was Heaven's gate ever thrown open twice?"[7] So that light spoke, and I stared at him wide-eyed. Then I glanced at my Lady and was equally dumb-founded there; for such a smile was blazing in her eyes that I thought my eyes had touched the limits of my blessedness and my Paradise.

Then, looking as joyful as he sounded, the spirit added things to his opening that I could not understand because they were so deep. He did not intend to hide his meaning from me this way, but his thoughts were far beyond human comprehension.[8] And when his bow of burning affection was relaxed enough that his message descended to the target of mortal understanding, the first I understood was "Blessed be Thou, Thou Three and One, Who art so gracious to my seed."

Then he continued, "Thanks to her who gave you wings to soar this high, you have satisfied an old, dearly-cherished hunger that I acquired (here in the light in which I speak) from reading the great book where black and white will never change.[9]

"You believe that your thoughts flow into me from the First Thought, as fives and sixes flow from the number one if one is understood;[10] therefore you do not ask who I am or why I seem

---

Dante about his future. Now in the Heaven of Mars Dante will learn the full import of those warnings.

[7] This formal salutation is spoken in Latin and assures Dante that he will someday return to Paradise.

[8] Robert Hollander reasons in his collection *Studies in Dante* that the sounds Dante could not comprehend must have been either the language of Adam or glossolalia (speaking in tongues). He also suggests that Dante might have identified the glossolalia in Acts 2 with the language of Adam. I suspect that if Dante meant to suggest glossolalia (I am not at all sure he did), he probably had Romans 8:26 in mind: "the Spirit himself intercedes for us with groans too deep for words."

[9] The eternal book that caused this spirit to yearn for Dante's arrival is a metaphor for divine foreknowledge, which the blessed spirits share with God. This spirit had foreknowledge that Dante was going to come, and he is thankful to Beatrice for bringing him.

[10] The existence of the number one and our awareness of it make

even more joyful than others in this festive throng. You are correct; the least and greatest of us here look into the mirror that reveals thoughts before they exist. But to most fully slake the thirst of my sweet longing, the sacred love with which I ceaselessly watch and wait for you, let your voice—assured, bold, and glad—proclaim your will and your desire, for which my answer is already decreed."

I turned to Beatrice, and because she heard me before I spoke she gave me a smiling signal that lifted the wings of my desire. So I began, "Once you entered Perfect Equality, love and wisdom were equally balanced in each of you, because the Sun that enlightens you and warms you with brightness and heat is so balanced that no analogy is adequate.[11] But for reasons that are evident to you, the feelings of mortals and the wisdom to express them are like two unequally feathered wings. Therefore I, a mortal, feel this imbalance deeply, and only in my heart can I thank you for your fatherly welcome. But I may and do implore you, living topaz within this precious jewelry, to satisfy my desire for your name."[12]

"O branch of mine, in whom I took delight while only expecting you, I was your root" was the beginning of his answer. Then he said, "He from whom your family received its name was my son and your grandfather's father, who has been circling the first ledge on the Mount for more than a hundred years. It would be fitting for good work from you to shorten his long task.[13]

---

possible the existence of higher numbers and our awareness of them. Similarly, it is unity that enables us to comprehend diversity.

[11] The spirit has addressed Dante in a stately way, and Dante responds in a stately way. What he means is that the spirits in Paradise have knowledge and love in equal amounts, because God (their sun) sheds light (knowledge and wisdom) and warmth (love and desire) equally. In Dante's theological parallel, Christ and the Holy Spirit emanate equally from God the Father.

[12] This spirit is like a gem, and the cross constellation is like a glowing cluster of similar gems. The topaz is a yellow stone that turns red when heated.

[13] Cacciaguida was Dante's paternal great-great-grandfather. His son, Alighiero, has been dead more than a century and is still strug-

"Florence, within the ancient walls from which she still hears the nine o'clock and twelve o'clock bells,[14] then lived in peace, sober and pure. For her no golden chain or crown, no elaborate gown or belts that are more impressive than the one who wears them.[15] The birth of a daughter did not strike a father with fear then, because her wedding date and dowry had not gone to extremes in opposite directions.[16] There were no empty mansions.[17] Sardanapalus had not yet arrived to teach what can be done in the bedroom.[18] Montemalo had not yet been surpassed by your Uccellatoio, which shall also surpass it in its decline.[19]

"I have seen Bellincion Bertil wear a leather belt with a bone clasp, and his wife come away from her mirror with her face unpainted.[20] I have seen de'Nerlo and de'Vecchio content in

---

gling around the terrace of pride with a heavy stone on his back, and so Cacciaguida suggests that Dante pray for him to hasten his ascent to Paradise.

[14] Cacciaguida is referring to the accurate bells of La Badia church, which was built at the old Roman wall. By Dante's time, a new city wall or two had been added to supplement the oldest one. According to Allen Mandelbaum, the 9 a.m. and 3 p.m. bells of La Badia marked the beginning and end of an artisan's normal work day in central Florence.

[15] In Cacciaguida's day Florence was not extravagant and ostentatious.

[16] In Dante's day the bride's age had shrunk and her dowry had expanded, to the point that fathers had to give their daughters away in marriage when they were little children and had to pay the grooms' families immense dowries. According to John Ciardi, "it was said that a man with one daughter was impoverished and a man with two ruined."

[17] In Dante's day some decadent heirs of family fortunes squandered their assets and closed ancestral homes they couldn't maintain; other owners of mansions had been exiled like Dante.

[18] Sardanapalus, King of Assyria in 667-626 B.C., was notorious for waste, extravagance, and sexual debauchery. Cacciaguida claims that in Dante's day the Florentines were following his example.

[19] Montemalo was a hill overlooking Rome, and Uccellatoio was a hill overlooking Florence. Cacciaguida predicts that just as the ascendency of Florence to ostentatious wealth has been more spectacular than that of Rome, so its descent will also be more spectacular.

[20] This honorable and wholesome Florentine contemporary of

simple leather, and their wives working with spindle and flax.
How happy they were—each one of them sure of her burial
place, and none left alone in her bed because of France.[21] One
woman would keep watch over the cradle and tenderly croon
the baby talk that is a pleasure to new parents;[22] another would
tell her children stories about the Trojans and Fiesole and Rome
as she drew out the thread she was spinning. At that time a
Cianghella or a Lapo Salterello would have been as great a
marvel as Cincinnatus or Cornelia would be now.[23]

"Beseeched during birth pains,[24] Mary placed me in this
serene city and its pleasant way of life, in such a good com-
munity, in such a sweet home. In your ancient baptistery I
became a Christian and Cacciaguida.[25] Moronto and Eliseo were

---

Cacciaguida did not parade his wealth by wearing ostentatious
jeweled belts. His daughter, "good Gualdrada," was mentioned in
Inferno, Canto 16, where her grandson in Hell was deeply concerned
about the welfare of Florence. Dante's bad news for him was "O
Florence, your aggressive riffraff and quick profits have brought
arrogance and excess, and you are weeping within." Now in Paradise
Dante's great-great-grandfather is expressing the same sentiment.

[21] These were leading families in Florence who enjoyed wholesome
domestic tranquillity, neither threatened by exile nor fractured by the
lure of lucrative business opportunities in France. (According to John
Ciardi, in Dante's day some husbands acquired new vices in France
and never honored their marital obligations again.)

[22] In his essay "Babytalk in Dante's 'Commedia'" Robert Hollander
points out that Dante had obviously spoken babytalk to his own
children before his exile and taken a serious interest in both individual
and universal language development. (Contemporary researchers have
ascertained the neurological need for babytalk and the instinctive
similarity of parental babytalk in all times and places.)

[23] Cianghella was a woman in Dante's Florence with a terrible
reputation, and Lapo Salterello was a corrupt lawyer and judge in
Dante's political party. In contrast, Cincinnatus and Cornelia were
historical Romans of noble character. (Quintius Cincinnatus was
mentioned in Canto 6 of *Paradise*, and Cornelia was mentioned in
Canto 4 of *Inferno*.)

[24] It was customary for women to pray to Mary for a safe childbirth,
as Cacciaguida's mother did.

[25] Cacciaguida received his name when he was baptized. This is how

my brothers, and my wife came to me from Po valley; and your surname came from her.

"Later I followed Emperor Conrad, who knighted me because my courage served him so well. In his ranks I marched against the evil of that creed whose people, to the shame of your shepherds, have seized what should be yours.[26] There I was freed by that foul race from the deceitful world, the love of which ruins many a soul; and I came from martyrdom into this peace."[27]

---

he finally tells Dante his name.

[26] Conrad III, who ruled from 1138 to 1152, took part in the disastrous Second Crusade against the Saracens (1147-1149), and that is where Cacciaguida died violently in an attempt to win back the Holy Land ("your heritage"). According to Richard Kay, Cacciaguida is condemning both Roman church leaders ("your shepherds") and Islam ("the evil of that creed") for fostering undue love of things of this world.

[27] The nature of Cacciaguida's courageous death transported him directly to the Heaven of Mars without a period in Purgatory. Courage (fortitude) is in a sense the most important of the four cardinal virtues, because without it people abandon the other virtues when threatened. Courage is manifested in many ways, but Aristotle taught that the ultimate form of courage is bravery in the face of death, particularly in battle. Dante's mentor Aquinas agreed with Aristotle, although Aquinas included other dangerous emergencies along with war.

CANTO SIXTEEN

Fine Families

Trifling nobility of family bloodlines! Your ability to make men glory in you down here where our affections are faulty won't amaze me anymore, because even in Heaven, where appetites are straightened out, I still did so. Yet you are indeed a cloak that quickly shrinks, so that if no cloth is added day after day, the shears of time will trim you all the way around.[1]

I began to speak again with the form of the word *you* that Romans used to use, although their descendants use it much less.[2] A short way from us, Beatrice smiled at that, reminding me of the one who coughed at the scene of Guinevere's first recorded misdeed.[3] I began, "You are my father. You make me bold to speak. You uplift me so that I am more than I.[4]

---

[1] Cacciaguida's first words to Dante were "O blood of mine!" Dante's exclamation here about bloodlines is his comment as a storyteller on earth, not his response as a visitor to Heaven who still has more to learn. Dante the visitor is proud to find such a worthy ancestor there, but in fact such a heritage is no credit to him. The only real aristocracy is the aristocracy of merit, and merit must be achieved independently in every generation. Cacciaguida's litany of fallen families in Canto 16 will make that clear.

[2] Dante accepts the common belief that to show respect to Julius Caesar Romans began to use the plural form of *you* when speaking to him. Although this form was commonly used throughout Italy in Dante's day, it was out of fashion in Rome.

[3] This smile is Beatrice's delicately humorous response to overhearing Dante's great deference for his illustrious ancestor, because he seems to be foolishly basking in Cacciaguida's glory. According to Mark Musa, Dante likens himself here to Guinevere when she kissed Lancelot and was gently warned by the cough of her lady in waiting that the two illicit lovers were not alone. So Beatrice gently warns Dante to check what he is doing.

[4] In my opinion this statement by Dante is significant. Dante uses the

"My mind is filled with joy from so many streams that I am glad it can hold it all without bursting. Tell me, then, dear root source from which I spring, what was your ancestry and which years entered history in your boyhood. Tell me about the sheepfold of St. John, how large it was then, and who were worthy of high positions there."[5]

As a coal flares into flame when the wind breathes on it, so I saw that light flare brighter at my loving words. And even as it grew more beautiful to my eyes, so in a sweeter and gentler voice (but not in modern Florentine)[6] he said: "From the day on which 'ave' was declared[7] to the day my mother, now a saint, was relieved of the heavy burden of my weight, this star returned five hundred, fifty, and thirty times to its Lion to be renewed beneath his paws.[8] My forefathers and I were born on the spot where a runner in your annual horse race first enters the last section.[9] About my ancestors let that much information

---

plural form of *you* to Cacciaguida three times in a row, then claims that (the plural) Cacciaguida has made Dante more than himself alone. Dante feels figuratively expanded by his connection to this illustrious ancestor, foreshadowing Cacciaguida's warning about dangers of hubris and over-expansion.

[5] Florence is called the sheepfold of St. John because he is the city's patron saint. The rest of Canto 16 is composed of Cacciaguida's answer to Dante's request, an answer designed to discourage inordinate love of things that pass away.

[6] Dante uses modern (fourteenth-century) Florentine Italian to report what Cacciaguida said in twelfth-century Florentine Italian.

[7] The angel's annunciation to Mary supposedly took place on March 25 (known in England as Lady Day), nine months before the birth of Christ — which supposedly took place on December 25. If Cacciaguida was born on March 25, he was born in the month named for Mars, under the sign of Mars in the Zodiac. Dante meets him in the Heaven of Mars.

[8] "This star" is Mars. When this planet had returned 580 times to the constellation of Leo after the annunciation to Mary, the date was A.D. 1091.

[9] This means that the Alighieri family home was located in the heart of Florence, which suggests both ancient Roman heritage and fine family pedigree.

suffice; silence about who they were and where they came from is more suitable than talk about it.[10]

"At that time all the men of arms-bearing age who lived between Mars and the Baptist were only a fifth of those there now.[11] And the citizenry that is polluted now by those from Campi, Certaldo, and Figlin was purebred then, down to the humblest worker. Oh, how much better it would be if your boundaries were back at Galluzzo and Trespiano! If only those I mentioned were still your neighbors instead of your having them within and enduring the stench of the cur from Aguglione and the one from Signa with such a sharp eye for swindling![12]

"If those who are the most astray in the world had not been like a stepmother to Caesar, but kind, like a mother to her son, then one who is now a Florentine moneychanger and trader would still be in Semifonte, where his grandfather was a scavenger. The Counts would still be in Montemurlo, the Cerchi in the parish of Acone, and perhaps the Buondelmonti would still be in Valdigreve.[13]

"A mixed population has always made a city-state sick, just as piling food on food will make a body sick.[14] A blind bull is

---

[10] The speaker, Cacciaguida, has it both ways here; he acknowledges his distinguished family line and lays claim to tasteful modesty as well. Did Dante write these lines as gentle self-mockery?

[11] Adult males from one end of Florence to the other (from the statue of Mars on the Ponte Vecchio to the baptistery of St. John) totaled perhaps 6000 in Cacciaguida's day and 30,000 in Dante's. Military references and references to swords, blood, and the color red are especially appropriate in the sphere of Mars.

[12] Many residents of neighboring localities had moved into Florence, which greatly expanded its borders. Cacciaguida mentions two politically powerful newcomers who were enemies of both Dante and his potential benefactor Emperor Henry VII.

[13] Dante blames church leaders in Rome for undermining the emperors (like an envious stepmother) rather than supporting them (like a kindly mother). This resulted in much disruption around Florence, causing many outsiders to move into the city. The unidentified moneychanger is an example of the undesirable newcomers. So are the Counts, the Cerchi, and the Buondelmonti.

[14] Cacciaguida is not lamenting racial intermarriage; he is lamenting

more apt to fall than a blind lamb, and one sword often cuts better than five.[15]

"If you consider how Luni and Urbisaglia have perished and how Chiusi and Sinigaglia are following them,[16] it won't seem unusual or puzzling to hear how families pass away, since even cities come to an end. Your affairs are all going to die, just as you are; but in cities that last a long time that fact escapes your notice because your lives are short.

"And just as the cycle of the moon endlessly covers and lays bare the shores, so fortune changes Florence.[17] Therefore, when I tell about some prominent Florentines whose fame is now covered over by time, it should not be surprising. I have seen the Ughi and the Catellini, Filippi, Greci Ormanni, and Alberichi, illustrious citizens even in their decline. I have seen

---

the damage that an influx of opportunistic newcomers can do to a well-regulated, cohesive community. It was believed that to eat again when the last meal is not yet digested will cause illness. In Dante's parallel, adding more immigrants before the last ones are assimilated will cause social illness.

[15] To deplore Florence's over-expansion between his day and Dante's, Cacciaguida cites sayings about disadvantages of large quantities and large size. An equivalent saying in English is "The bigger they come, the harder they fall."

[16] These were all important cities that died.

[17] Appraisals of the city's fortunes went on changing after Dante wrote this, and his very complaint added to its pride. In 1400 Coluccio Salutati wrote in *Invective against Antonio Loschi of Vicenze* "what city, not merely in Italy, but in all the world, is more securely placed within its circle of walls, more proud of its *palazzi*, more bedecked with churches, more beautiful in its architecture, more imposing in its gates, richer in piazzas, happier in its wide streets, greater in its people, more glorious in its citizenry, more inexhaustible in its wealth, more fertile in its fields? ... What city has been more active in professions, more admirable generally, in all things? What city without a seaport ships out so much goods? Where is business a greater enterprise, or richer in variety of stuffs, or carried on with more astuteness and sagacity? Where are men more illustrious? And — let me not be tiresome — more distinguished in affairs, valiant in arms, strong in just rule, and renowned? Where can you find a Dante, a Petrarch, a Boccaccio?"

the Sannella, Arca, Soldanieri, Ardinghi, and Bostichi families, as great as they were old.[18]

"The Ravignani (from whom Count Guido and all who inherited noble Bellincione's name are descended) used to live near the gate that is now burdened with such heavy treason that it will soon sink the ship.[19] Back then the Della Pressa family knew how to govern well, and in his mansion Galigaio's sword's hilt and pommel were gilded.[20] Back then the family of the fur stripe was great, the Sacchetti, the Giuochi, the Fifanti, the Barucci, the Galli,[21] and those who blush red because of a barrel stave.[22] Back then the stock from whom the Calfucci branched was great; and the Sizii and the Arrigucci were set in high office.[23]

"How great I saw those who are now undone by pride![24] And the balls of gold used to beautify Florence in all her great deeds.[25] So did the fathers of those who now fatten themselves at leisure in church council whenever the bishopric is vacant.[26]

---

[18] These were all noble families of Florence that had died out by 1300.

[19] The noble Ravignani family died out, and the Cerchi family inhabited that house in Dante's day. Their treacheries were weighing Florence down like a foundering ship.

[20] These families were both exiled in 1258.

[21] The Pigli family had a stripe of ermine on its coat of arms. These fine Florentine families all fled, declined, or died out by the time Dante wrote *Paradise*.

[22] The Chiaramontesi family was disgraced in Dante's day when one of its members betrayed his post in city government by removing a stave in the barrel used to measure salt for the public. For this fraud he was executed.

[23] The Calfucci family died out; and both the Sizii and the Arrigucci had to flee from Florence in 1260.

[24] Commentators agree that this is a reference to the Uberti family, especially Farinata, who appeared in Canto ten of *Inferno*..

[25] Gold balls were in the coat of arms of the Lamberti family and later appeared in that of the Medicis, who were powerful bankers. This eventually led to three gold balls becoming the ensignia of pawnbrokers.

[26] The Visdomini and Tosinghi families once enhanced Florence

The outrageous tribe that is a dragon pursuing anyone who flees—but quiet as a lamb to anyone who bares his teeth or his purse to them—was on the rise, but so contemptible that Ubertin Donato was displeased when his father-in-law made him a relative of theirs.[27] The Caponsacco family had long ago come down from Fiesole into the marketplace, and back then the Giuda and Infangato families were good citizens.[28]

"I will tell you something incredible but true: a person used to enter the inner wall through a gate named after the della Pera family.[29] Everyone who bears the coat of arms of the great baron whose fame and nobility are recalled on the feast day of Thomas received knighthood and privilege from him; but one with a fringe around that coat of arms has joined the commoners.[30]

"The Gaulterotti and Importuni families were there, and their Borgo would have remained a quieter place if they had not acquired new neighbors.[31] The house where your grief began (because of the righteous anger that has killed you and ended your happy years) was honored then along with its

---

along with the Lambertis, but later members used their administrative posts for personal gain. They profited financially by failing to appoint new bishops promptly when they were needed.

[27] A member of the Admiri family, enemies of Dante, obtained Dante's property when he was exiled and actively opposed his wish to return. Ubertin Donato was chagrined when his wife's father gave his wife's sister to an Admiri.

[28] These three fine families had decayed somewhat by Dante's day. According to John Ciardi, their names meant head-in-a-sack, Judas, and covered-with-mud.

[29] That family's past honor was no longer remembered.

[30] Hugh of Brandenbourg, Imperial Vicar of Tuscany, died on St. Thomas' Day in 1006; from then on, prayers were offered for him annually at the abbey he had built in Florence. Although Giano della Bella bore Hugh's coat of arms (with a gold fringe around it) on his shield, he joined the movement to curb the privileges of the nobility.

[31] The climax of Cacciaguida's litany of fallen families begins here. The Buondelmonti family moved to the Borgo Santi Apostoli neighborhood in Florence after their castle beyond the Ema river was destroyed in 1135.

allies.[32] O Buondelmonte, what a wrong you did when you fled your wedding at the wish of another! Many who are sad now would have been joyful if God had deposited you in the Ema when you were moving to our city. It was appropriate that Florence should sacrifice a victim to the battered stone that guards the bridge, to commemorate the last she knew of peace.[33]

"With families like these, along with others, I used to see Florence in such tranquillity that she had no cause to grieve. With families like these I saw such a brave and just citizenry that the lily on the staff was never turned upside down or dyed red by factionalism."[34]

---

[32] The upwardly mobile Buondelmonti family was socially inferior, but young Buondelmonte dei Buondelmonti managed to win the hand of a daughter of the Amidei family anyway. The Amidei family and its close associates were members of the Florentine elite.

[33] Prompted by a member of the elite Donati family, the bridegroom, who was evidently unaware of the seriousness of his obligation not to disgrace his fiancée, publicly jilted her in order to marry a more attractive Donati instead. Members of the devastated Amidei family murdered him at the foot of the statue of Mars at the Ponte Vecchio on Easter Sunday, 1216. That launched the feuding and hatreds that would wrack Florence for over a century.

[34] In its golden age Florence prospered peacefully and happily. Back then the lily on her flag was never displayed upside down to signify defeat and was never changed from white on red to red on white. (It was changed to red on white to signify the victory of the Guelph political faction in 1251.)

Cacciaguida
Gustave Doré (Canto 16)

CANTO SEVENTEEN

Footnotes on the Future

I was like Phaëthon, who came to Clymene for reassurance when he heard a claim about himself (and who still makes fathers cautious about indulging their sons);[1] that's how I was perceived by both Beatrice and the sacred light who had changed his location for me.[2]

Therefore my Lady continued. "Show forth the flame of your wish," she said, "that it may show clearly your internal design; not that we may learn anything from what you say, but that you may learn to reveal your thirst so your cup will be filled."

"Dear ground where I am rooted (set up so high that as you gaze upon the Point to which all times are present[3] you can see likely possibilities before they happen, just as earthly minds perceive that one triangle cannot contain two obtuse angles[4]),

---

[1] Phaëthon consulted his mother because he was worried about the claim that he was not really the son of Apollo. She told him to ask Apollo, who assured him the claim was false. (Next, Phaëthon asked permission to drive the chariot of the sun across the sky, and Apollo foolishly agreed; the resulting accident killed Phaëthon.) Dante resembled Phaëthon because he was worried about the claim that he would suffer disaster, and he hoped for assurance from his new father-figure, Cacciaguida. Unfortunately, in Dante's case the ominous claim was true.

[2] Cacciaguida had moved from the arm of the starry cross to the foot of the cross to talk with Dante.

[3] Here Dante refers to God as the First Point, meaning the origin of everything. In *Convito* Dante wrote "...as Euclid says, the point is the beginning of Geometry." (In laymen's terms, geometric points can be conceived of as minuscule spots that fill no space and have no material existence; but they are the most basic components of geometry, which is the mathematics of the properties, measurement, and relationships of points, lines, angles, surfaces, and solids.)

[4] There can never be two angles, each larger than a right angle, in one

while I was accompanied by Virgil up the mountain that cures souls and down through the world of death, ominous words were said to me about my future life.[5] Although I feel I am set foursquare to withstand the assaults of fate,[6] my wish would be fulfilled if I could hear what disaster is approaching; for the arrow that is expected hits with less impact." So I spoke to the same light who had been talking to me, and my wish was confessed as Beatrice had wished.

The fatherly love that was contained and revealed in the light of his smile answered me with plain words and clear thought—not in the kind of enigmas that ensnared foolish people before the Lamb of God was slain who takes away sin.[7] "Ephemeral things that do not continue beyond the pages of the material world are all on display in God's view; but this does not make them inevitable any more than watching a ship sail downstream makes it happen. Thus a vision of what time is preparing for you appears to me in the same way that sweet organ music arrives at the ear.

"As Hippolytus was forced to leave Athens by his cruel and crafty stepmother, so you will be forced to leave Florence.[8] This

---

triangle. That is so obvious to the eye that one doesn't have to be trained in geometry to understand it.

[5] Dante was warned about impending doom in the *Inferno*, Cantos 10, 15, and 24, and in *Purgatory*, Cantos 8 and 11.

[6] Using the term *tetragon*, which suggests the English adjective *foursquare*, Dante refers to geometry for the third time in this paragraph. Longfellow is unique among commentators I have consulted in pointing out that Dante must be alluding to the following statement from Aristotle's *Ethics*, "Always and everywhere the virtuous man bears prosperous and adverse fortune prudently, as a perfect tetragon." Neither Longfellow nor other commentators I consulted mention the second definition of *tetragon* in the *Oxford English Dictionary*, a square fortress. That little-known definition would fit Dante's hope to be like a tetragon in withstanding the assaults of fate.

[7] Cacciaguida foretells the future clearly, not in the kind of vague, ambiguous terms employed by pagan oracles.

[8] When Hippolytus refused to be seduced by Phaedra, his stepmother, she claimed that he was the spurned seducer, which led to his exile.

is willed and plotted and will soon be accomplished by some-
one who is arranging it in the place where Christ is up for sale
every day.[9] The public will blame the victim, as usual; but
truth dictates that the truth will become apparent in retri-
bution.[10]

"This is the first arrow that the bow of exile will shoot: you
will leave behind everything you love most dearly. You will
sample how salt tastes in someone else's bread, and how hard
the path is down and up another person's stairs.[11] And what
will weigh down your shoulders the most will be the spiteful,
senseless companions with whom you fell into this valley, for
they will become ungrateful, irrational, and blasphemous
against you. But before long their cheeks, not yours, shall
redden for it. The results of their actions will prove their brut-
ishness, so it shall be to your credit that you have made
yourself into a party of one.[12]

"Your first refuge and first dwelling place shall be the
courtesy of the great Lombard who carries the sacred bird on a
ladder; and he will hold you in such high regard that what
comes first for you two in the area of giving and requesting is
what comes second for other people.[13] With him you shall meet

---

(This is like the story of Joseph and Potiphar's wife in Genesis.) Dante
resembled Hippolytus because lies about him would cause him to be
banished also. Dante was to be falsely accused of graft.

[9] Pope Boniface VIII, in the corrupt, greedy Vatican in Rome, has set
events in motion that will enable Dante's enemies to banish him.

[10] Corso Donati, a Black Guelph leader who served Boniface, was
most responsible for the exile of Dante and other leaders of the White
Guelph party. Donati was condemned to death as a traitor in 1308 and
was speared in the throat as he tried to flee the city. Boniface also died
in disgrace. Cacciaguida sees these events as divine retribution.

[11] This passage is famous for its understated poignancy.

[12] Fellow members of the white Guelph party who were exiled along
with Dante launched an ill-conceived attack on the black Guelphs in
1304. By then Dante had already disassociated himself from them, and
they soon disbanded.

[13] This is the very center of *Paradise*, and Dante almost surely placed
his tribute to the Della Scala family here intentionally. The coat of arms
of Bartolommeo Della Scala showed an imperial eagle on a ladder (la

someone who was so stamped at birth by this strong star that his deeds will be outstanding. People have not yet become aware of him because of his youth, for these spheres have only rolled around him for nine years.[14] But before the Gascon deceives noble Henry, his virtue will start to sparkle in his indifference to silver and in his hard work.[15] His generous deeds will become so well known that even his enemies will not be able to keep quiet about it. Look to him and to his benefits; many people will be changed by him, the wealthy and the poor trading places; and you must record the following in your mind, but don't broadcast it." Then he told me things that will seem incredible even to first-hand witnesses.[16]

Then he added: "Son, these were the footnotes for what was said to you; these are the snares out of sight on the other side of a few rotations. But I don't want you to envy your neighbors,

---

scala). According to Cacciaguida, Bartolommeo and Dante would be such good friends that they would grant each other's requests before they were spoken.

[14] Bartolommeo's younger brother Can Grande (Francesco) was born in the month of Mars in 1291, nine years before Dante's trip to Paradise. (Nine is a special number to Dante, and the circle is a special shape to him. In *Convito* he wrote "... I call in general everything round, whether a solid or a surface, a circle; for, as Euclid says, the point is the beginning of Geometry, and, as he says, the circle is its most perfect figure, and may therefore be considered its end....") Can Grande became the Lord of Verona and Dante's chief patron. Dante discussed *Paradise* with him and dedicated it to him.

[15] Dante saw Henry VII as Italy's main hope for peace and his own main hope for return from exile. Pope Clement V, the French Pope, invited Henry VII to Rome to try to impose peace on Italy, but gave him a hostile reception when he arrived in 1312 (when Can Grande was 21). Henry died, and some suspected Clement of poisoning him. It is not surprising, therefore, that Clement burned in a baptismal font in Canto 19 of *Inferno*.

[16] The evidence that Dante had Can Grande in mind when he wrote about the Greyhound in Canto 1 of *Inferno* is highly persuasive. Dante evidently hoped that Can Grande would be able to restore order and decency to Italy.

since your life will persist long after they are punished for their crimes."[17]

When that blessed soul revealed by his silence that he had finished weaving his woof thread through the warp I had arranged for him, like a man in doubt who seeks advice from someone who sees and rightly wills and loves,[18] I said: "I see clearly, Father, that time rushes toward me to deliver the kind of blow that hits someone unprepared the hardest; therefore it is good for me to be armed with foresight so that if my most cherished place is torn from me, I won't lose every place else because of my poetry. Down through the infinitely bitter world, up the mountain from whose lovely summit my Lady's eyes have lifted me, and then from light to light through Heaven, I have learned things that will taste harsh and acrid to many if I tell. But if I shrink from being a friend to truth, I fear I won't live on for those who will call this present time ancient."[19]

The light in which my new-found treasure was smiling began to sparkle like a golden mirror struck by sunbeams:

---

[17] Cacciaguida has provided an explanation of the doom Dante was warned about in Hell and Purgatory, doom that would become manifest in less than two years. But Cacciaguida assures Dante that he will prevail in the long run.

[18] In my opinion this description of a good man is highly significant. I think Dante assumed that man is designed to reflect the triple nature of God: the Son (wisdom) sees, the Father (power) wills, and the Spirit (love) rejoices. This divine and human triad is implicit in the following prayer of St. Augustine: "O God, you are the light of minds that know you, the joy of hearts that love you, and the strength of wills that serve you. Grant us so to know you that we may truly love you, and so to love you that we may freely serve you, whom to serve is perfect freedom."

[19] Here Dante recapitulates his pilgrimage and sets forth the unavoidable choice he has to make between discretion and truth telling. The more he offends people with his future poem, the more he risks having nowhere to live; but if he leaves out harsh truths about evildoing, he forfeits his value to posterity. Ironically, when Dante the pilgrim consults Cacciaguida about the choice, Dante the poet has already written and circulated all of his *Inferno* and *Purgatory* and is halfway through *Paradise*. So Cacciaguida's answer is really Dante's self-justification.

"The conscience darkened by its own shame or someone else's will indeed find your words harsh. Nevertheless, avoid all falsehood and reveal all you have seen; let them scratch where they are scabby. Even if your words offend people's taste buds at first, when they are digested they will become vital nutrition.[20]

"Your outcry will be like the wind that hits the loftiest peaks the hardest; and this shall be no little cause for honor. That is why only souls known by their fame have been shown to you in these spheres, on the mountain, and in the miserable valley; for a hearer's mind does not settle on or trust an illustration if its root is unfamiliar and hidden, or on other evidence that is less than impressive."[21]

---

[20] Although truth will offend people with bad consciences, Cacciaguida instructs Dante to tell all because it will be healthful and is his civic duty.

[21] It has been remarked that although Dante selected the personalities in *The Divine Comedy* because they were famous, the overwhelming majority are remembered since then only because Dante selected them.

CANTO EIGHTEEN

The Eighth Heaven, Jupiter

Now as that holy mirror[1] was rejoicing in his own thoughts
and I was digesting mine (the sweet mixed with the bitter), the
Lady who was leading me to God said, "Change your perspec-
tive; remember that I am close to the One who lightens every
unfair burden."[2] I turned toward the loving sound of my
comforter, and the love I beheld then in her holy eyes I won't
attempt to tell here; not only because I distrust my speech, but
also because my memory cannot scale such heights unless
Another guides it.

I can report this much, that as I gazed upon her my heart
was freed from every other longing, because the Eternal Joy
that was shining directly on Beatrice satiated me with its
reflection from her face. Vanquishing me with the light of her
smile, she said, "Turn back to him and listen, for Paradise is not
only in my eyes."

Just as down here we can sometimes read a person's wish in
his face if it is so intense that it entirely fills his mind, so I could
see, in the flaring of the holy light I turned to, his wish to say
more to me. He began, "The blessed spirits in this fifth section
of the tree that is nourished from its top, that always bears fruit
and never sheds its leaves,[3] are those who down below, before

---

[1] Blessed souls in heaven are sometimes called mirrors because they
reflect the light of God. As Gregory Nuttall notes, Dante sometimes
refers to a soul as glass, diamond, ruby, crystal, amber, gold, or a
rainbow.

[2] I think Dante may have had in mind words of Jesus in Luke 11:46,
"Woe to you authorities in the law, because you weigh people down
with burdens they can hardly carry....", and in Matthew 11:30, "My
yoke is easy and my burden is light." Beatrice is assuring Dante that
she will pray for him in his exile.

[3] The Heaven of Mars is like the fifth branch on a tree that is

they came to heaven, were so admired that any poet would be enriched by them. Therefore, look at the arms of the cross; whoever I name there will be like lightning flashing through a cloud."

I saw a light shoot along the cross the instant Joshua was named, and I did not hear the name before I saw the fact.[4] At the name of the great Maccabee I saw another light spinning, and ecstasy was the cord that whirled it.[5] The same was true for Charlemagne and Roland, two more that I eagerly followed with my eyes the way one watches his falcon as it flies.[6] Then William and Renouard and Duke Godfrey, followed by Robert Guiscard, drew my sight along that cross.[7] Finally the soul who had been talking to me moved and mingled with the other lights and showed me his art in heavenly song.[8]

I turned to my right to Beatrice, to see if she indicated by words or gesture what I should do; and I saw her eyes so clear,

---

nourished from its top (the Crystalline sphere) rather than from below (the earth). Dante is alluding to the heavenly tree in Revelation 22:2 ("that yielded its fruit every month, and its leaves were for the healing of nations") and the ones in Ezekiel 47:12 ("Their leaves will not wither and their fruit will not fail. Every month they will bear, because the water from the sanctuary flows to them. Their fruit will provide food and their leaves will provide healing").

[4] Joshua is the first of eight warriors named by Cacciaguida in the starry cross. He led the Hebrews in their conquest of the Promised Land, as described in the Old Testament book of Joshua.

[5] In the second century before Christ, Judas Maccabaeus defeated Syria in its attempt to oppress the Jews, as described in the book of I Maccabees (between the Old and New Testaments).

[6] Charlemagne (742-814) restored the Holy Roman Empire. His nephew Roland, according to the French epic *Song of Roland*, saved Charlemagne and his army and died a heroic death.

[7] William of Orange and Renouard were heroes of a French epic. William was a real hero in the eighth century, but Renouard was legendary. Godfrey of Bouillon (1058-1100) led the First Crusade and became King of Jerusalem; Robert Guiscard (1015-1085) drove the Byzantines from Southern Italy.

[8] In Cantos 15-18 Cacciaguida has spoken more lines of poetry to Dante than any other soul in *Paradise*. Now he rejoins the choir and sings.

so blissful, that her face surpassed all its former appearances including the last one. And as a man gradually becomes aware that his virtue is increasing when he takes more pleasure in doing good, so when this miracle grew even more beautiful I realized that the circuit of the spheres I was following had expanded.[9] And the kind of change that occurs in a fair-skinned lady as soon as she is relieved of some embarrassment is what I saw when I turned, because the pure white glow of the temperate sixth star had received me.[10]

I saw the sparkling of the love within that Jovial torch[11] forming words that spoke to my eyes. Just as birds soar from a river bank as if rejoicing together over their food, and form first a round cluster, then a long line,[12] so in their lights the sacred spirits sang as they flew—and in their formations made first D, then I, then L. They moved with the rhythm of their song, forming themselves into a letter and then pausing briefly and quietly.

Holy Muse of Pegasus—you who give glory and long life to genius, as with your help genius does the same for cities and kingdoms—shed your light on me so that I may set forth these letters as distinctly as I inscribed them in my mind. Let your power appear in these brief verses.[13]

They arranged themselves in five-times-seven vowels and consonants, and I registered those letters in my mind so they appeared as words to me.[14] The verb and noun DILIGITE

---

[9] In earthly perspective, Dante and Beatrice rotate westward along with the heavenly bodies, and each sphere is larger as they travel upward (outward) from earth.

[10] According to medieval authorities, Jupiter is neither hot like Mars nor cold like Saturn. Thus the Heaven of Jupiter is cool and white in contrast to the warm red of Mars.

[11] Jove is a synonym for Jupiter, and the mood here is jovial.

[12] Dante is apparently referring to a passage from Lucan about the flight patterns of cranes.

[13] This invocation indicates that the following lines will demand more than Dante's usual skill. He appeals to Calliope, the muse of epic poetry, who drinks with other muses at the sacred spring that flowed from the hoofmark of the winged horse Pegasus.

[14] The thirty-five letters appeared one at a time. Dante kept them all

IUSTITIAM appeared first, then QUI IUDICATIS TERRAM.[15] At the end they stayed in place in the M of the fifth word so that Jove's silver looked as if it were embossed with gold. Then I saw other lights descending and settling on top of the M, where they sang, I take it, about the Good that drew them to Itself.[16]

Then like countless sparks that fly upward when burning logs are poked (which some foolish people have taken to be omens), I saw more than a thousand lights ascend—some more, some less, however the Sun from which they sprang ordained it.[17] And when they had all settled into place, I saw an eagle's head and neck outlined by the pattern of the lights.[18] (He who paints with them needs no guide, for He is the Guide; we see in Him the designer of every bird nest.)[19] The other spirits, who

---

in mind to see what message they would spell.

[15] The Latin quotation "Love justice, you who judge the earth" (the opening of the Book of Wisdom of Solomon in the Apocrypha) was spelled out by golden lights on a silver background. Jupiter is the Heaven for just and merciful rulers.

[16] The M formation (a rounded [uncial] M, not a pointed one) with a flock of newly descended lights perching on top of it, will remain in place and change into another formation. Dante has intentionally foreshadowed this shifting image with his description of the shifting formations of flying cranes. M is the exact center of the Latin and Italian alphabets, and most commentators point out that for Dante M stands for Monarchy.

[17] This display obviously resembles some contemporary fireworks.

[18] The eagle is the symbol of the Roman Empire, which to Dante meant the world's only hope for peace and justice; good government was always one of his chief concerns. According to Richard Kay, the astrological association between Jupiter and the urge for power (often resulting in political preeminence) accounts for Jupiter being the sphere for good rulers.

[19] Henry Wadsworth Longfellow responded to this sentence with the following:

The power which built the starry dome on high,
And poised the vaulted rafters of the sky,
Teaches the linnet with unconscious breast
To round the inverted heaven of her nest.

John Ciardi responded to Dante's sentence with the following: "So,

had seemed content to turn the M into a lily, made a slight adjustment to complete the eagle design.[20]

O lovely star, what quality and quantity of gems declared that justice depends on the Heaven you bejewel![21] Therefore I pray to the Mind in which your movement and power began, to watch the place that issues smoke that dims your rays;[22] then His wrath will be kindled again against the buying and selling in the temple whose walls are built by miracles and martyrdoms.[23]

O Heaven's soldiery that I'm recalling now, pray for all those who have gone astray on earth because of bad example.[24] Wars used to be fought with swords; now it is done by withholding, here and there, the bread the tender Father

---

by extension, are all the arts of this world derived from the guidance of the Unguided."

[20] The spirits composing the M had modified it slightly to form the heraldic lily design (fleur-de-lys) that symbolized the French monarchy; but that passing phase is only mentioned by Dante as an afterthought. The Dorothy Sayers and Mark Musa translations of *Paradise* both include illustrations of all four formations in their notes.

[21] Jupiter is like a jewel decorating Heaven, and the spirits are like jewels decorating Jupiter.

[22] Dante prays to God to watch the Vatican, which was issuing the smoke of injustice. Although I am not aware of other commentators saying so, it seems obvious to me that Dante is alluding to a custom that began in his own lifetime: white smoke is issued from the Vatican by the College of Cardinals when they select a new pope. Dante is saying that some of these selections obscured and diminished justice.

[23] Dante is referring to the wrath of Jesus in Matthew 21:12-13, "Jesus entered the temple area and drove out all who were buying and selling there. He overturned the tables of the money changers and the benches of those selling doves." (Jesus told them the temple was supposed to be a house of prayer but they had made it a den of thieves.) The Christian church in Dante's day was misused as badly as the Hebrew temple had been in Christ's day.

[24] There is some disagreement about Dante's location and orientation when he expresses this sentiment. Is Dante the poet back on earth recalling the spirits in the Heaven of Jupiter? Not in my opinion. I think that Dante the pilgrim is in the Heaven of Jupiter recalling the soldier spirits he left recently in the Heaven of Mars.

withholds from no one. But you who write in order to delete,[25] remember Peter and Paul, who died for the vineyard you spoil; they are still alive.[26] Well may you plead, "I am so intent on the one who lived alone and was led to martyrdom by a dance, that I don't know the fisherman or Pauley."[27]

---

[25] Dante is addressing Pope John XXII and accusing him of arbitrarily excommunicating church members so they will pay to have the excommunication revoked.

[26] Dante may be insinuating that Peter and Paul have reason to pray to God for this pope's downfall.

[27] Dante identifies John the Baptist by his lonely life as a desert prophet and his brutal death. (Because Salome delighted Herod with her dance, he granted her wish for the head of John the Baptist on a platter. See Matthew 14:3-12.) Dante bitterly accuses the pope of caring so much about the image of John the Baptist on gold florins that he has forgotten about two great Christian leaders who lived sacrificially and died as martyrs — Peter (a fisherman) and Paul. By putting words into the pope's mouth, Dante has him refer to Peter and Paul with casual contempt. The last word in Canto 18, *Polo*, is a kind of nickname. Elsewhere Dante refers to Paul properly, as *Paulo*. Thus Canto 18 ends with Dante railing against disgraceful church leadership.

CANTO NINETEEN

The Eagle's Beak

Now the beautiful image appeared with wings outstretched, composed of interwoven souls rejoicing in their sweet fruition. Each soul looked like a ruby burning in sunlight, lit so that the full sun was reflected into my eyes.

Never before has any voice told or ink written or imagination conceived of what I must now recount; I watched and listened to the beak talk and heard it say *I* and *mine*, when the meaning was *we* and *our*.[1]

It began: "Because I was just and merciful, I am lifted up to this glory that cannot be surpassed by any longing; and on earth my memory is such that even evildoers praise it in spite of the fact that they don't follow my example." Just as we feel one warm glow from many coals, so from those many loving souls a single sound issued from that image.

At that I answered, "O everlasting blossoms of eternal joy, you whose many fragrances are perceived as one perfume, with your breath please relieve the lack that has long famished me because on earth I found no food for it. I realize that although another realm of Heaven is the mirror of God's justice,[2] yours perceives it unveiled. You know how eager I am to listen; you know the question that has tantalized me so long."[3]

---

[1] The many souls composing the Eagle spoke in unison, referring to themselves with singular pronouns rather than plural because all righteous rulers function as one. The Eagle represents all good rulers, as well as the Roman Empire at its best.

[2] The realm of Saturn is the sphere of God's judgments.

[3] Dante is still deeply troubled about the fate of righteous non-Christians like Virgil. In my opinion he expects the souls who lovingly dispensed justice and mercy on earth to understand how the loving justice and mercy of God can exclude righteous non-Christians from Heaven.

The emblem composed of praises of divine grace[4] responded
with songs of the kind known to those who rejoice on high—as
a falcon released from its hood[5] shakes its head and flaps its
wings, preening itself and showing its eagerness.

Then it began, "He who turned His compass around the cir-
cumference of the universe,[6] and set within it all that is hidden
and all that is revealed, could not include enough of His
goodness in His creation that there would not be an infinite
amount of His Word left out. And this is demonstrated by the
first proud being, who was the highest of all creatures; because
he would not wait for the light, he fell before he was ripe.[7]
Thus it is clear that each lesser being is a container too small for
that boundless good which can be measured only by itself.

"As a result of its very nature, our perception—which has to
be only one of the rays of the Mind that penetrates every-

---

[4] The emblem is the Eagle on the flag of the Roman Empire, and the
praises of divine grace are joyful souls.

[5] A falconer would put a hood on the falcon's head while trans-
porting it, then remove the hood when they arrived where it would be
allowed to fly. Here the Eagle is likened to a joyful falcon, and Dante
will soon liken it to a nurturing stork.

[6] The Eagle refers to creation as described in Proverbs 8:23-29, in
which Wisdom says, "I was appointed ages ago, at the beginning before
the world began.... I was there when He set the heavens in their place,
when He set a compass to mark the horizon on the face of the deep...." It
also refers to the related passage in Job 38: 4-7, in which God answers
Job's complaint about injustice with a startling reply: "Where were you
when I laid the foundations of the earth? Tell me about it, if you know
so much. Who marked off its dimensions? Surely you know all about it!
Who stretched his measuring line across it? On what do its supports
rest, and who laid its cornerstone in place, while the morning stars
sang together and all the angels shouted for joy?" The finite mind of a
mere mortal cannot begin to fully understand God's nature and His
justice. Psalm 104 contains a similar passage.

[7] The first proud being was the angel Lucifer (Satan), who rebelled
because he wanted immediate power and glory equal to God's and did
not realize how limited his capacity for it was. As Gregory Nuttall
points out, Dante likens pride to unripeness; thus Lucifer is the opposite
of the blessed souls in the Heaven of Jupiter "rejoicing in their sweet
fruition." (Medieval astrologers associated Jupiter with fruit.)

thing—must realize that it lacks enough power to understand as much as our Source does. Therefore when it comes to eternal justice the amount of perception available to those in your world is inadequate, like the eye's inadequacy to see through ocean water. Although the eye can see the ocean bottom near the shore, in the open sea it cannot; for although the ocean bottom is still there, the depth conceals it.[8] There is no light except from that Serenity which never is disturbed; the rest is darkness or the shadow of the flesh or its poisoner.[9]

"Now the labyrinth that hid the living Justice that you frequently questioned has been opened enough for you. For you used to say, 'A man is born near the banks of the Indus where there is no one to tell about Christ, and no one to read, and no one to write;[10] and all the man's desires and deeds are good so far as human reason can make out—sinless in deed and word. He dies unbaptized and without faith—how can justice condemn him? How he can be blamed for not believing?'

"Who are you to sit in a judgment seat a thousand miles away when you can't see farther than a handbreadth? Surely the man who engages me in subtleties would have serious grounds for his doubting, if it weren't for the authority of Scripture. O earthly animals! O doltish minds! The Primal Will, goodness itself, never deviates from itself, which is Supreme Good. All that is just harmonizes with it;[11] it does not

---

[8] The Eagle seems to allude to Psalm 36:6, "Your righteousness is like the mighty mountains, your justice like the great deep...." Thus man cannot possibly penetrate God's justice.

[9] The only true intellectual light for humans is the serene light of God's grace; everything else mistaken for light is darkness—either the shadow of ignorance or the poison of sin. In Canto 19 Dante may have in mind John 1:1-5, 9: "In the beginning was the Word, and the Word was with God, and the Word was God. He was with God in the beginning. Through him all things were made; without him nothing was made that has been made. In him was life, and that life was the light of men. The light shines in the darkness, but the darkness has not understood it.... The true light that gives light to every man was coming into the world."

[10] India represents any place where people lack access to Christianity.

[11] Conformity with the will of God is the perfect standard of

approximate any created good, but gives rise to that good by beaming forth its rays."

As a stork circles above her nest after feeding her brood, and as the chick she fed looks up at her, so the blessed image did— its wings moved by many wills—and so I did.[12] As it wheeled, it sang; and then it said, "As my songs are beyond your understanding, so divine justice is beyond mortal understanding."

When these bright flames of the Holy Spirit fell silent, still forming the emblem that gained the Romans reverence all over the world, the emblem began again: "No one has risen to this kingdom who lacked faith in Christ, either before or after He was nailed to the tree. But many cry 'Christ, Christ,' who at the judgment shall be even farther from Him than those who don't know Christ;[13] and the Ethiopians shall put them to shame when the two groups are separated, the one forever rich, the

---

goodness and the ultimate test of justice.

[12] Dante asked the Eagle "to relieve the lack that has long famished me because on earth I found no food for it." I have not seen Psalm 104 mentioned by others who analyze Canto 19, but I consider it central here and in all of *Paradise*. In the midst of the Psalmist's jubilant song about the amazing diversity of God's creation, which is beyond human comprehension, he mentions the nest of the stork and says of God's creatures "These all look to you to give them their food at the proper time." The food Dante hungers for is true understanding, and the food the Eagle gives him is much like God's trans-rational answer to Job—a demand for faith in God's goodness. This is also the outcome for Orual in C. S. Lewis's finest novel, *Till We Have Faces*: "I know now, Lord, why you utter no answer. You are yourself the answer. Before your face questions die away. What other answer would suffice?" Job, Dante, and Orual are all satisfied—because although they did not get the kind of explanation they sought, their real underlying question was answered: "God, are you good? Do you love us? Can I trust you?"

[13] Here for the third time in *Paradise* Dante has ended three lines with *Cristo*, for a total of nine. His point is that insincere professing Christians are much farther from Christ than the virtuous unbelievers. He is referring to Matthew 7:21, "Not everyone who says to me Lord, Lord, shall enter the kingdom of heaven, but he who does the will of my Father in heaven," and Matthew 25, which says that disregard of the humble and needy counts as neglect of Christ Himself, and kindness to the humble and needy counts as kindness to Christ.

other poor.[14] What will the Persians[15] say to your kings when they see the volume opened in which all your rulers' misdeeds are recorded?[16]

"There shall be seen[17] among the deeds of Albert something to make all the realm of Prague a desert and set the pen in motion.[18]

---

[14] Ethiopians are those who have not heard about Christ. In my opinion the riches described here are those described by Wisdom in Proverbs 8, a chapter that in its entirety must have been dear to Dante's heart. Wisdom declares, "To you, O men, I call out; I raise my voice to all mankind …. Counsel and sound judgment are mine; I have understanding and power. By me kings reign and rulers make laws that are just; by me princes govern, and all nobles who rule on earth. I love those who love me, and those who seek me find me. With me are riches and honor, enduring wealth and prosperity. My fruit is better than fine gold; what I yield surpasses choice silver. I walk in the way of righteousness, along the paths of justice, bestowing wealth on those who love me and making their treasuries full. For whoever finds me finds life and receives favor from the Lord. But whoever fails to find me harms himself; all who hate me love death." This teaching and the teaching that faith in Christ is the only way to Heaven seem mutually exclusive; but the Bible has it both ways—and so does Dante.

[15] Like the aforementioned Indians and Ethiopians, Persians have not heard about Christ. The eagle has included representatives of three major regions where most people never heard of Christ in Dante's day: the Indian subcontinent, what we now call the Middle East, and Africa.

[16] Virtuous unbelievers will be shocked by misdeeds of Christians revealed at the Final Judgment as described in Revelation 20:12. (Richard Kay points out that because astrologers associated Jupiter with the act of writing, Dante refers to it several times in Cantos 18-20—most notably in golden words spelled out letter by letter and by the writing in the book of judgment.)

[17] Rulers are described in three triple sets of tercets (three-line stanzas), with nine lines in each set. The first lines of the first three tercets begin with *Li si vedrà*; the first lines of the fourth through sixth tercets begin with *Vedrassi*, and the first lines of the seventh through ninth tercets begin with the Italian word for *and*, which is *E*. Thus the initials of the first lines form an acrostic, spelling the Italian word for pestilence. (Jupiter is traditionally connected to good nutrition and health, and the eagle has mentioned wrong choices leading to green

"There shall be seen how the one who will die from a wild boar's thrust brought grief on the Seine by making false coinage.[19]

"There shall be seen the pride that so parches and maddens the Scot and Englishman that they won't stay within their borders.[20]

"That book will show the licentious and indolent life of the Spaniard and the Bohemian, who knew nothing about valor and never wanted to.[21]

"That book will show the cripple of Jerusalem, his good deeds totaling I and his bad deeds totaling M.[22]

"That book will show the greed and cowardice of the ruler of the Isle of Fire, where Anchises ended his long life.[23]

"And to make clear how little he is worth, his record shall be written in miniature to squeeze much data into very little space.[24]

---

fruit, poison, and pestilence,) Although most readers are skeptical about Walter Arensberg's ambitious volume *The Cryptography of Dante* (see the second footnote in *Dante's Divine Comedy, Inferno*), commentators are agreed about this acrostic and the earlier one spelling *uom* (man) in Canto 12 of *Purgatory*.

[18] "German Albert" was castigated by Dante in Cantos 6 and 7 of *Purgatory*, and he comes first in the Eagle's list of contemporary rulers (all professing Christians) whose misdeeds will be exposed at the Final Judgment. The Roman Emperor, Albert I, would cause the recording angel to enter his ruthless invasion of Bohemia (1304) in the book of judgment.

[19] Philip the Fair of France allegedly debased the coinage to one third of its value in order to meet the expenses of his Flemish campaigns. He died in 1314 in a boarhunting accident.

[20] This is a reference to Dante's contemporaries Robert the Bruce and William Wallace, who fought Edward I and Edward II in the Border Wars.

[21] The Spaniard was King Ferdinand IV, and the Bohemian was Wenceslaus IV.

[22] Charles II of Anjou (Charles the Lame) titled himself King of Jerusalem. In the angel's record book he will get credit for one good deed for every 1000 bad deeds.

[23] Frederick II ruled Sicily (land of an active volcano), where the father of Aeneas died.

"And plain to all shall be the foul deeds of his uncle and his brother, who cuckolded a fine family and two crowns.[25]

"And the Portuguese and the Norwegian shall be exposed there, and the Rascian who to his misfortune saw the coin of Venice.[26]

"O happy Hungary, if she avoids further abuse![27] And happy Navarre, if she is armored by her mountain range![28] For everyone should take warning from Nicosia and Famagosta, which already wail and shriek because of their own beast, who runs with all the rest of this pack."[29]

---

[24] Frederick's manifold misdeeds were recorded by the angel in shorthand.

[25] Frederick's uncle was King James of Majorca, and his brother was King James II of Aragon. They were both a disgrace.

[26] The king of Norway was Hacon VII, the king of Portugal was Dionysus, and the king of Rascia (part of Serbia) was Orosius II. The latter counterfeited the Venetian ducat, and John Ciardi points out that this will earn him a place with other counterfeiters down in the tenth ditch of Hell (see *Inferno.*, Canto 30).

[27] The king of long-suffering Hungary was Andrew III.

[28] The king of Navarre (located in what is now southern France and Spain) was Louis, who inherited the throne of France in 1314. This led to Navarre's unfortunate domination by France, which lay beyond the Pyrenees.

[29] Nicosia and Famagosta were towns in Cyprus already suffering under the misrule of "their own beast," Henry II of France.

The Eagle
Gustave Doré (Canto 20)

CANTO TWENTY

The Eagle's Eye

When the one who illuminates all the world sinks from our hemisphere and on every side daylight is ending, the sky that was lit by him alone promptly reappears lit by many lights in which he shines afresh.[1] This sky change came to my mind when the blessed beak of the emblem of the world and its leaders fell silent—because all the living lights, shining much brighter, launched into songs that escape my memory. O sweet love, wrapped in a smile, how fervently you were expressed by those flutes filled with nothing but the breath of sacred thoughts![2]

When the precious, shining stones that gemmed the Sixth Heaven had silenced their angelic chimes, I heard what sounded like the murmuring of a clear river dropping from rock to rock, indicating the copiousness of its spring. As notes are formed in the neck of a lute or the air vent of bagpipes, so to end my suspense the Eagle's murmuring rose up through its neck as if it were hollow; and there it became a voice that emerged from its beak in the form of words my heart was waiting for—and there I wrote them down.[3]

"Now watch closely the part of me that sees (and in mortal eagles can endure) the Sun," it began, "for of all the fires that

---

[1] In Dante's time it was commonly believed that, like moonlight, the light of all the stars was reflected sunlight.

[2] According to Richard Kay, the reason Dante related the souls in Jupiter to several musical instruments (flutes, chimes, guitar, bagpipe, and lute) is that according to medieval astrology Jupiter influenced people to enjoy musical instruments.

[3] Dante wanted to know who the souls were in the Eagle, and he memorized the names.

compose my form, those that make my eye[4] shine in my head are of the highest rank.

"The one who shines in the center, the pupil, was the Holy Spirit's songwriter who carried the ark from city to city.[5] Now he knows the value of his songs, insofar as they were his, because of his commensurate reward.[6]

"Of the five who compose the eyebrow's arch, the one closest to the beak consoled the Widow for her son. Now he knows

---

[4] The Roman Eagle has only one eye because its head is seen only in profile. The eye is composed of six souls, and each will be identified by two tercets. In each case, the second tercet begins with the phrase "And now he knows ...."

[5] King David (circa 1000 B.C.) brought the ark—the chest where the Spirit of God was manifest in a special way—into the city of Jerusalem, as recorded in 2 Samuel 6. There is no question that in Dante's mind Jerusalem was connected to the Roman Empire; as noted by Barbara Reynolds, in *Convivio (The Banquet)* Dante said, "It was in the very same age that David was born and Rome was born, that is, that Aeneas came from Troy to Italy, which was the origin of the most noble city of Rome, as the records testify; so that the divine choice of the Roman Empire is manifest from the birth of the holy city being contemporaneous with the root of Mary's race."

[6] What David inherited, presumably, was joy about the role his art played in God's plan for blessing the world. Dante was interested in the mysterious way that God's will and human will work together in creativity. It seems to me that although Dante was concentrating on David here, he was also commenting on all artists and artisans and on his *Comedy* in particular. Furthermore, in my opinion, when Dorothy Sayers translated this tercet into English *terza rima* in 1957, she had her own writing in mind as well as David's and Dante's. She had written an entire play, "The Zeal of Thy House," about this topic. Her translation of this tercet is "And now he knows how much his own songs merit/ So far as 'twas his art that shaped the strain/ For even as he deserved, he doth inherit." There is extraordinary poignancy in these three lines in light of the fact that shortly after completing Canto 20, she suddenly collapsed and died, on December 17, 1957. Instead of completing her *Divine Comedy*, she experienced for herself what truth is in the words "And now she knows how much her own songs merit/ So far as 'twas her art that shaped the strain/ For even as she deserved, she doth inherit."

from his experience of this sweet life and its opposite the price of not following Christ.[7]

"And the next one on the upswing of the curved line I am describing delayed his death with his true penitence. Now he knows that when a worthy prayer delays until tomorrow what would have happened today, the eternal judgment is not changed.[8]

The next who follows, whose good intention bore evil fruit, made himself and the laws and me all Greek in order to position the Shepherd. Now he knows that the evil result of his good deed does him no harm, even if it wrecks the world.[9]

And the one you see on the downslope of the curve is William, mourned by the same land that grieves because Charles and Frederick live. Now he knows how Heaven is in love with a righteous king, and he also makes that visible with his radiance.[10]

---

[7] This is the pagan emperor Trajan (ruler from 98 to 117 A.D.) whose kindness to a widow was depicted in Canto 10 of *Purgatory*. His inclusion here and his experiences of Hell and Heaven will be soon be explained by the Eagle. (In *The Great Divorce* C. S. Lewis had George MacDonald refer to Lewis's familiarity with this passage. Lewis asked MacDonald if visitors from Hell to Heaven can really stay, and he answered, "Aye. Ye'll have heard that the emperor Trajan did.")

[8] King Hezekiah of Judah (circa 700 B.C.) prayed for his life when he would have died, and thus received an extra fifteen years. (See 2 Kings 18-20 and 2 Chronicles 29-32. Hezekiah's humility and gratitude are expressed in Isaiah 38:1-22.) As John Ciardi points out, in Canto 6 of *Purgatory* Dante dealt with the apparent paradox of God's preordained will and the efficacy of prayer.

[9] The first Christian Emperor, Constantine (ruler from 306 to 337), is at the crest of the eyebrow; on earth he moved himself, the government, and the flag of the Empire east to Byzantium (Constantinople). As a result, the Church hierarchy in Rome was able to acquire great secular power and wealth, which promptly corrupted it. Dante has already deplored this disaster in Canto 19 of the *Inferno*, Canto 32 of *Purgatory*, and Canto 6 of *Paradise*. [10] After William the Good of southern Italy and Sicily (ruler from 1166 to 1189), Charles II of Anjou and Frederick II of Aragon took his place. They were condemned in Canto 19.

"Who would believe, down in the erring world, that Ripheus the Trojan could be the fifth sacred light in this curve? Now he knows much of the divine grace that the world cannot comprehend, although his sight cannot reach the bottom of it."[11]

That emblem—stamped by the eternal Will by which love makes everything what it really is—seemed to me like a lark that soars in the air, first singing and then silent, satisfied with the last sweetness that has satiated her. And although my question showed through me as clearly as color shows through glass that covers it, yet it could not bear to wait silently; the pressure of its weight thrust it from my lips—"How can this be?" And at that I saw a glad festival of flashing lights.

With its eye even brighter, the blessed emblem answered me immediately to avoid prolonging my suspense: "I see that you believe these things because I tell them to you, but you don't see how they can be true; thus, although you believe them, they are obscured. You are like one who knows something by its name but cannot see its essence unless someone else explains it. The Kingdom of Heaven suffers violence from ardent love and living hope that can overcome the eternal Will—not in the way men overcome each other, but because it wants to be overcome, and, being overcome, overcomes with benevolence.[12]

---

[11] Ripheus (circa 1200 B.C.), who died in battle, was described by Virgil as the most just and zealous for good of all the Trojans. Although there is no evidence that he ever existed, Dante treats him as a historical character and, more important, an example of a pagan saved by God's inscrutable grace. In my opinion, C. S. Lewis had Ripheus in mind when he described a virtuous pagan soldier named Emeth dying in *The Last Battle* and finding himself in Heaven.

[12] See Matthew 11:12, "From the days of John the Baptist until now the kingdom of heaven suffers violence, and the violent take it by force." Although this verse refers to evil powers, the Eagle quotes from it to explain that God wills that human love and faith in Him can prevail over the justice that excludes all unbelievers from Heaven. (I suspect that Dante was also alluding here to Revelation 17:14, "They will war against the Lamb, but the Lamb will overcome them because He is Lord of lords and King of kings; and His called, chosen and faithful

"The first and fifth souls in the eyebrow amaze you because you see them beautifying the angelic realm. They did not leave their bodies as pagans, but as Christians, trusting in the wounded Feet and the Feet that would be wounded.[13]

"One of them returned to his bones from Hell (where none get another chance at right choices), and this was the reward of living hope; the living hope that empowered the prayers made to God to raise him up so that his will could be reactivated. This glorious soul I'm speaking of, returning to the flesh where it lived again briefly, believed in Him who had the power to rescue him; and that belief kindled such a great flame of true love that at his second death he was fit to enter this festivity.[14]

"The other, by the grace that wells up from such a deep spring that no created eye has ever plumbed the depths of its source, set all his love below on righteousness; and therefore, by grace on grace, God let him see our future redemption.[15] Thus he believed; from then on he could not bear the stench of paganism, and he warned the obstinate people about perversity. More than a thousand years before baptism, the three ladies you saw by the right wheel were his baptism for him.[16]

---

followers will be with Him."

[13] The first and fifth souls both died as Christians because of faith in Christ's atoning sacrifice (before or after His feet were wounded on the cross).

[14] Thomas Aquinas recounted the popular medieval story about Gregory (Pope from 590 to 606) praying to God for the salvation of Trajan, and God granting the prayer; according to this story, God had predestined him to be saved by Gregory's prayers. Because no one in Hell can be saved, Thomas thought Trajan's salvation was probably accomplished by a brief return to his body, in which he chose to trust Christ.

[15] The first kind of grace is God's actively reaching out to His beloved creature, and the second kind of grace is His helping the beloved creature to reach back. C. S. Lewis described this paradoxical relationship in his untitled poem about prayer in his final book, *Letters to Malcolm*. (Unfortunately, in Lewis's posthumous poetry collection, where this poem is titled "Prayer," over half the lines were changed by the editor.)

[16] By special revelation, God enabled Ripheus to become a Christian

'O predestination, how far you are rooted from any vision that does not see the First Cause in its entirety! And you mortals, restrain yourselves from judging; for even we who see God do not know yet all the roll of His elect. Yet our limitation is sweet to us, because our good is perfected in this good: that what God wills, we also will."[17]

So this is how the divine emblem gave me sweet medicine to cure my shortsightedness. And just as a skillful lutanist[18] will make his quivering strings accompany a good singer to increase the pleasure of the song, so while he spoke I remember seeing the two blessed lights, like two eyes that blink of one accord, moving their flames to accompany his words.

---

more than a millennium before Christ, midway between the lives of Joshua and David. His baptism was accomplished by the three virtues that accompanied Beatrice in Canto 29 of *Purgatory*, Faith, Hope and Charity. (At this point in Canto 20 both Trajan and Ripheus have been individually commemorated in a total of six tercets each. There are, of course, six souls in the eye of the Eagle.)

[17] The Eagle finally uses the plural pronouns *we, us* and *our* here because this time he is speaking for all souls in Heaven, not just those in the Heaven of Jupiter.

[18] A lute is a stringed instrument rather similar to a guitar.

CANTO TWENTY-ONE

The Seventh Heaven: Saturn

My eyes were set on my Lady's face again now, and my mind with them, removed from everything else; but she did not smile.

"If I were to smile," she began, "you would be like Semele when she was burned to ashes;[1] for my beauty (which blazes brighter when we ascend higher, as you have seen) radiates so brilliantly that your mortal senses would be like foliage shattered by a thunderbolt if it were not subdued. We have arisen to the seventh splendor, which beneath the burning Lion's breast joins with his power beaming down.[2] Focus your mind along with your eyes so they reflect the figure that this mirror shall reflect to you."[3]

Anyone who could understand what it was like for my sight to pasture in her blessed face would realize what joy it was to obey my heavenly guide by transferring elsewhere, because one joy balanced the other.[4] Inside the crystal that carries around the world the name of its dear ruler beneath whom all evil lay dead,[5] I saw a ladder the color of light-reflecting gold, raised so high that my sight could not follow it. And I saw so

---

[1] Semele insisted upon seeing the full splendor of her lover, Jupiter, and it incinerated her with a thunderbolt.

[2] The Seventh Heaven is that of the "cold" planet, Saturn. In March and April of 1300 Saturn was in conjunction with the constellation of Leo.

[3] Each of the lower Heavens is like a mirror reflecting aspects of the Highest Heaven to Dante.

[4] The pleasure of gazing at Beatrice was matched by the pleasure of obeying her.

[5] The god Saturn, father of Jupiter, ruled in the mythical golden age of history.

many splendors coming down its rungs that I thought every light that shines in heaven was pouring down.[6]

As crows instinctively take off in a flock at the beginning of the day to warm their chilled feathers—then some depart without returning, others come back to where they started, and others wheel around—it seemed to me that so did those luminescences as soon as they had descended together to a certain level. The one who was closest to us became so bright that in my mind I said, "I see the love you are signaling to me. But she from whom I await the how and when of speech and silence pauses, and thus I rightly refrain from asking, although I would like to."

At that she who saw my silence in the sight of the One who sees everything said to me, "Give way to your eager desire."

So I began, "I am not worthy of an answer from you; but for the sake of her who gave me permission to ask, O blessed soul hidden inside your bliss, let me know why you have come so close to me. And tell me why the sweet symphony of Paradise that rang so prayerfully in the realms below is silent here."

"You have mortal hearing and sight," he answered me, "and thus there is no song for the same reason that Beatrice doesn't smile. I came down the steps of the sacred ladder this far just to welcome you with my words and the light that surrounds me. And my eager descent is not the utmost in love; for the flaming here gives you an idea of how the love up higher burns.[7] The high love that causes us to eagerly serve the Wisdom that governs the world assigns us as you see us."

---

[6] This is the famous image that Jacob saw in a dream in Genesis 28:12. It is the third symbol of this kind presented to Dante. (He already saw the Cross of martyrs in Mars and the Eagle of just rulers in Jupiter.) The Ladder is the symbol of contemplatives, Christians devoted to quietly nurturing a direct spiritual experience of God. Some Roman Catholics have taught that the angels descending Jacob's ladder symbolized contemplatives who descend from spiritual heights to teach ordinary Christians what they have learned.

[7] This soul's great love for Dante is evident in his eagerness and his brilliance, but that much love and more exists in the still higher Heavens.

"O sacred lamp," I said, "I see that in this dominion unfettered love is enough to cause conformity to eternal providence, but here is what I find hard to understand: why you alone among your companions have been predestined to this task."

Before I came to my last word, the light made his center point into an axle and whirled himself around it like a swift millstone.[8] Then the love within him answered, "The divine light focuses itself on me, piercing into the light in which I am embodied. The power of this, added to my sight, lifts me so far above myself that I can see the Supreme Essence that is its source.[9] The joy with which I flame comes from this: its brilliance is equivalent to the clarity of my sight. But even the spirit in heaven that is most illuminated, the Seraph whose eye is most focused on God, could not satisfy your question—because the thing you ask lies so deep in the abyss of eternal Wisdom that it is hidden from all created sight. So when you return to the mortal world, take the message that it should no longer presume to move its feet toward such an exalted goal. The mind that is aflame here is only smoky there; consider, therefore, how it could have an ability down there that it doesn't have even when received into heaven."

His words imposed such restriction on me that I abandoned that question and was limited to humbly asking who he was. "'Between the two shores of Italy, not far from your birthplace, cliffs rise so high that thunder booms far lower down; they form a humped ridge called Catria, beneath which a consecrated hermitage used to be devoted to worship."[10]

---

[8] The soul spins with joy in response to Dante's question about predestination. The center of his ecstatic spinning is love, and John Ciardi makes a good case for his theory that the soul continues to spin through the entire canto.

[9] As Sheila Ralphs explains in *Etterno Spiro: A Study of the Nature of Dante's Paradise*, "Dante distinguishes three words in particular which refer to light—*luce*, which is light itself, *raggio*, which is the raying forth of light, and *splendore*, which is the glory of the light revealing itself in created beings. *Splendore* is what results from the raying forth of light."

[10] The monastery of Fonte Avellana is located on the Apennines.

Thus he began his third discourse for me and continued, "There I became so rooted in serving God that I bore heat and cold easily, with only olive juice, content with contemplation.[11] That cloister used to produce ample harvest for these heavens, but now it has become so unproductive that this will soon have to be revealed. I, Peter Damian, was in that very place; and I, Peter the Sinner, was in the house of Our Lady on the Adriatic shore.[12]

"Not much of my mortal life remained when I was called and dragged to the hat that goes from bad to worse recipients.[13] Cephas and the great vessel of the Holy Spirit came lean and barefooted, finding their food wherever they could lodge.[14] But today's pastors are so obese that they must have someone to brace them on either side, and one in front and one to hoist behind. With their cloaks spread over their horses, two beasts move along under one hide.[15] O heavenly patience, how much longer will you continue!"[16]

---

[11] The extremely abstemious diet at this monastery included common olive oil for the bread rather than butterfat or animal fat. Those monks were required to go barefoot with no protection from heat and cold.

[12] There is no question about the identity of Peter Damien; he was a brilliant and zealous reform-minded monk of the monastery of Fonte Avellana on the slope of Monte Catria and became the abbot in 1043. Scholars disagree about his reference to Peter the Sinner. As John Ciardi concludes, all that most readers need to know is that Peter Damian went by both names and lived for two years in the monastery of Santa Maria Pomposa in Ravenna ("by the Adriatic").

[13] In 1057 Peter Damian was reluctantly installed as Cardinal bishop of Ostia. In fact, the traditional Cardinal's red hat did not exist until 200 years after Peter, but the point is clear: by 1300 the office of Cardinal had started passing from unworthy recipients to even worse ones.

[14] Peter (John 1:42) and Paul (Acts 9:15) were willing to forego the comforts of materialism in order to serve Christ (Luke 10:4-7).

[15] Peter Damien contrasts the selfless dedication of early church leaders with the greed, sloth, and arrogance of decadent church leaders in 1300, bitterly lampooning the latter. In *Paradise* perfect bliss does not preclude righteous indignation, and the common assumption that

At these words I saw many precious flames descend from step to step and whirl, and every whirl made them more beautiful. They came and gathered around this soul and raised such a deep cry that there is nothing similar; but I could not understand it because I was stunned by the thunder.[17]

---

blessed spirits in *Paradise* have turned into some kind of bland, mindless entities is utterly wrong.

[16] This exclamation is a cry for punishment of the corrupt church hierarchy, and Mark Musa suggests that it echoes Romans 9:22.

[17] Other joyfully whirling souls thundered their agreement with Peter Damien so loudly that Dante could not make out their words.

Beatrice
Gustave Doré (Canto 21)

CANTO TWENTY-TWO

St. Benedict's Answer

Overwhelmed with astonishment, I turned to my guide—
like a startled child who always runs to the one with whom he
feels safest.

And she, like a mother who is quick to soothe her pale and
panting child with her calming voice, said to me, "Don't you
know that you are in Heaven? And don't you know that
Heaven is completely holy, and that everything done here is
done in righteous zeal? Since this cry has shaken you, imagine
how you would have been undone by my smile. If you had
understood their prayer, you would already know about the
vengeance you will see before you die. (The sword of Heaven
does not cut too early or too late, except in the opinion of one
who longs for it or dreads it.) But turn and look at the others; for
if you follow my suggestion you will see many great souls."

I looked in the direction she indicated and saw a hundred
precious globes shining together, made more beautiful by each
other's glow. I stood still there like one resisting a strong urge,
not venturing to ask a question for fear of being too bold. Then
the largest and most luminous of these pearls came forward to
satisfy my desire to know about him.

Next I heard from within it, "If you could see as I do the love
that burns in us, you would speak your thoughts. But to avoid
delay on your way to your high destination, I will answer the
question that you are too discreet to ask. The summit upon
whose slope Cassino lies was once inhabited by deluded and ill-
disposed people; and I am the one who first carried up there the
name of the One who brought to earth the truth that lifts us on
high.[1] Such great grace shone upon me that I converted those
villages from the false religion that had seduced everyone.[2]

---

[1] Dante's readers would realize from the geography that this con-
templative was St. Benedict (480-543), founder of the Benedictine Order

"These other flames were all contemplatives kindled by that warmth which produces holy flowers and fruits. This one is Maccario, this one is Romoaldo, and these are my brothers who kept their footsteps in the cloisters and kept their hearts pure."[3]

I answered, "The affection you show in speaking with me — and the kind appearance I see and note in the fires of all of you — expand my confidence just as the sun expands a rose in full bloom. Therefore I pray, Father, for you to reassure me if I may I receive enough grace to behold your face uncovered."

At that he said, "Brother, your lofty desire shall be fulfilled in the final sphere, along with all the others and my own; there and there alone every desire is perfect, ripe, and whole.[4] There everything is where it always was, because it is not in space, nor does it have poles.[5] And our ladder goes clear up there, which is why it soars beyond your sight.[6] The patriarch Jacob saw its topmost part reaching that high when it appeared to him laden with angels.[7]

---

and monasticism in the West. In about 525 he and his followers moved to Monte Cassino.

[2] A temple of Apollo and a grove of Venus existed at the town of Cassino, and Benedict turned that pagan site into the site of his great central monastery.

[3] Maccario was probably St. Maccario the Younger of Alexandria (died in 404), founder of monasticism in the East. Romoaldo (956-1027) was founder of the Camaldoli or Reformed Benedictines; he reportedly changed their black robes to white after a vision of monks climbing a ladder to heaven. Benedict contrasts these two to the kind of wandering mendicant monks who preceded Benedict's rules.

[4] Although he is extremely illustrious, St. Benedict corrects Dante about how to address him; in Heaven he answers to the egalitarian term "Brother" rather than the deferential "Father." Dante won't see Benedict directly until they are in the Empyrean, the very Highest Heaven.

[5] The Highest Heaven does not move or revolve (around poles), because it is not in space; it exists in the mind of God.

[6] Benedict refers to the symbolic golden ladder composed of contemplative Christians described in Canto 21.

[7] Genesis 27 tells how Abraham's grandson Jacob cheated his twin brother Essau out of his birthright and had to leave home for his own

"But now no one lifts his feet from the earth to climb it, and my Rule serves only to waste the parchment it is written on. The walls that used to house an abbey have become dens; and the monks' hoods, sacks of rancid meal.[8] Even compound usury is not so offensive to God as the fruit that makes the hearts of monks go mad; for anything entrusted to the Church belongs to the needy who request it in God's name — and not to monks' family members or worse relations.[9]

"Human flesh is so weak that down on earth a good beginning is not enough to reach from the sprouting of an oak tree to when it bears acorns. Peter began his gathering without gold or silver, I began mine with prayers and fasting, and Francis began his with humility; but if you look at the beginning of each one and look at how it has strayed, you will see how the whiteness has darkened. Yet a rescue here would not be such an amazing sight as the Jordan flowing backwards and the parting of the sea at God's will."[10]

---

safety. Genesis 28:12 tells how Jacob slept on the ground and dreamed of a ladder reaching to heaven. God was at the top of the ladder and spoke to Jacob, blessing him. The next day Jacob piled up a landmark of stones on that spot and planned to name it Bethel. His famous dream probably occurred circa 1950 B.C.

[8] Monks no longer cared about the symbolic ladder of contemplation included in St. Benedict's *Rules of Monks*, which was no longer worth the paper it was written on. The Benedictine house of prayer had become a den of thieves (see Christ's denunciation of the Temple in Matthew 21:13). Although I have come across no commentary suggesting a Biblical reference for the symbolic sacks of rotten meal, I think Dante is alluding to Exodus 16, in which the children of Israel were ordered to trust God by gathering fresh manna each morning and by not storing any. When they disobeyed, their day-old manna was rotten and crawling with maggots. That is in contrast to Numbers 15:20-21 and Ezekiel 44:30, in which God's people are told to give an offering of their best meal, "...so that a blessing may rest on your household."

[9] Monks were not only siphoning off donations for the poor to their families of origin, but also to mistresses and illegitimate offspring.

[10] Dante was surely referring to the opening verses of Psalm 114: "When Israel came out of Egypt, the house of Jacob from a people of

So He spoke to me. Then he moved back into his company, and they all drew close; and they were swept upward like a whirlwind. My gentle Lady's power overcame my physical nature so fully that she thrust me after them up that ladder with no more than a signal. Here below, where we arise and descend according to the laws of nature, there has never been a motion swift enough to compare to my wing.[11] Reader, you could not have drawn back and plunged your finger into the flame so quickly as I saw the sign that follows the Bull then and was inside it (as I hope to return to that holy triumph for which I often bewail my sins and beat my breast).[12]

O glorious stars—O light that is pregnant with mighty power, to which I owe whatever genius I have—when I first felt the air of Tuscany, the one who is father of every mortal life was rising with you and sinking out of sight with you.[13] Then

---

foreign tongue, Judah became God's sanctuary, Israel his dominion. The sea looked and fled, the Jordan turned back; the mountains skipped like rams, the hills like lambs. Why was it, O sea, that you fled, O Jordan, that you turned back ..." (NIV). The two separate acts of God cited here rescued His people from apparently hopeless situations (see Joshua 3:14-17 and Exodus 14:21-29 for details), demonstrating that He could possibly rescue His Church after 1300 A.D. I suspect that Dante's chronological reversal of the two exodus events (reversing the flow of time) might be meant to correlate with the reversal of the tragic course of monasticism so desirable about 2,800 years after the reversal of the flow of the Jordan. (According to recent findings, a volcanic explosion that destroyed the great Agaean civilization on Santorini in about 1500 B.C., the source of the Atlantis legend, coincides with events in the exodus from Egypt and probably accounts for some of them in terms of natural science—which does not, of course, preclude divine will.)

[11] Although *wing* obviously means flight here, John Ciardi suggests that it may also signify faith: on earth our two wings are reason and faith, but in Heaven faith suffices

[12] Beatrice and Dante have instantaneously arrived at the Heaven of the Stationary Stars and entered the constellation of Gemini (the Twins), which follows that of Taurus (the Bull). Dante refers to Heaven as the holy triumph over sin and death.

[13] This sentence shows that Dante's birthday was sometime between May 18 and June 17 in 1265. That part of the year is when the sun rises and sets in the astronomical sign of Gemini, and so Dante attributes his

when by grace I entered the lofty sphere that rolls you round, I was assigned to your part. To you now my soul sighs prayerfully for the power I need for the great passage that is drawing me to itself.[14]

"You are so near to the Supreme Good," Beatrice began, "that your eyes should be clear and keen. Therefore, before you progress further toward Him, look down and see what a great universe I have already put beneath your feet—so that your heart, rejoicing to its utmost, may meet the triumphant throng that is approaching gladly through this ethereal sphere."

My eyes looked back through all the seven spheres and saw this globe, so puny that its appearance made me smile; and I value most the teaching that values it least, for one who sets his heart elsewhere can be called truly wise. I saw Latona's bright daughter without the dark patches that used to make me think that her density varied.[15] Hyperion, I looked full at the face of your son and saw how Maia and Dione move about near him.[16] Next I saw the moderation of Jove between his father and his son,[17] and I could see clearly how they move in their orbits. All seven were visible to me, along with how large and swift they are and how distant they are from each other.

And as I circled with the eternal Twins, the little threshing-floor[18] that incites our ferocity[19] was entirely visible to me, from

---

salient characteristics astrologically to this constellation. Ultimately, of course, he attributes them to the providence of God, the source of all beneficial environmental influences.

[14] Instead of appealing to the muses for creative support, at this point Dante appeals to his native constellation, which has enhanced his talent in arts and letters.

[15] In Canto 2 Dante wondered about the dark spots on the moon, and Beatrice corrected him. Now Dante sees the moon (identified by the name of her mythological mother) from the side that is always turned away from the earth and always consistent.

[16] Dante sees the sun, identified by the name of his mythological father; and he sees Mercury and Venus, identified here by the names of their mythological mothers.

[17] Dante sees Jupiter, which is neither hot nor cold, between its mythological father, Saturn, and its mythological son, Mars.

[18] A threshing floor is a small circle of land where the grain harvest is

hills to shores. Then I turned my eyes again to those beauteous
eyes.

---

brought to be winnowed (separated from the chaff) by agricultural
workers. All the commentators I have consulted assume that a thresh-
ing floor is mentioned here simply because it is a small and humble
area, as the earth is a small and humble planet; but I believe this misses
Dante's main point, which is the overwhelming cosmic significance of
the earth. There are almost 40 references to threshing floors in the Bible,
both historical and symbolic; and an amazing array of biblical events
took place at these little plots of land—ranging from courtship and
human slaughter to angelic visitations. In fact, the great Jewish temple
was built on a threshing floor. The final mention of a threshing floor in
the Bible is Christ's warning in Luke 3:17: "His winnowing fork is in
his hand to clear his threshing floor and to gather the wheat into his
barn, but he will burn up the chaff with unquenchable fire" (NIV).
Clearly, in my opinion, the threshing floor is the earth (seen from
above), the farmer is God, the grain is human souls, the fire is Hell, and
the barn is Paradise itself.

[19] Although the Italian word *feroci* is commonly translated as
savagery, it can also mean pride; and in my opinion Dante had that in
mind if the word had that alternative definition in his day. Dante
considered pride his own besetting sin and the most basic sin of all
humanity. *The Divine Comedy* teaches that souls will be completely
cleansed of the taint of pride on their way to Paradise.

CANTO TWENTY-THREE

The Eighth Heaven, Stationary Stars

Like a bird[1] who has sheltered the nest of her sweet brood within the foliage she loves all through the night that hides everything, who (eager to look at them and begin the heavy labor of finding food for them, which is a pleasure for her) on an open bough anticipates the sun with ardent longing and faithfully watches for the dawn to rise[2] — so my Lady was standing, erect and vigilant, looking toward the region where the sun seems to slow its pace;[3] so that as I beheld her in her suspense and longing, I became like one who yearns for something he does not yet have, feeding on hope.[4]

But the span of the interim was brief — I refer to the interim between starting to wait and seeing the heavens grow more and more brilliant. Then Beatrice said, "Behold Christ's triumphant army and all the fruit harvested by the circling of these spheres."[5]

---

[1] In his essay "Imagery in the Last Eleven Cantos of Dante's *Comedy*," C. S. Lewis points out that from here to the end of *Paradise* there are nine references to birds, "usually by the mere suggestion of wings and feathers which symbolize spiritual movement."

[2] Dante's long, tender simile about a mother bird was preceded in Canto 22 by his likening Beatrice to the mother of a frightened child (himself). There she soothed him, and here she is eager to feed him. The bird's attention is on the approach of the sunlight, and that of Beatrice is on the approach of Christ's light. This simile is laden with allusions to older literary passages.

[3] Beatrice is gazing upward in the same posture that she would use if she were on earth looking up at the noon sun.

[4] Beatrice's suspense inspires the same in Dante, and his suspense inspires the same in his reader.

[5] The spheres are the seven planetary spheres, and the gathered fruit includes all the blessed souls in Heaven. C. S. Lewis notes, "Dante looks at vegetation with the eyes of a gardener more often than with those of a

I saw her face shining and her eyes so full of gladness that I have to leave the matter behind unanalyzed. As Trivia smiles serenely during full moons in clear skies among the eternal nymphs who decorate every bit of the sky,[6] I saw the one Sun above thousands of lights, all of which it kindles as our own sun kindles a heavenly display;[7] and the resplendent Essence radiated through its living light so brightly that my eyes could not endure it.[8]

O Beatrice, dear sweet guide! She said to me, "That which overwhelms you is a power against which no one has any defense. Within it is the wisdom and the strength which opened the pathway between heaven and earth that had been desired so long."[9] Just as lightning breaks out of a cloud when it expands so much that it cannot be contained and, counter to its nature, shoots down to earth—so my mind, expanded by this feast,[10] broke out of itself; and what it then became it can't recall.[11]

---

tourist: he is interested in becoming, in process." Lewis felt that here Dante was regarding the planetary spheres as the embodiment of time and almost identifying them with time. "The gathering of the Church Triumphant in Heaven is the final cause of the whole historical process and may thus be called the fruit of Time, or of the Spheres."

[6] Trivia (indicating the number three) was another name for the moon, a triple-goddess whose temple was at a three-way intersection. "The eternal nymphs" are the stars. Dante is using the relationship of the nymphs to Trivia to describe that of the stars to the moon, and using the relationship of the stars to the moon to describe the relationship of all the blessed souls to God.

[7] People used to believe that the sun was the source of light for stars as well as planets. Here Christ is the source of light for all the souls in Paradise.

[8] At the end of Canto 22 Dante was able to look directly at the sun. In contrast, in Canto 23 he finds the light of Christ too bright for his eyes.

[9] See 1 Corinthians 1:24-25, "... but to those whom God has called, both Jews and Greeks, Christ the power of God and the wisdom of God. For the foolishness of God is wiser than man's wisdom, and the weakness of God is stronger than man's strength"(NIV).

[10] C. S. Lewis points out that in *Paradise* references to food usually symbolize satisfaction of spiritual or intellectual desire—"if indeed we

"Open your eyes and look at what I am; you have seen things by which you are made strong enough to bear my smile."

I was like a person who comes back to himself from a dream he can't remember and strives in vain to bring it to mind, when I heard this offer—deserving so much gratitude that it will never be blotted out in the book that chronicles my past. If at this moment all the voices that Polyhymnia and her sisters have ever enriched with their sweetest milk were to sound forth to help me praise the sacred smile that lit that sacred face, it would not amount to one one-thousandth of the truth.[12]

Therefore, in describing Paradise this sacred poem must take a leap the way a person does who finds his pathway interrupted; but whoever considers the human shoulders bearing such weighty subject matter will cast no blame if they tremble beneath it.[13] The seapath that my daring prow cleaves is no voyage for a little boat, nor for a helmsman who is easy on himself.

"Why does my face so enamor you that you fail to turn toward the fair garden that blooms beneath the radiance of Christ?[14] There is the Rose in which the Divine Word made itself flesh; there are the Lilies whose fragrance guided people to the right path."[15]

---

can, in Dante, distinguish the two."

[11] Dante's mind more or less bursts in response to the intense light and the realization that the light is Christ. While unconscious he undergoes some kind of transformative spiritual experience.

[12] Even if all the greatest poets who were ever helped by the Muses were now to help Dante, their combined efforts to praise Beatrice's smile would be grossly inadequate.

[13] C. S. Lewis points out that Dante's images of weight are noteworthy in "a poem where we are steadily moving away from the Earth to the rim of the universe .... I have always felt that no poet—least of all any poet whose theme is so unearthly as Dante's—has such admirable solidity."

[14] John Ciardi refers to this garden in the Eighth Heaven as the Garden of Christ's Triumph.

[15] This is an allusion to the Song of Solomon 2:1, "I am the rose of Sharon, the lily of the valley," and 2 Corinthians 2:14, "But thanks be to

Thus spoke Beatrice; and I, eager to follow her guidance, again committed my feeble eyes to the encounter. When my eyes were in the shade once, they saw a meadow full of flowers illumined by a beam of Sunlight that emerged through a break in the clouds;[16] so it was when I beheld troops of splendors now, lit from above by burning rays of Light, the source of which was hidden from my view. O Kindly Power, imprinting them that way! You lifted yourself higher to make allowance for my eyes that were not strong enough.[17]

The name of the beautiful flower whom I praise morning and evening concentrated my mind upon the brightest of the flames. And when both my eyes had been shown the quality and greatness of this living star who reigns up there the same as down here, a torch in the shape of a ring, like a crown, descended from the sky, encircling her and wheeling around her.[18] The sweetest and most captivating melody on earth would sound like the rumble of thunder when lightning rips a

---

God, who always leads us in triumphal procession in Christ and through us spreads everywhere the fragrance of the knowledge of him (NIV)." For Dante the rose represents Mary and the lilies represent apostles.

[16] C. S. Lewis points out that in these cantos Dante mentions only three landscapes. "Medieval poets are interested in trees, flowers, beasts, birds, and rivers: not often, I think, in landscape. When they are, they are usually of Germanic stock." Later in his essay Lewis remarks, "The poetry of the *Paradiso* is as full of roots and leaves and growth as it is of lights—and far fuller of both than of jewels or crowns. It is worth noticing that very few of these images are merely images of visible beauty." He cites the flowery meadow as nearest to the merely visual; "but then it is a garden 'blossoming under the rays of Christ'— one feels the light drawing up those flowers."

[17] Because Dante's eyes are not strong enough to endure Christ's direct light, He lifted Himself up out of Dante's line of vision so that Dante can enjoy the sight of His close followers who reflect His light.

[18] Beatrice's mention of Mary, often referred to as a rose, has focused Dante's mind on the blessed soul of Mary, whose traditional Roman Catholic titles also include "morning star," "star of the sea," and "Queen of Heaven." The torch that descends upon her and crowns her is an angel.

cloud apart if it were compared to the sound of the lyre which crowned this beautiful sapphire that ensapphires the brightest Heaven.[19]

"I am angelic love who circles the sublime joy inspired by the womb that was once the abode of our desire; and I will circle, Lady of Heaven, until you follow your Son and make the Highest Heaven even holier by your being there."[20] Thus the circling melody signed off, and all the other lights sang out the name of Mary.[21]

The inner surface of the royal cloak wrapped around the revolving layers of the universe,[22] the layer most burning and alive with the spirit and in the ways of God, was so far above us that the sight of it was inaccessible to me where I was.[23] Therefore my eyes lacked the power to follow that crowned flame as she ascended after her Son.

Like an infant who stretches his arms toward his mother when he has had his milk, because his inner feelings flame forth in outward gestures, so each one of these white brilliances reached upward with its tip, demonstrating for me their deep love for Mary. Then they lingered in my sight, singing "O

---

[19] Mary is likened to a blue sapphire (blue is her traditional color), and as a sapphire she is a jewel that beautifies the Highest Heaven, the Empyrean.

[20] This angel is encircling Mary until she leaves the Eighth Heaven and follows Christ (who is the true desire of all of creation) back to their dwelling place in the Tenth Heaven, the Empyrean.

[21] In my opinion, they are all mirroring Christ's innate love for His mother.

[22] According to this image, the Empyrean is the robe of the cosmos, and the Crystalline Heaven (the Primum Mobile) is its lining. Dante habitually uses images of being robed, swathed, and enfolded — along with images of encountering bright light, receiving food and drink, and learning to see. Needless to say, aside from breathing, these are the most dramatic experiences of a newborn baby; but that parallel does not make Dante a candidate for Freudian analysis. I venture to claim that at heart his entire consciously constructed allegory is about spiritual birth.

[23] Dante cannot watch Mary's return journey because even the Crystalline Heaven, which is closer than the Empyrean, is far out of sight.

Queen of heaven" so sweetly that the delight has never left me.[24]

What great wealth is stored in these treasure chests for those who were faithful seedsowers on earth![25] Here they live in joy with the treasure they earned by weeping in exile in Babylon, where gold was scorned.[26] Here below the exalted Son of God and Mary, along with the blessed of the old and new dispen-

---

[24] The song the angel sings is the Latin Easter hymn "*Regina coeli.*" As part of the riot of metaphors in this canto, Dante likens a baby's expression of tender love for its mother to fire breaking out, and likens the white-hot flames of the souls of the apostles who are expressing love for Mary to babies who love their mothers. According to Mark Musa, Dante is also likening the relationship of Mary and the apostles to the relationship of a mother bird and her nestlings at the beginning of the canto. I personally suspect that Dante might be contrasting the bliss of these flame-souls with the despair of flame-souls in Cantos 26-27 of *Inferno*. There (in contrast to the faithful apostles who stretch the crests of their flames to express love) one reads the story of Guido da Montefeltro, an unfaithful Franciscan monk who had to bellow hideously inside his flame when he started to talk. "'Therefore, as you can see, I am lost—and clothed in flame, I grieve at heart.' When he had ended his story, the flame departed in sorrow, writhing and flickering its pointed crest."

[25] Although the commentators I have consulted do not mention the idea, it would be fitting for the treasure chests to symbolize the various realms of Paradise. In any case, Dante seems to have Galatians 6:8 in mind: "Be not deceived; God is not mocked. For whatever a man sows, that he will also reap."

[26] The Babylonian exile represents life on earth, where we are aliens and strangers. Although I don't see it mentioned by other commentators, I believe that Dante has to be referring here to the famous passage about Old and New Testament heroes of the faith in Hebrews 11:13, "All these people were still living by faith when they died. They did not receive the things promised; they only saw them and welcomed them from a distance. And they admitted that they were aliens and strangers on earth"(NIV). 1 Peter 2:11 is a fitting corollary: "Dear friends, I urge you, as aliens and strangers in the world, to abstain from sinful desires, which war against your soul" (NIV).

sations, the one who holds the keys of glory triumphs in His victory.[27]

---

[27] Barbara Reynolds points out the contrast between the painful portrayal of the Church Militant in the Garden of Eden at the top of Mount Purgatory and the glad portrayal of the Church Triumphant in the Eighth Heaven, the realm of the Stationary Stars. In the final two lines of poetry in Canto 23 (lines 138 and 139) Dante mentions St. Peter, the soul who will dominate Canto 24.

CANTO TWENTY-FOUR

St. Peter's Questions about Faith

"O fellowship of those invited to the great supper of the blessed Lamb who feeds you so that your desire is always fulfilled—if, before death delimits his life span, by the grace of God this man is receiving a foretaste of what falls from your table—consider his immense longing and bedew him somewhat; you drink forever from the fountain that flows with what he is thinking of."[1]

Thus spoke Beatrice; and those glad souls, blazing like comets, formed rings revolving around a fixed axis. Like synchronized wheels turning in a clockwork, in which to an observer's eye the first wheel seems motionless and the last one flies,[2] these dancers showed me their ecstasy by circling at different rates of speed. From the richest ring I saw a flame approach so joyfully that none it left behind were brighter; and it spun in a circuit around Beatrice three times with such a divine song that memory fails me.[3] Therefore my pen skips

---

[1] Beatrice's request to the blessed apostles to enlighten Dante is a medley of New Testament images. See (in this order) Revelation 19:9, John 1:29, Matthew 15:27, and John 4:14. In addition, the end of Beatrice's sentence alludes to three more verses: Revelation 21:6, "He said to me: 'I am the Alpha and the Omega, the Beginning and the End. To him who is thirsty I will give to drink without cost from the spring of the water of life.'" Revelation 22:1, "Then the angel showed me the river of the water of life, as clear as crystal, flowing from the throne of God and of the Lamb." Revelation 22:17, "The Spirit and the bride say, 'Come!' And let him who hears say, 'Come!' Whoever is thirsty, let him come; and whoever wishes, let him take the free gift of the water of life."

[2] Mechanical clocks, one of the latest wonders of advanced technology, were such a new invention when Dante wrote this that few people had seen one or learned about the cogged wheels inside. The first (largest and slowest) wheel drove a series of smaller and faster wheels.

[3] This spirit is wrapping Beatrice in beautiful music, as if in a cloak. C. S. Lewis points out that in this example and others, "[Dante's] mind (and therefore ours while we read) is apparently very sensitive to the

ahead and I don't write about it; not only our language but our imagination is too flat to paint such folds.[4]

"O holy sister of mine, praying to us devoutly, by your glowing love you detach me from that beautiful ring."[5] As soon as the blessed flame halted, he addressed my Lady just as I report it here.

She answered, "O light eternal of that great man to whom our Lord brought down and entrusted the keys to this miraculous joy,[6] test this man, as it pleases you, on light and heavy principles of the faith that once enabled you to walk upon the

---

experience of putting on, being enfolded, swathed, enveloped."

[4] Timekeeping is not the only thing that was changing radically in Dante's lifetime; so was Western art. I take the phrase that I translate as "too flat to paint such folds" to be a reference to Dante's witty friend Giotto (sometimes called the first great creative personality of European painting, and celebrated in Canto 11 of *Purgatory*). Giotto consciously created a revolution by replacing the conventional flat, linear, Byzantine-style pattern pictures with softly colored three-dimensional realism; his robed saints and angels were rounded figures that had weight and depth. Thus Dante seems to be likening his own inability to describe the contours of apostles' songs to a conventional Christian painter's inability to portray the deep contours of folds in apostles' robes.

In *A Concise History of Painting from Giotto to Cézanne*, Michael Levy notes the similarity between Giotto's painting and Dante's writing: "The elevated tone, the restricted gesture, and monumental grouping, do not inhibit powerful observation of ordinary things. Everywhere are images—like the girl carding wool—as commonplace and as memorable as those in Dante: dogs plagued by flies, a shepherd waiting for the frost to break, a woman fleeing naked with her child at the alarm of fire. Poet and painter share the ability to pare down their images to a compact essence, all the more vivid because of its brevity."

[5] C. S. Lewis points out that this is the first of eight references to binding (in contrast to simply wrapping) and unbinding in the last eleven cantos of *Paradise*. "The world of Dante's imagination, like that of Ptolemaic science, is a world of knots, cords, and envelopes."

[6] In my opinion, Beatrice asks this spirit to question Dante about his faith because he is St. Peter, the most famous person who ever answered a question about his faith. When Christ asked the disciples who they believed He was, Peter answered, "You are the Christ, the Son of the living God," and Christ responded by announcing that Peter would receive the keys to the Kingdom of Heaven. See Matthew 16.

sea.[7] Whether he loves and hopes and believes correctly is not unknown to you, for your eyes see where everything is known.[8] But since this realm is peopled by the true faith, it is good for him to have the opportunity to speak about it in order to glorify it."

Just as a doctoral candidate musters his defenses and refrains from speaking until his examiner asks him a question for discussion (not for settling the matter),[9] while she was speaking I prepared myself with solid reasoning, so that I might be ready for such an examiner and such attestation.

"Good Christian, speak up and reveal yourself; what is faith?" At that I raised my eyes toward the light that breathed forth these words; then I turned to Beatrice, and she gladly signaled me to pour out water from my inner fountain.[10]

I began, "May the grace that permits me to make my confession to the highest-ranking captain[11] help me to express my belief!" Then I continued, "O Father, as the truthful pen of your dear brother—who, along with you, set Rome on the right road—wrote for us, faith is the substance of things hoped for and the evidence of things not seen. I take this to be its essence."[12]

---

[7] It seems to me that Beatrice injected the terms *light* and *heavy* into this sentence because the faith of Peter (whose name meant stone) once made him light enough to walk on water. See Matthew 14. (Before the crucifixion and resurrection Peter's faith was not always consistent, as biblically literate readers would have known.)

[8] Dante will be examined orally on faith, hope, and love. His answers are already known by God and all the blessed who can see what is in the mind of God. As Dorothy Sayers has said, "Eternity is not an unmeaning stretch of endless time: it is all times and all places known perfectly in one deathless and ecstatic present."

[9] Dante quickly gathers his thoughts about faith. The kind of examination that led to a doctorate required discussion, and so Dante is going to have the awesome privilege of discussing some basic tenets of the Christian faith with St. Peter himself.

[10] This figure of speech is from Christ's words in John 4;14 and John 7:37-38, in which He says there will be a fountain of living water in those who believe in Him. Dante takes the water to be theological truth.

[11] Dante refers to Peter as the chief centurion in the army of God.

[12] Dante refers to Paul as Peter's dear brother because Peter referred to him that way in 2 Peter 3:15. Dante quotes the famous description of

Next I heard "You are correct, if you adequately understand why he classified it first as a substance and then as evidence."[13]

Upon that I said, "The deep things that reveal themselves to me here are hidden from the eyes of people down below; there their existence is a matter of faith, upon which high hope is built. There we must reason from faith without further revelation, and so reasoning is inherent in the substance of faith; that is why faith has the character of evidence."[14]

Next I heard, "If all the doctrine that is taught down below were understood this well, there would be no room for the repartee of sophists."[15] That burning love breathed this forth; then he added, "You have covered well the content and weight of the coin; now tell me if you have it in your purse."

I responded, "Yes, I have it—so bright and round that for me there is no question about its marked value."[16]

Next to flow from the deep light glowing there was "This dear gem that is the basis for all virtue, where did you get it?"

And I answered, "The bountiful rain of the Holy Spirit that showers on the old and new scriptures is proof that has convinced me—so sharply that in comparison all other evidence seems blunt."[17]

---

faith in Hebrews 11:1, attributing it to Paul; but the weight of recent scholarship is against Pauline authorship, and the letter is now attributed to some other early church leader.

[13] Notes by H. Oelsner and Philip Wicksteed in the Carlyle-Wicksteed edition observe, "The Catholic Church has always maintained that faith is an *intellectual* virtue, hence the rationalistic colouring of this canto, from which the Protestant reader will miss much that comes under his conception of faith (based on the really Pauline Epistles to the Galatians and Romans), and which he will find elsewhere in the *Comedy*, but not here."

[14] On earth faith (rather than visible evidence) is the basis for belief in the reality of Heaven. In its full complexity, this passage involves esoterica of scholastic philosophy.

[15] "Sophists' repartee" is elaborate and misleading philosophical argumentation.

[16] Dante likens his faith to a coin of genuine gold that has not been shaved down at all.

[17] The Bible, inspired by the Holy Spirit, is the source of Dante's faith. (This is the first of the "good rain images" in *Paradise* that C. S. Lewis points out.) From Genesis to Revelation, including the Apocrypha, there

Then I heard, "The old and new expositions that bring you to this conclusion, why do you hold them to be the word of God?"

And I said, "The proof of this revelation of truth is in its miraculous results, the likes of which nature never forged with red-hot iron and a hammered anvil."[18]

I was answered, "Tell me, what assurance do you have that these miracles happened? No source confirms them except the very one that they supposedly confirm."[19]

"If the world had turned to Christianity without these miracles," I said, "this in itself would be a hundred times more miraculous; because when you were poor and fasting you entered the field and sowed the good plant that was a vine — but has now become a thorn."[20]

This ended, throughout the spheres the high and holy choir rang out "God, we praise Thee"[21] in the kind of melody that is sung up there.

---

are by one count 124 references to rain in the Bible. In my opinion, two that Dante could have had in mind here are Deuteronomy 32:2, "Let my teaching fall like rain and my words descend like dew, like showers on new grass, like abundant rain on tender plants" (NIV) and Ecclesiasticus 1:19, "She [wisdom] showers down knowledge and ability..." (Jerusalem Bible).

[18] Nature cannot produce miracles; they are by definition supernatural.

[19] It would be illogical to believe accounts of miracles because they are in the Bible if one's reason for believing the Bible is those same accounts of miracles.

[20] Dante acknowledges Peter's role in the wonderful growth of the Christian Church, but he laments again (as he did at the end of Canto 23) its corruption. In my opinion he draws this vineyard image from Jeremiah 2:21, "I had planted you like a choice vine of sound and reliable stock. How then did you turn against me into a corrupt, wild vine?" (NIV) and Micah 7:-1-4, "What misery is mine! I am like one who gathers summer fruit at the gleaning of the vineyard; there is no cluster of grapes to eat .... The godly have been swept from the land; not one upright man remains .... Both hands are skilled in doing evil; the ruler demands gifts, the judge accepts bribes, the powerful dictate what they desire — they all conspire together. The best of them is like a brier, the most upright worse than a thorn hedge ...." (NIV).

[21] Because of Dante's answers, the choir sang "*Te Deum laudamus*," opening words of a famous hymn of thanks.

And that nobleman who had drawn me from branch to branch while examining me, so that we were approaching the topmost leaves, began again: "So far, the grace that speaks to your mind like a lover has caused your lips to open correctly,[22] so that I approve of what has emerged from them. But now it behooves you to state what you believe and how you came to believe it."

"O holy father whose spirit is seeing now what you believed so strongly long ago that you moved beyond younger feet in coming to the sepulcher,"[23] I began, "you want me to make the shape of my unhesitating faith and its source clear.[24] Therefore I answer: I believe in one God, sole and eternal, himself unmoved, who moves all the Heavens with love and desire.[25] And for this belief I not only have the evidence of physics and metaphysics, but also that provided by the truth showering on us through Moses, the Prophets, the Psalms, the Gospels, and through those of you who wrote after the flaming Spirit turned you into foster fathers.[26] And I believe in three eternal Persons; I believe these to be one essence—so single and so triple that both *are* and *is* sound correct. Evangelical teaching often impresses my mind with the reality of the profound condition of God of which I speak. This is the beginning; this is the spark

---

[22] The credit for Dante's right answers belongs to God, who provided them to Dante.

[23] As recorded in John 20:1-9, as soon as John and Peter heard that the body of Jesus was not in His tomb, they ran there to see for themselves. John arrived first, because he was younger, and peered inside; but as soon as Peter arrived he rushed inside ahead of John.

[24] After referring to Peter's unhesitating rush into the tomb, Dante mentions that his own faith is now unhesitating.

[25] Being in love with God is what makes the Ninth Heaven (Crystalline Heaven or Primum Mobile) and all the lessers spheres of Heaven revolve. (Hence the secularized saying "Love makes the world go around.")

[26] Dante refers to the Bible by citing first the three parts of the Old Testament mentioned by Christ in the New Testament Gospels (Luke 24:44); then he adds the New Testament epistles written by Peter and other apostles. The apostles fostered the early Church after the Holy Spirit descended upon them with tongues of fire as described in Acts 2.

that expands into a living flame and shines in me like a star in heaven."[27]

Like a master who embraces his servant as soon as he hears good news that causes him to rejoice,[28] so the light of that apostle at whose command I had spoken circled me three times, blessing me in song. That is how much my answer pleased him.[29]

---

[27] Dante's concept of the nature of God is based upon various Bible passages. In turn, this concept is the basis for the rest of his beliefs and serves as his guiding star.

[28] C. S. Lewis points out the psychological significance of this happy social image and others like it. "We have all read books which place philanthropic and optimistic sentiments in the foreground, but betray, as it were in odd corners, how few people the author likes. In Dante the tension is reversed. Terrible denunciations are hurled at persons and abuses; but at the roots of his mind we discover an easy and unemphasized enjoyment of 'towered cities' and the 'busy hum of men'. He is not an oddity or a misfit; hence springs some at least of the security and exhilaration with which we read his severe and in some ways appalling poem."

[29] Is it immodest for Dante to report that his "test score" caused St. Peter to glorify him with song and dance? In his famous 1941 sermon "The Weight of Glory," C. S. Lewis explains at length personal glory in Heaven. "I suddenly remembered that no one can enter heaven except as a child; and nothing is so obvious in a child — not in a conceited child, but in a good child — as its great and undisguised pleasure in being praised. Not only in a child, either, but even in a dog or a horse.... Perfect humility dispenses with modesty."

CANTO TWENTY-FIVE

St. James's Questions about Hope

If it ever comes to pass that this sacred poem (to which both heaven and earth have set my hand, so that for many years it has been making me lean)[1] should overcome the cruelty that bars me from the lovely sheepfold where I, an enemy to the wolves that prey upon it, used to sleep like a lamb—then with changed voice and changed fleece I shall return as a poet,[2] and at the very font where I was baptized I shall be crowned with laurel, because that is where I entered into the faith that brings souls to God and for which Peter has just now crowned my brow.[3]

Then a light moved toward us from the sphere from which the first vicar of Christ had approached us.[4] Full of gladness, my Lady said to me, "Look! look! Behold the nobleman for whose sake, down below, people go to Galicia."[5]

---

[1] The opening of Canto 25 is famous for its pathos and for Dante's hope that he would be allowed to return to Florence because of his successful labor on this poem. Charles Singleton points out that at this point Dante is within nine cantos of completion (after at least nine years of intense work).

[2] Dante's poetic voice had matured during his exile, and his hair had turned gray. He had been exiled as a political activist, and he hoped to be welcomed back as a major poet.

[3] Dante hoped to receive a wreath of laurel (equivalent to an honorary doctorate) in the church of San Giovani, where he had been baptized into the Christian faith. (He was offered the laurel wreath in Bologna, but he held out for receiving one in Florence instead.) Dante connected the symbolic laurel wreath to the symbolic wreath of light, song, and dance that Peter had just bestowed upon him.

[4] A second spirit approached as Peter had done.

[5] In the Middle Ages the tomb of St. James in northwest Spain was second only to Rome as the destination of pilgrims.

As it is when a dove alights by its mate and they express their love for each other by circling and cooing, so I saw one great, glorious prince greeting the other, praising the banquet that they feast on above. But when their greeting was completed they both settled silently before me, burning so brightly that they overwhelmed my eyes.[6]

Smiling, Beatrice said, "Illustrious life, you who wrote about the generosity of this palace, cause hope to sound up here; you know that is what you personified when Jesus[7] gave extra light to the chosen three."[8]

"Look up and be confident, for it befits anyone who ascends here from the mortal world to ripen in our radiance." This comforting word from the second flame caused me to lift my head up toward the mountains that had bent me down with their great weight.[9]

---

[6] I am convinced that this image is designed to contrast with the image of lovers Paolo and Francesca in Canto 5 of *Inferno*, who were like doves swept hither and yon by a dark wind amidst the noisy screaming and crying of other unrepentant souls. Hell is all darkness, misery, and noise; Heaven is all light, joy, and (in the words of Jeffrey Burton Russell) singing silence.

[7] Joseph Gallagher points out that this is the first appearance of the name Jesus in the entire *Divine Comedy*, and there will be only one more. "The name Christ never appears in *Inferno*, but appears five times in the *Purgatorio* and thirty-four times in the *Paradiso*."

[8] Beatrice is probably referring to at least three memorable verses about the generosity of God in the Epistle of James: 1:5, 1:17, and 2:5. James, along with Peter and John, was granted the privilege of being present at three special events in the ministry of Christ: the raising of the daughter of Jairus (Mark 5 and Luke 8), the Transfiguration (Matthew 17), and the Garden of Gethsemene (Matthew 26). Peter, James, and John are sometimes thought of as symbolizing faith, hope, and charity. (Beatrice assumes that the Epistle of James was written by this favored disciple, but it is usually attributed instead to James the brother of Jesus.)

[9] This image is an allusion to Psalm 120:1, "I will lift up my eyes to the mountains, the source of my help." Peter and James are the mountains Dante is looking to for help, but he is in such awe of their radiant majesty that he bends his head as if the weight of their light is more than he could bear. In my opinion this is an allusion to 2

"Since by His grace our Emperor wills that before your death you are personally encountering the noblemen in His inner chamber—so that having seen the truth of this royal residence, you may thus strengthen in yourself and others the hope that causes people to love rightly—tell me what hope is and how your mind blossoms with it, and tell me where you acquired it." So the second light continued.

And the compassionate one who guided the feathers of my wings on such high flight prefaced my reply: "It is written in

---

Corinthians 4:17, "For this slight momentary affliction is preparing for us an eternal weight of glory beyond all comparison ...."

In Lewis's essay "Imagery in the Last Eleven Cantos of Dante's 'Comedy,'" he says, "... the weight of the mountains (or of the Apostles, for they are momentarily one) which weighs upon the soul is equated with the actual weight which bends the bearer double." He continues, "... how immensely venerable the Apostles have become first by the mountain image and then by the image of weight which, as it were, grows from it. No direct praise of their wisdom or sanctity could have made us respect them half so much." In "The Weight of Glory" Lewis warns that it may be possible to think too much of one's future glory in Heaven, but it is hardly possible to think too often or too deeply of the future glory of other people ("everlasting splendours"). "The load, or weight, or burden of my neighbour's glory should be laid daily on my back, a load so heavy that only humility can carry it, and the backs of the proud will be broken." (Few readers of "The Weight of Glory" realize that it is based upon 2 Corinthians 4:17, and almost none realize that it is based upon Dante's allusion to 2 Corinthians 4:17.) In the last book he wrote before he died, *Letters to Malcolm*, Lewis reflected, "But when Dante saw the great apostles in heaven they affected him like *mountains*. There's lots to be said against devotions to saints; but at least they keep on reminding us that we are very small people compared to them. How much smaller before their Master?"

Lewis also connected the crushing weight of the mountains' light with the intolerable weight on the backs of the proud on the First Terrace of Mount Purgatory (see Canto 13 of *Purgatory*). There Dante feared that his own back would be bent double someday because of pride, his besetting sin. In my opinion, the comforting words of St. James in Canto 25 of *Paradise* are an assurance to Dante that his pride had been replaced by humility, obviating his need to be cleansed of pride after death.

the Sun that enlightens all our ranks that no child in the Church Militant possesses more hope than this one; that is why he was allowed to come from Egypt to Jerusalem to see it before his assignment on the battleground is ended.[10] I leave to him your other two questions—asked not that you may learn from him, but so he may carry back word about how much you cherish this virtue[11]—for these will not be hard for him or make him sound boastful. So may he answer them, and may the grace of God assist him."

Like a pupil responding to his teacher, ready and willing to display his proficiency in a subject he knows well, I said, "Hope is a certain expectation of future glory, the result of divine grace preceded by merit.[12] This light came to me from many stars;[13] but the sublime singer of the Sublime Ruler first sprinkled my heart with it. 'Let those hope in you' he says in his divine song, 'who know your name'[14]—and who with my faith lacks that knowledge? You, also, sprinkled me with it in your letter, so that I am brim full and in turn sprinkle others with it."[15]

While I was speaking, a sudden series of flashes like lightning trembled within the living heart of that flame. Then he breathed to me, "The love that still burns in me for that virtue which accompanied me all the way to the palm and my

---

[10] To spare Dante the problem of sounding boastful by answering James's second question, Beatrice answers for him. Egypt, where the Israelites were slaves for 400 years, represents life on earth; and Jerusalem, the city of the Promised Land, represents Heaven. The church on earth is the Church Militant (engaged in spiritual conflict), and the church in Heaven is the Church Triumphant.

[11] There is no more use for hope in Heaven, but it is still precious in itself.

[12] Dante is quoting Peter Lombard's definition of a specific theological concept of hope, not the general meaning of the term.

[13] See Daniel 12:3, "Those who are wise will shine like the brightness of the heavens, and those who lead many to righteousness, like the stars for ever and ever" (NIV).

[14] Dante is quoting Psalm 9:10 by David, the King of Jerusalem.

[15] Dante refers to the New Testament epistle by James. As Allen Mandelbaum recommends, see James 1:12, 2:5, 4:7-10, and 5:8.

departure from the battlefield[16] leads me to breathe again to
you who delight in hope; so it will please me to have you state
what it is that hope promises to you."

I answered, "The New and Old Testaments set up the target
for the souls God has befriended,[17] and they enable me to point
to it. Isaiah says that everyone shall wear two garments in his
true homeland, which is this sweet life.[18] And your brother was
more explicit for us in his revelation where he wrote about
white robes."[19]

After I had concluded my words, "Let those hope in You"
rang out next above us with all the choral groups answering.[20]
Then from their midst such a light flashed out that if the Crab
contained one crystal like it the darkest month of winter would
be one unbroken day.[21] And just as a glad maiden rises and

---

[16] Hope for Heaven accompanied James all the way to his martyr-
dom, traditionally symbolized by the palm. (It was probably in 44 A.D.
that Herod had James executed as recorded in Acts 12.) At that point
James departed from the battlefield of earthly life.

[17] Dante may have been alluding to James 2:5, "... and he [Abraham]
was called God's friend."

[18] As I see it, Dante is referring to Isaiah 61:10: "I delight greatly in
the LORD; my soul rejoices in my God. For he has clothed me with
garments of salvation and arrayed me in a robe of righteousness, as a
bridegroom adorns his head like a priest, and as a bride adorns herself
with her jewels" (NIV). Thus the blessed in Heaven are to be adorned
with both their salvation and their sanctification, and will eventually
be clothed in both spiritual light and resurrected bodies. Needless to
say, if he had chosen to do so Dante could have provided a far more
direct scriptural basis for the resurrection of the body, 1 Corinthians 15.

[19] It was commonly assumed that James's brother John, who wrote
three New Testament epistles, was the same John who wrote the book of
Revelation. Dante is referring to Revelation 7:9, "After this I looked and
there before me was a great multitude that no one could count, from
every nation, tribe, people and language, standing before the throne and
in front of the Lamb. They were wearing white robes and were holding
palm branches in their hands" (NIV). Those were all the blessed saved
by the sacrificial death of Christ, the Lamb.

[20] This scene is reminiscent of Job 38:7, "the morning stars sang
together and all the angels shouted for joy."

[21] In the darkest month of winter, the Crab constellation (the sign of

unselfconsciously makes her way to join the dance in honor of the bride, so I saw this brilliant splendor join the other two in the wheeling dance that expressed their burning love. There he entered into their singing and dancing; and like a bride my Lady aptly watched them, silent and motionless.

"This is the one who leaned on the breast of our Pelican,[22] and the one chosen at the cross for the great assignment."[23] Thus spoke my Lady; but she did not shift her gaze after she spoke any more than before.

Like one who stares and squints to see the sun during a partial eclipse and by looking blinds himself,[24] so I peered at this last flame until I heard "Why do you blind yourself trying to see what is not here?[25] My body is now earth in the earth, and there it shall remain with all the rest until our number reaches what is eternally ordained.[26] Only two lights arose to

---

Cancer) is above the horizon all night long, and if it had just one star as bright as this light it would make the night as bright as day.

[22] In some translations of Psalm 102, which begins with painful lamentation and ends in triumphant faith, in verse 7 the psalmist likens himself to a pelican. In the Middle Ages the pelican was believed to pierce its own breast in order to provide blood to nourish or revive its offspring; therefore it became a symbol of Christ, who shed his blood for the sake of mortals. At the crucial point during the Last Supper when Christ foretold his betrayal, "there was leaning on Jesus' bosom one of his disciples, whom Jesus loved." That was how John described his proximity to Christ in John 13:23 (KJV).

[23] When Christ was dying on the cross He asked John to take care of Mary.

[24] There were five partial eclipses of the sun (and two full ones) in Dante's lifetime that he might have seen.

[25] John knows that Dante is trying to see if the story is true that when John died his body went directly to Heaven with his spirit. The answer is no. In my opinion, John's words are meant to be a mirror image of Luke 24: 5-6, in which the women who went to Christ's tomb to anoint His body were addressed by two shining men who said, "Why do you look for the living among the dead? He is not here; he has risen!" Christ's followers who thought His body was earthbound were mistaken, and later followers who thought John's body was not earthbound were mistaken.

[26] When the total number of blessed spirits fulfills God's purpose

this blessed cloister with both their robes, and you are to report this back on earth."[27]

At the sound of his words the flaming circle had halted its dance along with the sweet harmony of the three combined voices, just as oars that were slicing the water all stop in unison when the whistle sounds to avert fatigue or danger. Ah! How upset I was when—turning to look at Beatrice—although I was close to her and in the Realm of Bliss, I could not see her!

(Dante believed that it would equal the number of angels that fell with Lucifer), the Resurrection and the Day of Judgment will occur.

[27] John means that the only two humans whose physical bodies entered Heaven along with their spirits at the time of their physical deaths were Christ and Mary. All the rest of the blessed await the resurrection of their earthly bodies. (In the Middle Ages the Old Testament accounts about Enoch and Elijah ascending in their physical bodies were taken to mean that the bodies of these two prophets went to the summit of Mount Purgatory rather than directly to Paradise.)

The Heaven of the Fixed Stars
Gustave Doré (Canto 26)

CANTO TWENTY-SIX

St. John's Questions about Love

Right after I was alarmed by my inability to see, I became aware of a voice exhaled from the brilliant flame that had blinded me. It said, "Until you regain your vision, which you squandered by staring at me, it is best to fill in with discourse. So begin, and state what your heart is set on. (Rest assured that your sight is stunned but not destroyed, because the lady who is conducting you through this divine region has in her glance the power that used to exist in the hand of Ananias.)"[1]

I answered, "Sooner or later, at her good pleasure, may healing come to these eyes that were the gates through which she entered, bringing the fire with which I always burn.[2] The Good that fills this royal residence is the Alpha and Omega of all the writings that love has read to me, whether softly or loudly."[3]

The same voice that had calmed my terror caused by the sudden dazzlement directed me to further discourse by saying

---

[1] John is referring to Acts 9, which tells how Paul's vision, which he lost when Christ appeared to him in a blinding light on the road to Damascus, was restored three days later when Ananias laid hands on him. Beatrice will heal Dante by touching him with her eyes rather than her hands when she finally turns from Peter, James and John and looks back at Dante again.

[2] It was through seeing Beatrice with his eyes that Dante had fallen in love with her (hence, with goodness) in the first place. Now it is through seeing Dante that Beatrice will restore his eyes.

[3] God is the true beginning and end, the A and Z, of all there is to know about love. As I see it, Dante is referring to John's teachings about love in his epistles (such as "God is love" in 1 John 4:8), and he is also referring to John's report in Revelation 1:8 and 21:6 that God is the Alpha and Omega, the beginning and the end. (It was assumed that these were all by one author.)

"Now you must strain through a finer sieve. You must explain what aimed your bow at such a target."[4]

I responded, "By philosophical reasoning and by the authority that descends from here,[5] such love was bound to stamp its seal on me because so far as good is perceived, it kindles love; and the more good there is, the more love there is. Therefore the mind of anyone who discerns the basic truth underlying this principle must fall most in love with the Essence so unmatched that any goodness found outside Him is nothing but a reflection of His own light.[6] This truth is made plain to me by the one who shows me the primal love of all eternal beings.[7] It is made plain to me by the voice of that truthful Author who said of Himself to Moses, 'I will show you all goodness.'[8] It is made plain to me by you also, at the beginning of the sublime proclamation that, better than any other, declares on earth the mysteries of this place."[9]

Then I heard "As human wisdom and authorities concur, of all your loves the highest is for God. But tell me also if you feel other cords pulling you toward Him, in order to identify the various teeth with which this correct love bites you."[10]

---

[4] Now Dante is required to answer more specifically and to explain what caused him to aim at love.

[5] Dante cites philosophy and divine revelation in Scripture as the sources of his belief.

[6] Anyone who perceives that God is the supreme good is bound to love him more than anything else, because His supreme goodness makes Him the supreme object of love. John wrote in 1 John 1:5 "This is the message we have heard from him and declare to you: God is light; in him there is no darkness at all." C.S. Lewis remarks that Dante's portrayal of this theme is traditional; however, at this point "we not only understand the doctrine but see the picture."

[7] Dante is referring to Aristotle.

[8] Exodus 33:19, as translated by Dante from the Latin Vulgate.

[9] Some hold that Dante is referring to the book of Revelation, but others hold that he is referring to the Gospel of John. A strong case can be made for either opinion.

[10] Mark Musa notes the origin of this metaphor in the writings of mystics. (It brings to my mind Francis Thompson's 1893 poem "The Hound of Heaven.") I find it odd that none of the commentators I

The sacred purpose of Christ's eagle was not hidden;[11] indeed, I perceived where he was leading my explanation. Therefore I resumed, "All the bites which have power to make the heart turn to God work together in my love—the world's existence and my own existence, the death He endured that I might live,[12] and every believer's hope, along with mine, together with the living awareness I mentioned—drawing me from the sea of wrong love and placing me on the shore of correct love.[13] I love all the leaves that make the eternal Gardener's garden green, according to the amount of His goodness in each one.[14]

As soon as I fell silent, Heaven rang with sweet music; and my Lady cried out "Holy, Holy, Holy!" with the others.[15] Then just as a bright light awakens someone from slumber by causing his visual system to react to light penetrating the layers of his lids, and thus he awakens confused by what he sees until full consciousness comes to his aid, so Beatrice removed every bit of blur from my eyes with light from her own that shone for more than a thousand miles. After that I saw better than before,

---

consulted mention what seems obvious to me: that St. John is referring to the ministrations of a sheepdog, which nips at the animal it is herding in order to guide it safely in the right direction.

[11] Based upon Revelation 4:7, the authors of the four Gospels (Mark, Luke, Matthew, and John) were traditionally portrayed as a lion, an ox, a man, and an eagle. John had such keen spiritual vision (like an eagle) that he saw the mysteries of Heaven.

[12] Because Dante is speaking to John, he seems to be alluding to John's most famous teachings about love, John 3:16 and 1 John 4.

[13] At the beginning of Canto 1 of *Inferno* Dante spoke about straying from the right path and likened himself to a nearly-drowned survivor who has struggled to shore and looks back at the dangerous lake (of inordinate loves) in his heart.

[14] C. S. Lewis pointed out that "Dante looks at vegetation with the eyes of a gardener more often than with those of a tourist: he is interested in becoming, in process." Dante ends his oral examination on love by expressing his love for everything created by God in ratio to how much of God's goodness is in it.

[15] See Isaiah 6:2-3. Heaven rejoices in Dante's understanding of faith, hope, and love.

and like someone startled I wanted to know about a fourth light that I saw with us now.

My Lady said, "The first soul created by the First Power contemplates his Maker within that light."

Like a bough that bends its crown when the wind passes over and then lifts itself back up by its own power, so I did in awe while she was speaking. Then, emboldened by the desire to speak that was burning in me, I began, "O you who are the one and only fruit ever begun fully mature[16]—O ancient father for whom every bride is both a daughter and a daughter-in-law[17]—as reverently as possible I implore you to speak to me. You see my wish, and so I leave it unspoken in order to hear you sooner."

Sometimes when an animal moves inside a covering its eagerness is visible because what enfolds it moves with it;[18] and in similar manner that first soul showed through his covering how joyfully he came to give me pleasure.[19] Then he breathed forth, "Although you have not revealed it to me, I know your wish better than you know whatever is most certain to you, because I see it in the accurate Mirror that reflects everything else perfectly (and which is not Itself reflected perfectly in anything else).[20] You want to know how much time

---

[16] Tradition had it that Adam was created in a 30-year-old body. Eve, created from his rib, was considered a derivative of Adam rather than a separate creation.

[17] Every bride is a descendent of Adam, and every bride marries a descendent of Adam.

[18] Some think Dante is referring to an animal in a hood or sack, and others think he is referring to a silkworm making silk inside its cocoon. (In Canto 8 the spirit of Charles Martel was enfolded in light like a silkworm in a cocoon.) Because the movements of silkworms inside cocoons are said to be visible to observers, that interpretation seems appropriate.

[19] Although Adam is hidden in light, his movement shows his emotion.

[20] The Mind of God includes everything there is. I strongly suspect that Thornton Wilder (who did graduate study in Italy) had Dante's *Paradise* in mind when he wrote his Pulitzer Prize winner, "Our Town." At the end of the first act Rebecca said, "He wrote Jane a letter

has passed since God placed me in the garden on high where the lady prepared you for such a long stairway, how long my eyes were delighted there, the true cause of the great wrath, and what language I used and formed.[21]

"Now understand, my son, that the cause of such a long exile was not the tasting of the tree itself, but solely the violation of a boundary.[22]

"In the place from which your Lady sent Virgil to you, my longing for this assembly lasted four thousand three hundred and two cycles of the sun; and I beheld the sun run its course through all the constellations on its path nine hundred and thirty times while I lived on earth.[23]

"The language I spoke was completely extinct long before Nimrod's subjects undertook the work that could never be completed; for human preferences change with the movements of the heavens, and the human mind has never yet produced anything permanent. Nature designed humans to speak; but nature permits you to speak this way or that way, as it suits you.[24] Before I descended to Hell's anguish, J was the earthly

---

and on the envelope the address was like this. It said: Jane Crofut, The Crofut Farm, Grover's Corners, Sutton County, New Hampshire, United States of America.... Continent of North America, Western Hemisphere, the Earth, the Solar System, the Universe, the Mind of God—that's what it said on the envelope."

[21] Adam perceives four questions that Dante wants answered: How long ago was Adam created and placed in the Garden of Eden (where Beatrice prepared him to ascend to Paradise)? How long did Adam enjoy the Garden? Why was Adam exiled from the Garden? And what language did Adam speak?

[22] Adam means that the foolish pride that led him to transgress God's rule is what caused his banishment from the Garden of Eden.

[23] Adam lived 930 years on earth before he died, as stated in Genesis 5:5. He then spent 4,302 years in Limbo until he was delivered in 34 A.D. by Christ at the Harrowing of Hell. According to Allen Mandelbaum, Dante was following the chronological theory in a book written circa 300 A.D. by Eusebius of Casearea.

[24] Adam informs Dante of the mutability of languages that existed from the beginning of human history, long before Nimrod, the ruler of Babylon, contributed to language diversity by his proud, futile attempt

name of the Supreme Good that wraps me in gladness; but later He was called El. And this is fitting, for the words of mortals are like leaves upon a branch; one falls and another replaces it.[25]

"First innocently and then disgraced, for a quarter of a day I lived at the top of the tallest mountain that rises from the sea — from the first hour to the hour after the sixth."[26]

---

to build a tower to heaven (the Tower of Babel). (See Genesis 10-11.)

[25] J is the initial of Jehovah (in Hebrew Yahweh), and El is related to Elohim; both of these names for God are used in the Old Testament and refer to majesty. Adam, having devised the first human language, indicates that the specifics of language are mere accidents of history and not ordained by God or nature. Although I have not seen the idea elsewhere, I suspect that this foray into etymology is Dante's allusion to the following statement by Thomas Aquinas in *Summa contra Gentiles*: "… the reality of the names predicated of God and other things is first in God according to His mode, but the meaning of the name is on Him afterwards. Wherefore He is said to be named from his effects." This puts Dante's special deference for the names Jesus and Christ in *Commedia* into perspective; the words themselves are only earthly artifacts.

[26] Adam's life in the Garden of Eden lasted only a little over six hours, according to a book by Peter "The Eater" (circa 1100-1179). This scholar, chancellor of the University of Paris, appeared in Canto 12.

CANTO TWENTY-SEVEN

The Ninth Heaven: Crystalline Sphere

All Paradise began to ring with the sweet strain "Glory be to the Father, to the Son, and to the Holy Spirit!" — which intoxicated me. I seemed to see the entire universe smile, and I was enraptured by both sound and sight.[1] O joy! O indescribable ecstasy! O life of perfect love and peace! O endless unlimited riches![2]

The four torches kept on blazing before my eyes;[3] and the one who had come to me first began to increase, looking as Jupiter would look if he and Mars were birds that traded their

---

[1] Dante is portraying fictionally Psalm 19:1, "The heavens declare the glory of God; the skies proclaim the work of his hands." In *Reflections on the Psalms* C. S. Lewis said of Psalm 19, "I take this to be the greatest poem in the Psalter and one of the greatest lyrics in the world." In my opinion Lewis had both the beginning of Psalm 19 and the beginning of Canto 27 in mind when he described the heavens in the fifth chapter of *Out of the Silent Planet*: "He [Ransom] had read of 'Space': at the back of his thinking for years had lurked the dismal fancy of the black, cold vacuity, the utter deadness, which was supposed to separate the worlds. He had not known how much it affected him till now—now that the very name 'Space' seemed a blasphemous libel for this empyrean ocean of radiance in which they swam. He could not call it 'dead'; he felt life pouring into him from it every moment. He had thought it barren: he saw now that it was the womb of the worlds, whose blazing and innumerable offspring looked down nightly even upon the earth with many eyes.... Older thinkers had been wiser when they named it simply the heavens—the heavens which declared the glory...."

[2] Dante tastes the ecstasy of Paradise for himself. Ironically, much of the rest of Canto 27 is about the lack of love and peace caused by greed for ephemeral worldly riches.

[3] The four are Peter, James, John, and Adam.

plumage.[4] The Providence that orchestrates performances there imposed silence on all sections of the blessed choir, and then I heard "Do not marvel if I change colors, because as I speak you will see these others change also. On earth the one who usurps that place of mine—that place of mine—that place of mine, vacant before the Son of God—has made my burial-ground a sewer for blood and filth, pleasing to the outlaw down below who fell from up here."[5]

Then I saw all Heaven tinted with the color that the slanting sun paints on a cloud at evening or at morning; and Beatrice's appearance changed like that of a moral woman with a clear conscience who blushes with shame when she hears about someone else's immorality. I imagine that the solar eclipse was like that when the Supreme Power was suffering.[6]

Then he resumed his discourse, with his voice altered as much as his appearance. "The bride of Christ was not nourished by my blood and that of Linus and Cletus so that she might later be used for gain of gold;[7] it was for gain of this joyous life that Sixtus, Pius, Calixtus, and Urban shed their tears and shed their blood.[8] We did not intend for our successors to place one

---

[4] Peter's white light turns red with righteous indignation, causing it to resemble that of Mars instead of Jupiter. To account for these planets being likened to birds, some commentators point out that the rays from planets used to be referred to as their feathers.

[5] Peter declares that the current pope in 1300 (Boniface VIII) is no real pope; he defiles Rome and delights Satan. Allen Mandelbaum suggests that Peter's threefold utterance of "my place'" echoes Jeremiah's threefold utterance of the term "sanctuary of Yahweh" in Jeremiah 7:4. Because Jeremiah 7 is God's outraged denunciation of religious corruption and hypocrisy, I agree with Mandelbaum. Needless to say, the dramatic juxtaposition of blissful ecstasy ("perfect love and peace") with this denunciation of sin serves both theological and artistic purposes.

[6] Luke 23:44-45 reports that there was a three-hour eclipse during the crucifixion. Dante imagines that witnessing the crucifixion caused the sky to darken with shame.

[7] Like Peter, Linus and Cletus (second and third bishops of Rome) died because they were church leaders.

[8] Sixtus, Pius, Calixtus, and Urban were other very early popes who

group of Christians on their right side and a different group on the other;[9] nor for the keys entrusted to me to become the emblem on a battleflag warring against the baptized;[10] nor for my image to be an official stamp validating the sale of false promises which make me turn red and blaze with anger.[11]

"From up here we can see ravening wolves dressed like shepherds in all the pastures.[12] God's vengeance, how can you sleep?[13] Cahorsines and Gascons are preparing to drink our blood.[14] O good beginning, to what a vile ending you fall![15] But I perceive that the lofty Providence which used Scipio to

---

died because they were church leaders.

[9] Recent popes were fostering factionalism in the church and favoring one group (on their right side) over another.

[10] Boniface used the emblem of Peter's keys on his papal flag.

[11] Boniface used Peter's face on the seal that stamped documents for worthless indulgences and reinstatements into the church after excommunications.

[12] In my opinion, Peter is alluding to Paul's warning in Acts 20:29, "I know that after I leave, savage wolves will come in among you and will not spare the flock," and his related admonishment in verses 33-35, "I have not wanted anyone's silver or gold or valuable clothing. You all know that my manual labor has supplied my needs and those of my companions. In all that I did, I showed you that by hard work we must help those in need, remembering Jesus' words 'It is more blessed to give than to receive.'" When he said that, Paul was well aware that he was going to die soon for his faith. Thus Acts 20 is the most eloquent rebuke possible to greedy, worldly, hypocritical church leadership.

[13] Peter seems to be echoing Psalm 44:23, "Awake, O Lord! Why do you sleep? Rouse yourself!"

[14] Clement V (1305-1314) was a native of Gascony, and John XXII (1316-1334) was a native of Cahors. Inclusion of John XXII in this canto proves that Dante was writing or editing it after John ascended to the papacy in 1316.

[15] This exclamation about the papacy applies also to the human race and to Satan himself; all three began well but fell. In her commentary Barbara Reynolds remarks, "Men have become degenerate as a result of their abuse of time, so that progress is turned into regress, the innocence of childhood being quickly lost with the passing of the years." In my opinion this concept accounts for the way Canto 27 treats greed and time as if they are obviously related.

defend Rome as the glory of the world will soon bring help.[16]
And you my son, who will go back down again because of your
mortal weight, speak out there; and do not hide what I am not
hiding here."

Like flakes of frozen moisture drifting down through the air
in the season when the horn of the sky-goat reaches the sun,[17]
so I saw the flakes of triumphal flame that had been with us all
drifting upward, ornamenting the expanse.[18] My eyes followed
and followed them, until they could follow no farther. When
my Lady saw then that I had gazed upward enough, she said to
me, "Cast your eyes down and see how far you have circled."[19]

I saw that since the last time I looked down I had traveled
the second half of the semicircle of the first latitudinal band,[20] so
that now I could see beyond Cadiz the mad route of Ulysses,
and in the other direction almost to the shore where Europa

---

[16] Scipio led the Roman army against the attacker Hannibal in 202
B.C. Peter predicts that once again God will provide a rescuer.

[17] On December 21, the sun enters the zodiac's constellation of
Capricorn (the Goat), marking the beginning of winter and its snows.

[18] This upward snowfall of joyful spirits (called "Christ's
triumphant army" in Canto 23) is one of the famous images of reversal
in *Commedia*. In *The Soul's Journey*, Alan Jones wrote of the *Inferno*, "We
move through the sins of lust, gluttony, avarice and prodigality, anger,
heresy — to those of violence, fraud, and treachery at hell's cold heart ....
We end in the icescape of hell." In contrast, in *Paradise* spirits are
moving toward the lightscape of the Empyrean. Dante's image of
Heaven's snow is a symbol of weightlessness and freedom — in contrast
to Hell's ice, which is a symbol of weight and imprisonment.

[19] Canto 27 is closely related to Canto 22 in several ways, including
the denunciation of corrupt clergy, the ascent of the blessed, and Dante's
being instantly thrust up to the next sphere. In Canto 22 Dante enters the
Eighth Heaven and Beatrice tells him to look down at the earth; in
Canto 27 she tells him to look back down at the earth and he leaves the
Eighth Heaven.

[20] Because of the daily rotation of the sky around the earth, Dante is
rotating also. He can see that (according to medieval geography) he has
moved a quarter of the way around the earth since the last time he
looked down, which means that six hours have passed since he arrived
in the Eighth Heaven. During that six-hour period Dante has taken and
passed three oral examinations.

became a precious burden.[21] And even more of that part of the threshing floor would have been visible to me if it were not that the sun was lower than I was, ahead of me by a sign and more.[22]

My love-obsessed mind, which was always cherishing my Lady, burned with more desire than ever to feast my eyes on her. If all the bait ever designed by nature and art to catch the eyes and captivate the heart—in human flesh or in pictures—were added together, that would seem like nothing compared to the divine beauty that shone on me when I turned toward her smiling face. Then the power bestowed on me by that look plucked me from Leda's lovely nest[23] and thrust me up to the swiftest Heaven.[24]

The parts of this quickest and highest sphere are all so uniform that I cannot identify where Beatrice located me in it. But she saw my wish,[25] and smiling so joyfully that God

---

[21] Now Dante's view stretches from the Atlantic Ocean (where Ulysses perished) almost to Phoenicia (where according to myth Jupiter took the form of a white bull and carried Europa away to Crete on his back). Barbara Reynolds points out that Ulysses' disastrous venture westward was like Adam's sin in the Garden of Eden; in Adam's own words in Canto 26, "violation of a boundary." Phoenicia is as far east as Jerusalem, and Rome was thought of as the midpoint between the edge of the Atlantic and Jerusalem. John Ciardi points out that Dante may be suggesting that he finds himself directly above Rome.

[22] Dante could see more land to the east if it were not in the shadow of night because the sun was at least two hours to his west. In calling the earth a threshing floor he echoes the ending of Canto 22: "And as I circled with the eternal Twins, the little threshing-floor that incites our ferocity was entirely visible to me, from hills to shores." I notice that in Canto 27 Dante has written nine consecutive lines about details of time and space.

[23] According to myth, Leda was impregnated by Jupiter in the form of a swan and gave birth to twins. Thus Dante fancifully refers to the constellation of Gemini (the Twins) as Leda's nest.

[24] The power of Beatrice's smile catapults the two of them into the Ninth or Crystalline Heaven, the Primum Mobile.

[25] Once again Beatrice sees that Dante craves an explanation, this time of the Crystalline Heaven.

seemed to be rejoicing in her face, she began to speak. "It is the nature of the universe, which keeps its center still and moves everything else around it, to begin here as its starting point.[26] And this Heaven has no other location than the Mind of God, which kindles the love that spins it and the power that rains down from it.[27] Light and love surround it as it surrounds the other Heavens;[28] and the One who surrounds it is the only one who comprehends it.[29] No one measures out its movement; but it measures movement out to all the rest, as surely as ten can be divided by two and five.[30] And now you can see how it is that the taproot of time is in this container, and the leaves of time are in the lower Heavens.[31]

---

[26] In the Ptolomaic model of the universe, everything below the Empyrean revolved around the earth in nine concentric layers. The invisible Primum Mobile, the outermost layer, was right next to the Empyrean and indwelt by the Seraphim.

[27] The Crystalline Heaven, spinning with love and longing for God, serves as an electrical generator providing energy for the rest of the universe. Of course Dante could not use that analogy because electrical generators were not yet invented.

[28] It seems to me that Dante is suggesting in Canto 27 that humans experience historical reality in the created dimensions of time and space, but blessed spirits experience higher reality in the eternal dimensions of light and love, beyond time and space. Greed is a parasite of time and space.

[29] To comprehend can mean to understand or to include. The words contain, enfold, cloak, swath, enrobe, wrap, encircle, encase, and envelop all suggest what Dante means.

[30] Allen Mandelbaum points out that the numbers 5 and 2 generate 10, just as the Primum Mobile generates all the energy in the universe. Commentators differ on the exact meaning of Dante's mathematical analogy here.

[31] The root of time (its origin) is hidden where it is planted, in the Primum Mobile; and the leaves of time (the movements of the sun and other heavenly bodies) are visible in the lower Heavens. Without movement (change), all would be stasis and there would supposedly be no time at all. The image of time as a tree that grows downward (Charles Singleton calls the Primum Mobile time's flower-pot) is one of Dante's famous inversions, like the upward snowfall earlier in this canto. In his essay "Imagery in the Last Eleven Cantos of Dante's

"O greed, sinking mortals so deep that not one has the power to lift his eyes above your waves![32] The human will blossoms well; but a continuous downpour turns the fine plums into spoiled fruit. Faith and innocence are found only in little children, and they depart before boys' cheeks are bearded. A child is willing to fast while he still talks babytalk; but as soon as his tongue improves he starts eating everything all year long. And as soon as his tongue matures, a lisping child who loves and heeds his mother will long to see her buried. So the white skin of the lovely daughter of the one who brings the morning and leaves the evening immediately darkens.[33] And you, so you won't be taken off guard, remember that there is no one to govern on earth; and that is why the human family strays so far from the path.[34]

"But before January is unwintered by the day that men neglect every century,[35] the light of these spheres will cause a long-awaited storm to whirl the sterns around to where the

---

'Comedy'" C. S. Lewis refers to it as "the astonishing vision which reveals our race crawling along the topmost (or, if you will, the lowest) leaves of the great time-tree that grows head-downward from the Ninth Heaven."

[32] At the end of his examination in Canto 26 Dante spoke of Christian truth "drawing me from the sea of wrong love and placing me on the shore of correct love." Greed is a form of wrong love.

[33] Beatrice may simply mean that humanity, offspring of the sun (symbolizing God), quickly goes bad. John Ciardi and some others think that the lovely daughter is specifically the church.

[34] Dante lamented the fact that the Roman Empire was no longer restraining evil; without the balancing power of Imperial Rome, wealth and greed soon corrupted Roman church leadership. (That is one of the flaws in theocracy.) The image of straying from the right path recalls the opening of *The Divine Comedy* 94 cantos earlier: "Midway on life's journey, I woke up and found myself in a dark wood, for I had lost the path."

[35] An error of 13 minutes per year in the Julian calendar was gradually pushing January toward spring at the rate of one day a century. Dante obviously thought this could and should be corrected. (That finally happened in 1582 with adoption of the Gregorian calendar.)

prows are and straighten out the fleet.[36] Then blossoms will develop into good fruit."[37]

---

[36] Beatrice seems to be employing a kind of reverse hyperbole here by predicting that help will come in less than thousands of years. Peter had just predicted, "But I perceive that the lofty Providence...will soon bring help," and they agreed.

[37] C. S. Lewis observed, "The poetry of the *Paradiso* is as full of roots and leaves and growth as it is of lights — and far fuller of both than it is of jewels or crowns." "The gathering of the Church Triumphant in Heaven is the final cause of the whole historical process and may thus be called the fruit of Time, or of the Spheres."

CANTO TWENTY-EIGHT

Rings of Fire

After the Lady who imparadises my mind had laid bare this truth about the miserable state of mortal affairs, I looked into those eyes that had served as love's cord to capture me;[1] and I recall being like someone completely oblivious to a candle that is burning behind him, who discovers it in a mirror, turns around to see if the mirror is correct, and finds that the reflection matches the reality as closely as lyrics match the rhythm of a song.

When I turned, my own eyes were struck by what appears in that sphere whenever one looks.[2] I saw a Point radiating such bright light that any eyes seared by it must close because of its intensity; and whatever star seems smallest from here would look as large as the moon if placed next to it.[3]

Around that Point, at the approximate distance of a halo wrapping the light that creates it in the thickest kind of mist,[4] a ring of fire wheeled so rapidly that it exceeded the speed of the swiftest revolution around the earth.[5] And this was enclosed in

---

[1] C. S. Lewis observed, "The world of Dante's imagination, like that of Ptolemaic science, is a world of knots, cords, envelopes." A little later in this canto Beatrice will speak of a certain heavenly paradox as a knot.

[2] The light that Dante saw reflected in the eyes of Beatrice was the glory of God, which was directly visible to him in the transparency of the Ninth Heaven. Dante is referring to a kind of mystical experience sometimes reported by contemplatives and others.

[3] Once again Dante is using understatement. The brilliance and minuteness of the infinitesimal Point are so extreme that they are indescribable except perhaps in terminology of modern physics. The Point is indivisible and immaterial and not located in space.

[4] The thicker the mist, the closer a halo is to the source of light that emanates it.

[5] The first ring of fire is closest to the Point of Light and revolving around it more quickly than any heavenly bodies revolve around the

a second ring, that one in a third, the third in a fourth, the fourth in a fifth, and the fifth in a sixth. Next came the seventh, with such a span that if the messenger of Juno were completed it would still be too narrow for it.[6] And so with the eighth and ninth; and the farther each one was from the first, the more slowly it moved. The ring closest to the Pure Spark had the most crystalline flame, and I think that is because it absorbs more of the Point's truth.

Seeing my bewildered amazement, my Lady said "All of heaven and nature hang on that Point.[7] Look at the circle nearest it and realize that its rapid movement is due to the burning love that propels its spinning."

I answered, "If the universe were arranged in the same pattern as the pattern of these rings, then I would be satisfied with what I see.[8] But in the material universe we see that the farther the spheres are from the center, the more divine they are. So if my hunger is to be satisfied in this wonderful angelic temple with only love and light for its perimeter,[9] I need to hear why the copy and the original fail to match;[10] for by myself I scrutinize the matter in vain."

"If your fingers are unable to untie such a tight knot, don't be surprised; it is this tight because no one has ever tried to loosen it," my Lady answered.[11] Then she continued, "If you

---

earth.

[6] The seventh ring from the Point is so immense that if the rainbow were a compete circle around the earth it would be too small to hold this ring.

[7] Just as a geometric point is the center of a circle, God is the Point at the center of spiritual reality.

[8] Dante perceives that this nine-tiered angelic reality corresponds to the nine-tiered pattern of the universe, and so he is dismayed by the fact that the angelic rings closest to the center point revolve fastest of all.

[9] Dante likens the Crystalline Heaven to a temple with walls of light.

[10] Dante is in the Crystalline Heaven when he has this vision of nine concentric fiery rings with the Point at their center. Perhaps this depiction of Heaven influenced C. S. Lewis's depiction of Heaven at the end of his *Narnian Chronicles*. There one of the children said, "I see... world within world, Narnia within Narnia.... " "'Yes,' said Mr. Tumnus, 'like an onion: except that as you go in and in, each circle is larger than the last.'"

[11] Beatrice seems to be indicating that no theologian before Dante's

want to be satisfied, take what I will tell you now and sharpen your wits on it.[12] The material spheres are larger or smaller according to their share of the power that is spread among them. More goodness results in greater blessedness; and if things are in proportion, greater blessedness goes with greater size. Thus the sphere that sweeps all the rest of the universe along with it corresponds to the ring that knows and loves the most.[13] Therefore, if you count the power rather than the appearance of the beings perceived in these rings, you will see a marvelous correspondence of greater to more and smaller to less in every sphere,[14] according to its Intelligence."[15]

---

time has tried to make sense of this multi-layered paradox; thus Dante's reading has not prepared him to understand it.

[12] In her essay "The Meaning of Heaven and Hell" Dorothy Sayers warns against imagining that educated people in the Middle Ages were childish and credulous. "It was an age in which a great many people were illiterate, and when nobody knew as much as the twentieth-century person about the physical sciences. But the culture of a fourteenth-century city like Florence was extremely high, and the things that educated people did know, they knew very well indeed, and theology was one of those things. I have before now tried to explain Dante's conception of Heaven and Hell in simple terms to the kind of modern person who is brought up on smatterings of knowledge in popular digests, and have been told that my ideas were very sophisticated. The fourteenth century *does* seem sophisticated to the twentieth century when it is talking on its own subject. We have forgotten so much of our theology since Dante's time."

[13] Dante often focuses on spatial magnitude and intensity of speed. It seems to me that in *Paradise* these are physical (spatial and temporal) symbols of two spiritual qualities: magnitude of goodness and intensity of desire. Spiritual reality (the Empyrean) transcends space and time, and so perhaps knowledge (of goodness) and love could be called its real dimensions. I theorize that Beatrice was encouraging Dante to apply his wits to this "tight knot" and that her emphasis upon the nature of space and time in Canto 27 was preparation. She is helping Dante to understand the relationship of physical reality to spiritual reality.

[14] The angelic ring closest to the Point has the most divine power, and the physical sphere closest to the Empyrean is the largest. (The ninth physical sphere is the largest and corresponds to the first fiery ring; in contrast, the ninth angelic circle is the least powerful and corresponds to the first physical sphere.) Thus greater size and more power cohere in the physical and spiritual mirror-images of reality. Similarly, God is

Just as the earth's atmosphere becomes clear and serene when Boreas blows from his gentle cheek, clearing away cloudy obscurity and causing the sky to smile with farflung pageantry,[16] so my mind cleared when my Lady provided me with her clear answer; and the truth was seen like a star in the sky. When she finished speaking, the rings of fire sprayed sparks like those from molten iron when it boils and spurts forth a shower of sparks; and every spark went on circling with its ring.[17] Their numbers were far more than the doubling on a chessboard.[18]

From choir to choir I heard Hosanna sung to that fixed Point that holds them where they are and ever shall be and have been forever. And she who saw my mind's questioning thoughts said, "In the innermost rings you see the Seraphim and Cherubim. The swiftness with which they follow their guy lines enables them to resemble the Point as much as possible; and they do so in proportion to their sight.[19] The next Loves,

---

both the center-point of reality and the all-encompassing circumference of reality.

[15] Each sphere's Intelligence is its kind of angel.

[16] Boreas was the traditional personification of the north wind, and when he blew upon Italy from the north-east rather than the north-west (his gentler cheek rather than his harsher cheek) he cleared the sky.

[17] Each spark is an individual angel, and their numbers are countless.

[18] According to legend, the inventor of chess asked a Persian king to reward him with one grain of wheat for the first square, two for the second, four for the third, and so on to the sixty-fourth square on the chessboard. To his dismay, the king learned that there was not that much grain in his entire kingdom; simple calculation shows that the total comes to approximately 18.5 billion billion.

[19] The Bible is vague about the natures and names of various kinds of angels, but that has never stopped some people from trying to categorize and systematize them. According to the angelology used in *Paradise*, Seraphim are the angels of the Crystalline Heaven and Cherubim are the angels of the Stationary Stars; these two orders of angels are the closest to God and the most like God. (1John 3:2 " ... we shall be like him, for we shall see him as he is.") But, as Barbara Reynolds points out, fallen angels preside over the corresponding levels of Hell. Therefore in Canto 27 of *Inferno* a black Cherubim thrust a soul who had counseled fraud into the eighth ditch, where the suffering soul spoke to Dante from within a flame.

ringing those, are called Thrones of the divine appearance; and they complete the first set of three.[20]

"And you should know that bliss is allotted according to how deeply anyone sees into the truth in which every intellect finds rest. From that, one can see that being blessed is the result of seeing — not of loving, which is its result. And the allotment of sight is according to the righteousness bestowed by grace and by good will.[21] Thus the progression goes from grade to grade.

"The second triad blossoming in this eternal spring, never spoiled at night by Aries,[22] perpetually sings winter away with Hosanna in three interweaving melodies in its three rings of joy.[23] In this hierarchy there are three divinities: first Dominions and then Virtues, and the third order is Powers.[24]

"In the two next-to-last rings of dancers Principalities and Archangels whirl; and the last is made up of Angels frolicking.[25] These orders all gaze upward, and they have such

---

[20] Thrones are the angels of Saturn, the third order of angels in this system. In Canto 9 Cunniza mentioned them to Dante: "There are Mirrors above (you call them Thrones) where God's judgment shines on us so that we know the things we decided to tell you."

[21] In my opinion, Dante is referring to Paul's teaching in Philippians 1:9-11, "And this is my prayer: that your love may abound more and more in knowledge and depth of insight, so that you may be able to discern what is best and may be pure and blameless until the day of Christ, filled with the fruit of righteousness that comes through Jesus Christ — to the glory and praise of God." (NIV). Ultimately it is grace, the unmerited favor of God, that enables beings to see, understand. and love spiritual truth; but created beings must choose to cooperate with this grace. They are not forced to so.

[22] The sun entering the sign of the Ram on March 21 marks the beginning of spring. On earth spring can be unpredictable, destroying blossoms with night frosts; but heavenly spring is perfectly dependable.

[23] According to Mark Musa, in Dante's brief three-line stanza Beatrice has ingeniously painted a word-portrait of eternity and the Trinity. Unfortuately, there is no way to translate this kind of verbal artistry because it is a matter of the choice and arrangement of fifteen Italian words.

[24] Dominions are the angels of Jupiter, Virtues are the angels of Mars, and Powers are the angels of the Sun. They have some responsibility for the general order of nature.

[25] Principalities, the angels of Venus, deal with nations. Archangels are the angels of Mercury, and the last group, called Angels, are the

powerful influence downward that all are drawn toward God and draw to God.[26]

"Dionysius set himself to contemplate these orders with such zeal that he named them and described them just as I do.[27] (But eventually Gregory differed from him, and that is how it happened that as soon as Gregory's eyes opened in Heaven he laughed at himself.[28]) And you need not be amazed that a

---

angels of the Moon. Only the two lowest orders deal with individual humans on earth.

In a note at the end of her essay "Dante's Vision of Heaven" Barbara Reynolds states, "C. S. Lewis, who knew Dante's poem well, has used the concept of the Great Dance of the universe in the last chapter of *Perelandra*, which is in fact a descant upon *Paradise*."

[26] In her remarkable little prayer-poem "For Timothy, in the Coinherence" Dorothy Sayers playfully celebrates the life of a beloved pet from the perspective of Dante's *Paradise*, quoting line 129 of Canto 28 in Italian as an epigraph. Her sixth stanza follows:

> Dante in the Ninth Heaven beheld love's law
> Run up and down on the infinite golden stairway;
> Angels, men, brutes, plants, matter, up that fairway
> All by love's cords are drawn, said he, and draw.

In the context of Dante's joyful hierarchy of spiritual reality, Sayers contemplates her relationship to Timothy, and concludes with the eighth stanza:

> When the Ark of the new life grounds upon Ararat
> Grant us to carry into the rainbow's light,
> In a basket of gratitude, the small, milk-white
> Silken identity of Timothy, our cat.

[27] An anonymous mystic who used to be identified with the Athenian Dionysius (see Acts 17) wrote a book called *The Celestial Hierarchy* that was considered authoritative by medieval theologians. He probably wrote the book in the fifth or sixth century.

[28] It is unlikely that Pope Gregory I (590-604) ever heard of *The Celestial Hierarchy*, and he worked out the slightly different theory that Dante accepted and used when he wrote *Convivio (The Banquet)* shortly after his exile; but between *Convivio* and *Comedia* Dante obviously changed his mind. In my opinion, Beatrice's portrayal of Gregory gently laughing at his own error when he saw Heaven for himself is not only a tribute to Gregory's buoyant humility but also an intentional display of Dante's. And considering the errors in the medieval view of

mortal man dispensed such secret truth on earth; for one who saw it up here reported it to him, along with much more truth about these rings."[29]

the physical universe that Dante had to use in *Comedia*, I think it is fair to assume about Dante what he assumed about Gregory: "as soon as his eyes opened in Heaven he laughed at himself."

In her introduction to *Paradise* Barbara Reynolds ventured, "if Dante had now to re-write his poem in conformity with twentieth-century physics he would probably seize on the interesting numerical correspondence between the ten heavens of his cosmology and the ten dimensions of ours, and find little difficulty in adapting his picture accordingly. Nor would a centreless universe disconcert him; it would fit in conveniently enough with the famous dictum of the Schoolmen that 'God is a circle whose centre is everywhere and its circumference is nowhere.'"

[29] Beatrice indicates that Paul reported to Dionysius what he had observed in Heaven (see 2 Corinthians 12:1-4). Her seemingly contradictory attributions of *The Celestial Hierarchy* first to the author's hard work and then to revelation strike me as parallel to her previous statement "the allotment of sight is according to the righteousness bestowed by grace and by good will [correct choice]." In my opinion this is Dante's way of telling how he wrote *The Divine Comedy*: it was the product of years of extremely enthusiastic and intense labor, but it was also a gift of God's grace. Throughout, Dante depended upon divine assistance. At the beginning of *Paradise* he wrote " ... for this crowning task make me an adequate channel of your power ... Enter my heart and breathe ...."

The Empyrean
Gustave Doré (Canto 31)

CANTO TWENTY-NINE

All about Angels

Gazing intently at the Point that had overwhelmed me,[1]
Beatrice remained silent with a smile on her face for the length
of time that the children of Latona, when they are below the
Ram and the Scales,[2] are both belted by the horizon and held
in balance by the zenith — until they both move away from that
belt and that balance by changing hemispheres.[3]

Then she began: "I will tell without asking what you want to
hear,[4] for I see it where every *where* and every *when* is cen-
tered. Eternal Love blossomed into new Loves not to increase
His own good, which would have been impossible, but so that
reflections of His splendor might declare 'I am' in His eternity,
beyond all time and limitation.[5]

---

[1] Although it is impossible for Dante to keep his eyes on the Point,
Beatrice can do so.

[2] Here Dante launches into a rhetorically elegant reference to myth-
ology and astronomy. Latona's children were Apollo and Diana, the
Sun and the Moon, and at the Vernal Equinox the constellations of
Aries (the Ram) and Libra (the Scales) are above them.

[3] Beatrice gazes silently at the Point for as long as the Sun and Moon
remain simultaneously poised on the rim of the horizon at sunrise or
sundown at the Vernal Equinox. At such a moment half of each of these
two heavenly bodies is above the horizon and half is below (as if the
horizon were a belt), and they seem to hang evenly on a balancing scale
from the top of the sky. Then the imaginary scale tips, and one slides
above the horizon while the other slips below. I suspect that Beatrice
was silent for about as long as it would take to read Dante's nine lines
describing her pause.

[4] What Dante wants to hear about is the origin of the angels, a subject
that is not discussed in the Bible.

[5] God created angels (Loves, Intelligences, Movers, Mirrors) so they
could enjoy existing. In her essay "The Meaning of Heaven and Hell"
Dorothy Sayers summarizes this in one word: *generosity*. She elabo-

"And He did not rest inactively before this, because there was no after or before until God's moving on the waters.[6] Form, matter, and the combination of the two[7] sprang flawless into existence, like three arrows from a three-stringed bow and like a ray of light shining instantaneously through glass, amber, or crystal.[8] So the threefold creation of the Lord shot into existence all at once, with no delay between its beginning and completion.[9] The ranking of every essence was co-created along with it; those composed of pure actuality were at the pinnacle of the

---

rates, "He desired that there should be others, derived from Himself but distinguishable from Him, and with a dependent but genuine reality of their own, having each a true selfhood, which should reflect back to Him the joy and beauty and goodness that they received from Him. The image here, as throughout the *Paradiso*, is the familiar one of light; God is the light: the derived radiance of the creature is the *splendore*, the splendour. The right end [goal] of every creature is to shine back to God with that splendour, and to be able to say, thus shining (*risplendendo*); 'I am — *subsisto*'. This is a key passage to Dante's thought, and, indeed, to Catholic thought."

[6] For God there is no past or future; all time is present. The question "What did God do before creation?" is self-contradictory because "before" did not exist before creation. According to Beatrice, time began to exist after the process described in Genesis 1:2, "Now the earth was without form and empty, darkness was over the surface of the deep, and the Spirit of God was moving on the waters."

[7] These technical philosophical terms are from Aristotle. By pure form Dante means immaterial spirit (angels), by pure matter he means basic physical substance (perhaps like the concept of "primordial soup"), and by the combination of the two he means physical substance with a spiritual nature (all of mineral and organic nature, including mankind).

[8] All of creation came into existence instantly, at once. Dante's two analogies seem obscure today, but there used to be three-stringed bows for triple shots, and light appears to pass through translucent materials instantaneously.

[9] Beatrice may be referring primarily to Genesis 1:1, "In the beginning God created the heavens and the earth." Presumably the six stages of creation described in Genesis 1:3-31 were gradual developments presided over by the angels.

universe, pure potentiality was the lowest, and in middle the two were permanently tied together into potential actuality.[10]

"Jerome wrote to you of a long span of ages in which the angels were created before any other part of the universe was made; but the truth I tell is recorded in many passages by the Holy Spirit's scribes, and you will realize that if you look carefully.[11] Reasoning perceives it somewhat also, in that the angel forces would not be apt to have to wait so long to fulfill their function.[12] Now you know where and when and how these Loves were created, so three of your burning requests are already quenched.[13]

"In less time than it takes to count to twenty, a portion of the angels convulsed the earth's core.[14] But the rest remained and began their vocation that you observe, circling with such delight that they never pause. The beginning of the fall was the accursed pride of the one you saw imprisoned under all the weight of the world.[15] But those you see here modestly

---

[10] In "The Meaning of Heaven and Hell" Dorothy Sayers says, "The lowest and least of created things — the prime matter — is formless and homogeneous: and inorganic matter has very little individuality. Plants are much more; animals are real individuals; and a human being is more than that: he is a person. When we come to the angels, or 'Intelligences' in Dante's phrase, they are thought of as possessing such super-personalities that the Schoolmen refused to think of them as being merely so many members of a species; they said that every angel was a species all to himself."

[11] St. Jerome (340-420), the scholar who translated the Bible into Latin, taught that the angels were created long before the rest of the universe.

[12] According to Beatrice, it goes against reason that angels would exist for ages without a universe for them to move.

[13] The angels were created in the Empyrean before time began, simultaneously with the rest of creation, and they were created perfect.

[14] As soon as they were created, part of the angels fell as far as possible from Heaven, hurtling all the way into the center of the earth like an extraordinary meteorite.

[15] As Dorothy Sayers points out in "The Meaning of Heaven and Hell," a man's or angel's knowledge and enjoyment of existence is enhanced by his assent to the fact that he was created by God and can

acknowledged that they were a result of the very Goodness that gave them their great, swift intelligence;[16] that is how their vision was enhanced with illuminating grace and with their merit, so that their will is fully formed and firm. And I don't want you to doubt, but to know certainly that there is merit in receiving grace, in proportion to one's desire for it.

"If my words have been well absorbed, now you can surmise much more about this sacred place without further help. But since on earth some scholars teach that angelic nature understands, remembers, and wills, I will continue so that you may see clearly how truth is confused down there by the ambiguity of that kind of teaching.[17] Since these beings first gathered joy from the face of God where nothing is hidden, they have never glanced away from it; therefore their sight is never diverted to something new. They never have occasion to remember anything because their attention has never been diverted from anything.[18]

"So it is that whether asleep or awake (believing or disbelieving that they are telling the truth) down there men dream things up; and the sin and shame is worse in the latter case.[19] You on earth do not tread the narrow path of philosophy because you get turned aside by the desire to make a display of your cleverness. But even this is less of an offense to Heaven than the neglect or twisting of Holy Scripture. No one thinks

---

only enjoy or attain his true selfhood by letting his desire and will conform to God's will. "The fall of angels and men is, looked at from one point of view, a refusal of assent to this reality: or what the scientist would call 'a lack of humility in the face of the facts.'"

[16] Angels don't process information or think; they know everything instantaneously.

[17] Human souls in Heaven know, remember, and will. Beatrice agrees with teachers who claim that angels also know and will, but she argues that angels never remember anything. Memory is meaningless to the omniscient.

[18] Angels are always fully conscious of everything.

[19] Some false teachers are deluded (like dreamers), but others delude their followers intentionally. The latter is worse.

about how much blood is shed to plant it in the world, and how pleasing a person is who humbly keeps close to it.[20]

"Everyone strives to show off by inventing novelties; and preachers choose to discourse on these, thus silencing the Gospel.[21] One says the moon reversed its course when Christ was suffering, and that it blocked the sunlight from the earth; others say the light withdrew itself, causing the same eclipse for the Spaniards and Indians as for the Jews.[22] Florence does not have so many Lapis and Bindis[23] as it has fables of that kind proclaimed in just one year from pulpits on every hand. As a result, the know-nothing sheep return from their pasture fed with wind; and ignorance of their loss does not excuse them.[24]

"Christ did not say to his first apostles 'Go forth and preach drivel to all the world,'[25] but gave to them the true foundation.[26] That and only that is what sounded from their lips,

---

[20] As important as it is to follow the precepts of the sages like Aristotle and Aquinas, it is even more important to follow the Bible.

[21] As Barbara Reynolds has put it, " … in the Primum Mobile itself, on the very threshold of the abode of God, Beatrice rebukes the covetousness of mankind and pours scorn upon petty-minded and unworthy preachers who misrepresent or neglect the Gospel in their sermons."

[22] The crucifixion accounts in Matthew 27, Mark 15, and Luke 23 tell of darkness from the sixth hour to the ninth, but they don't mention these entertaining details, which are pure speculation or fabrication.

[23] Lapi and Bindi were extremely common nicknames, like Bill and Bob in the United States today.

[24] The preachers of Florence were flouting Christ's commandment in John 21:17, "Feed my sheep," but Beatrice also blames the laity for their silly ignorance that made them satisfied with frivolous preaching. (C. S. Lewis assumed that feeding on wind was a proverbial term in Dante's day.)

[25] Beatrice was parodying the Great Commission as recorded in Mark 16:15, "Go forth and preach the Gospel to all the world." See also Matthew 28:19-20 and Luke 24:47.

[26] Although I have not found any commentary that suggests it, I think Beatrice is alluding to Ephesians 2, a passage about "the true foundation." (Note the theology of Ephesians 2:8, "For it is by grace you have been saved, through faith—and this not from yourselves, it is the gift of God…." [NIV].)

and thus they used the Gospel as their shield and sword in the battle to spread the Faith.[27] But now men go forth to preach with jokes and buffoonery; and if they arouse hearty laughter their hoods puff up and that is all they want.[28] Such a bird is nesting down in the tip of that hood that if the people saw it they would realize what kind of pardons they are trusting in;[29] but gullibility has increased so much on earth that people rush after promises without any proof of validity. That is how St. Anthony's pig gets fat, along with others even more piggish — paying with forged coins.[30]

---

[27] This is the figurative language of Ephesians 6:16-17, "In addition to all this, take up the shield of faith, with which you can extinguish all the flaming arrows of the evil one. Take the helmet of salvation and the sword of the Spirit, which is the word of God" (NIV).

[28] In Dante's day, as in our day, some preachers were talented entertainers who craved popularity and acclaim. In today's vernacular, success made their heads swell.

[29] Beatrice rails against unscrupulous preachers who persuaded people to pay for worthless pardons for their sins. (The most notorious contemporary equivalents now would be unscrupulous televangelists who exploit their viewers.) The bird nesting in the hats of all these preachers was Satan, who used to be symbolized by a black bird.

[30] Herds of "consecrated" hogs owned by monks of the order of St. Anthony the Great were entitled to forage freely and to be treated like the sacred cows of India. Beatrice considers these monks more greedy and destructive than their hogs. In addition to dunning the public for charity, they sold indulgences worth no more than play money.

In Heaven Dante has already heard similar denunciations from St. Peter Damian, who lampooned fat clergymen and likened them to their horses; St. Benedict, who likened greedy clergymen to sacks of rancid meal; and St. Peter, who likened Rome to a sewer and clergymen to ravenous wolves. But some modern male critics find it unseemly for Beatrice (a Lady) to use "rather strong words" in this "extended harangue" and "diatribe" about clergymen, "calling some of them liars and connecting others with pigs and concubines." I suspect that Dorothy Sayers, author of the trenchant essay "Are Women Human?", would have been amused by these critics.

According to Sayers, "the blessed dead are deeply concerned with the living, whether to help, pity, pray for them, or to feel indignation at their sins, yet in Heaven the powers of anger and pity are experienced

"But now we have digressed enough, so turn your eyes back to the right path and we will fit our journey into the remaining time. Angelic nature amounts to such numbers that neither mortal speech nor thought can count that high: and if you look at the revelation from Daniel, you will see that in his thousands no definite number can be found.[31] The primal light that shines into them all is received in as many ways as there are splendors with which it mates. Therefore, since love comes after the act of conception,[32] the sweetness of love blazes or glows in them all differently.[33] And now you see the height and breadth of the Eternal Goodness that divides itself into so many mirrors and yet remains Itself, still only One."

---

pure, and not bound up with a whole complex of confused personal feelings. While God and His Saints are angry, anger does not tear them to pieces, distort their judgment and poison their lives... "

[31] See Daniel 7:9-10, "...the Ancient of Days took his seat. His clothing was as white as snow; the hair of his head was white like wool. His throne was flaming with fire, and its wheels were all ablaze. A river of fire was flowing, coming out from before him. Thousands upon thousands attended him; ten thousand times ten thousand stood before him. The court was seated, and the books were opened" (NIV).

[32] "Knowing" another person in what is called the Biblical sense causes physical conception. Beatrice claims that knowing (seeing) God as He is engenders love for Him, as in the common saying "To know him is to love him."

[33] As Dorothy Sayers put it, "an angel is so triumphantly and perfectly himself that one of those blessed beings differs from another not as one man from another but as one *class* of terrestrial beings from another."

The Queen of Heaven
Gustavé Doré (Canto 31)

CANTO THIRTY

The Empyrean

When about six thousand miles away from us noon is blazing and where we are the earth's shadow is already moving lower, toward its level bed — then the sky overhead begins to change so that here and there a star is too dim to shine down this far; and as the brightest handmaid of the Sun approaches, the sky extinguishes light after light, even to the most beautiful one of all.[1] Similarly, the triumph that dances perpetually around the Point that vanquished me (which seems to be enclosed by what It encloses)[2] faded from my sight little by little; at that, my seeing nothing and my love caused me to turn my eyes back to Beatrice.[3]

If everything said about her so far were compressed into a single expression of praise, it would be too weak to serve now.

---

[1] According to medieval calculations, when it is noon in India it is about an hour before dawn (the handmaid of the sun) in Italy. At that time of morning the shadow of night sinks toward the western horizon; then one by one the stars become dim and go out, until even Venus finally disappears.

[2] In *Letters to Malcolm* C. S. Lewis observed, "God is not in space, but space is in God." Gene Edward Veith observes in his 1998 article "Science Fiction's 'Still Point,'" "Dante's real tour de force as a science fiction writer came when he questioned his own conceptual model. After he broke through the last of the crystalline spheres, which, nested like matrushka dolls, constitute the Ptolomaic cosmology, he is in the Empyrean, the pure, light-filled realm outside of both space and time that is the true Heaven. From this vantage point, he looks back at the universe he has just traversed. Suddenly, the perspective shifts and he glimpses it differently. Dante then, in an outstanding act of imagination, turns his whole universe inside out."

[3] The nine angelic rings of fire (dancing around the Centerpoint that is also the Circumference) have gradually faded from sight like morning stars.

The beauty I beheld was immeasurable, beyond comprehension; I'm convinced that only her Maker can enjoy it completely. At this point I concede a greater defeat than any other suffered by a comic or tragic poet with a difficult theme;[4] for as the Sun dazzles even dim eyes, so the very memory of her lovely smile dazzles my mind. From the first time I saw her face on earth until this vision of her, nothing has stopped me from my quest in verse; but now I must end my poetic pursuit of her beauty, like every artist who has done his best.

With beauty that I leave now to a mightier trumpet fanfare than my own (which is drawing its laborious theme to a close), and with the voice and gesture of a successful guide, she began again.[5] "We have ascended from the largest sphere into the Heaven of pure light[6] — intellectual light, abounding in love;

---

[4] A "comic" poet wrote in the language of the people, as Dante did in *Commedia*. A "tragic" poet wrote in lofty, formal style, as Dante did in some of his other poetry. He has tried to praise the beauty of Beatrice in both styles.

[5] In *The Ladder of Vision*, Irma Brandeis points out that from their first earthly encounter, the beauty of Beatrice pointed beyond itself, snatched Dante out of preoccupation with himself, was his "first great *eye-opener*." Her beauty is a transcript of her light, and she leads Dante from sphere to sphere of sight. "With every apparent brightening we know that some further film of the human limitation has been lifted from his eyes."

[6] On Sunday, April 3, 1300, Dante enters the Empyrean and is beyond the cosmos. As C. S. Lewis observed in his essay "Imagination and Thought in the Middle Ages," the Empyrean is not the boundary of space in the absurd sense of there being more space beyond it; instead, it is the point at which the spatial mode of thought breaks down. Dante cannot make spacelessness imaginable, and so he has been turning space inside out to teach us that spatial thinking, as we ordinarily know it, has broken down. Lewis does the same thing when he portrays Heaven in *The Great Divorce* ("a larger *sort* of space") and *The Last Battle*. ("The inside is larger than the outside").

I suspect that for most people not schooled in science fiction or modern physics, the simplest and quickest illustration of spatial ambiguity is personal construction of an ordinary Möbius strip in a minute or two from a piece of paper and a bit of tape. (In a sense both sides of the paper become the same side, with only one edge; this

love of true goodness, abounding in ecstasy; ecstasy that surpasses every sweetness. Here you will see both hosts of Paradise, one of them as it will appear at the Last Judgment."[7]

Like a sudden flash of lightning that scatters the powers of vision and robs the eyes of the ability to recognize even the clearest objects, so a light burst around me—wrapping me in such a veil of radiance that I saw nothing. "This is how the Love that quiets this Heaven always welcomes those who enter, to prepare the candle for its flame."[8]

As soon as these brief words entered my ears, I felt myself empowered; and I began to see with new vision, so that there was no degree of brilliance my eyes could not endure. Then I saw a river of dusky golden light[9] flashing between two banks that were painted with a magical springtime.[10] Living sparks sprayed out of this river and dropped everywhere onto the blossoms, like rubies set in gold. Then, as if intoxicated with the fragrances, they plunged back into the marvelous current; and when one entered, another emerged.[11]

---

peculiar fact was discovered by a mathematician after 1800.) Dante would surely have included the Möbius strip somewhere in *The Divine Comedy* if he had known about it.

[7] Dante is now in the Empyrean, the Mind of God. The two triumphant throngs in Heaven are the redeemed saints and the angels. The former are going to appear to Dante in their superhuman bodily forms unlimited by earthly laws of nature.

[8] The Empyrean is not spinning like the other Heavens. The redeemed are like candles that will burn forever there with the joy they were made for. In the words of Sheila Ralphs, "The Blessed are in fact on fire with God's own 'triple light' whose nature may be summed up as being intellectual joy."

[9] The river of light is evidently honey colored.

[10] Near the end of Canto 29 Dante pointed readers toward the vision of Heaven in Daniel 7:9-10, which includes a river. The river in heaven also appears in Revelation 22:1.

[11] The frolicking sparks are angels, and the blossoms are souls of the blessed. (I think this is an intentional contrast to Cantos 21-22 of *Inferno*; there Dante visited a ditch where thick tar boiled and coated the rocky banks with glue. There malicious demons [fallen angels] tortured the souls of grafters. Two angry demons who fell into the

"The more it swells, the more pleasure I take in the great desire that enflames and impels you now to know more about the things you see. But before your great thirst can be quenched, first you must drink of this water."[12] So the sunshine of my eyes spoke to me; then she added, "The river and the topazes going in and out and the smiles of the foliage are only a shadowy preface to their reality.[13] Not that they are themselves deficient; for the defect is in you, that your vision has not yet fully improved."

No baby who awakens far later than usual ever turns his face toward his milk faster than I turned[14] in order to make my eyes still better mirrors,[15] bending down to the water that flows for our benefit. And no sooner had the fringe on my eyelids drunk some of it[16] than the river's straight line spread out into

---

boiling tar stuck fast, cooked within black crusts, and had to be fished out with grappling hooks.)

[12] I am sure that Dante's driving thirst, likened to that of a newborn baby for milk, is not for information, although it often appears that way. It is a thirst for reality.

[13] The angel sparks are also gems, and the blossoms are also smiles.

[14] Although I have not found this idea in other commentaries, I am convinced that when Dante wrote about the Empyrean he was greatly influenced by Isaiah 66:10-13, "Rejoice with Jerusalem and be glad for her, all you who love her; rejoice greatly with her, all you who mourn over her. For you will nurse and be satisfied at her comforting breasts; you will drink deeply and delight in her overflowing abundance. For this is what the LORD says: 'I will extend peace to her like a river, and the wealth of nations like a flooding stream; you will nurse and be carried on her arm and dandled on her knees. As a mother comforts her child, so will I comfort you; and you will be comforted over Jerusalem.'" For Dante this prophecy was about Heaven, the New Jerusalem, the eternal City of God. See also 1 Peter 2:2, "Like newborn babies, crave pure spiritual milk, so that by it you may grow up in your salvation" (NIV).

[15] Dante has repeatedly referred to Beatrice's eyes as mirrors of God, and now for the first time he refers to his own eyes that way because he is almost ready to look at God.

[16] It is not unusual to speak of drinking in information or surroundings or light; Dante drinks in the light of God by wetting his eyes.

a circle.[17] Then like people who have been wearing masks and
seem to change identities when they take off the masks that
used to hide their faces,[18] so the flowers and sparks before me
changed into a greater festival, and I saw both courts of heaven
made manifest.[19] O splendor of God by which I saw the su-
preme triumph of the true kingdom, give me the power to tell
about what I saw.[20]

There is a light on high that makes the Creator visible to the
creature who finds peace only in beholding Him. That light
expands into such a great circle that its circumference would be

---

[17] What had appeared to be a river of light has turned into an ocean
of light. In my opinion this ocean of light is the sea that Piccarda spoke
of in Canto 3. There she told Dante that the essence of Heaven is the
ocean of rest that is God's will. "In His will is our peace. It is that sea to
which everything moves."

C. S. Lewis, who first read *Paradise* in 1930 and wrote *The Pilgrim's
Regress* in 1932, was evidently alluding to Canto 30 when he wrote
Book 9, chapter 1 of *Regress*. There the sleeping pilgrim was awakened
by the light of a woman who introduced herself as Contemplation and
said "Rise and come with me." They traveled far through the air
together in a sphere of light that was finally swallowed up in an ocean
of light. There light ran down like a river too bright to look at, and it
sang with a very loud voice. Many people were traveling with them
with happiness on their faces, moving together toward great castle
gates at the summit. But all this was only a dream, and the pilgrim
awakened to his old terror of death; his real arrival at that destination
would come a bit later in the story, in Book 10. I propose that Lewis's
allegorical dream journey with Contemplation was a thinly veiled
account of his reading of *Paradise* shortly before he became a Christian
believer. (Hence, Lewis allegorized Dante's allegory.)

[18] The only face Dante has seen in all of Paradise is that of Beatrice.
(He saw only a hint of Piccarda's.) Now with stronger vision he will see
all the individual inhabitants of heaven no longer hidden by their light.

[19] This important paragraph (lines 82-90) contains an amazingly
potent combination of images and concentrated meanings. It ends with
what may be another reference to Daniel 7:9-10, "Thousands upon
thousands attended him; ten thousand times ten thousand stood before
him. The court was seated ...."

[20] Dante ends lines 95, 97, and 99 of Canto 30 with the verb *vidi*, "I
saw." Then he finally appeals to God to help him write what he saw.

far too large to serve as a belt for the sun. It is made in its entirety by a Ray of Light[21] beamed down to the highest part of the First Moved, which draws its energy and power from that radiance.[22] And like a mountainside that reflects itself in the water at its base as if to look at its rich adornment of grass and flowers,[23] so I saw everyone who has returned up there[24] in more than a thousand tiers that were mirrored in the light.[25]

---

[21] Although I don't find a discussion of this ray of light in other commentaries, I think it is Christ, the creator, sustainer, and redeemer of the universe. See Colossians 1:15-20, "He is the image of the invisible God, the firstborn over all creation. For by him all things were created: things in heaven and on earth, visible and invisible, whether thrones or powers or rulers or authorities; all things were created by him and for him. He is before all things, and in him all things hold together. And he is the head of the body, the church; he is the beginning and the firstborn from among the dead, so that in everything he might have the supremacy. For God was pleased to have all his fullness dwell in him, and through him to reconcile to himself all things, whether things on earth or things in heaven, by making peace through his blood, shed on the cross" (NIV).

[22] The river of light (from beyond space and time) flows to the top of the largest sphere, the Crystalline Heaven at the base of the Empyrean, and forms an immense sea that reflects the Empyrean. The tree of time described in Canto 27 is rooted in the Crystalline Heaven; in the words of C. S. Lewis, "a gigantic tree growing downward through those 118 million miles [the distance from the earth to the stars according to medieval calculation], its roots in the stars, its leaves being the days and minutes we live through on Earth." (Down means toward the earth, and up means toward the Empyrean.) It seems to me that the roots of the tree of time are watered by the ocean of light.

This sea is apparently the sea mentioned in Revelation 4:6, "Also before the throne there was what looked like a sea of glass, clear as crystal" (NIV).

[23] This image of a lush mountainside above a body of water fed by a river may have inspired C. S. Lewis's image of Paradise at the end of *The Last Battle*. There the children found themselves swimming joyfully up a river: "You went on, up and up, with all kinds of reflected lights flashing at you from the water and all manner of colored stones flashing through it, till it seemed as if you were climbing up light itself...." and "there were forests and green slopes and sweet orchards and

If the lowest row encircles such an immense light, what can the expanse of the rose's outermost petals be![26] My sight did not get lost in all its breadth and height, but absorbed the full magnitude and quality of that bliss. (Neither near nor far adds or subtracts anything there, for where God rules without any intermediary the laws of nature have no relevance.) [27]

Beatrice drew me, like one who is silent and wishes to speak, into the gold of the eternal rose that spreads itself open, row after row, and releases the fragrance of praise to the Sun that makes this perpetual spring.[28] And she said, "Behold how great this white-robed gathering is![29] See how vast our city spreads![30] See how the thrones are filled up except for the few souls who are still awaited. Before you join this wedding feast, the soul of Henry, predestined to become Emperor and come to

flashing waterfalls, one above the other, going up forever."

[24] The souls of the blessed have returned home from their sojourn on earth.

[25] Dante continues to look into the sea of light that reflects the entire Heavenly assembly, which rises around and above it like a measureless amphitheater full of blessed spirits. His characteristic use of inversions seems to me to present new conceptual difficulty here. It was hard enough to try to imagine a two-dimensional circle with its centerpoint as its circumference, and here we seem to have that image in three dimensions; the light at the base of the concave amphitheater may be the oceanic, nonspatial Empyrean that includes the concave amphitheater within itself. I have not located any commentary that touches on this particular complexity.

[26] When Dante saw a river, the saints were flowers on the river banks. After he wet his eyes in the river, he beheld a sea instead, surrounded by humans in an indescribably large amphitheater. Finally, he sees and enters the golden center of a white rose, and the saints are thousands upon thousands of rose petals.

[27] Neither time nor distance impedes the Heavenly sight of reality.

[28] God is like the sun somewhere above this rose.

[29] Dante beholds the multitudinous inhabitants of Heaven. Their white robes are indicated in Revelation 3:5 and 7:13.

[30] Heaven is most often likened to a city (the New Jerusalem) because it is a joyful community of distinct individuals, not an ocean of undifferentiated Spirit. In Canto 13 of *Purgatory* Sapia told Dante "My brother, every one of us is a citizen of the true city."

set Italy straight before she is ready for it, will sit on the great throne that you are looking at because a crown is already placed above it.[31]

"The blind greed that bewitches you has made you like a little child dying of hunger who pushes away his mother's breast;[32] and the man who presides over the holy court at that time will be the kind who will not walk along with him both in the open and in secret.[33] But God will endure that man in the sacred office only briefly after that,[34] and he shall be thrust down where Simon Magus is for his reward; and he shall shove the one from Anagni deeper down."[35]

---

[31] There are countless thrones in this amphitheater, and the people in them are crowned with light. There is immense poignancy in this sentence because in 1300 Henry of Luxembourg was still alive. He would become Emperor Henry VII from 1308 to 1313, when he died suddenly (perhaps from malaria or poison) during his valiant attempt to restore order to Italy. Before his unfortunate death, Henry was Dante's hope for the reform and restoration that would provide peace and justice in Italy and permit Dante to return home to Florence from exile.

[32] Beatrice suddenly prophesies against Italy, showing how it rejected help (portrayed in Isaiah 66 by the image of a baby nourished at its mother's breast).

[33] It seems that although Pope Clement outwardly supported Henry, he secretly betrayed and opposed him because of political developments.

[34] Henry died in August, 1313, and Clement died in April, 1314.

[35] The fates of Pope Clement and Pope Boniface (the one from Anagni) were described in Canto 19 of *Inferno*; they were consigned to a hole in the region of Hell reserved for Simoniacs, those who misuse what is holy for financial gain. Some critics have found Dante's repeated condemnations of greed too persistent and harsh for their taste; but others have pointed out that this is consistent with Dante's observation in Canto 1 of *Inferno* that of the three beasts that blocked his path, the third, the she-wolf, was the worst. I would add that Dante began Canto 15 by stating that benevolence is the essence of genuine love, "just as selfishness is the essence of malice."

CANTO THIRTY-ONE

The Celestial Rose

The holy throng that Christ made His bride with His own blood appeared to me in the form of a pure white rose. But like a swarm of bees that first plunge into flowers and then return to where their toil is turned into sweetness,[1] the other throng[2] (which, as they fly, see and sing the glory of the One who arouses their love and the goodness that made them what they are) were descending into the great many-petalled flower and then rising from there to where their love abides forever.[3] Their faces were all of living flame, their wings were gold, and the rest of them was whiter than snow.[4]

---

[1] In his elliptical style, Dante refers to honey and beehives without using the actual words. Commentators I consulted do not mention the Scriptural basis of his bee image; but honey (as well as light) is mentioned from Genesis to Revelation. Best known is the promise in Ezekiel 20:6 of "a land flowing with milk and honey, the most beautiful of all lands."

I find Song of Solomon 4:9-12 highly relevant to all of Canto 31. "You have stolen my heart, my sister, my bride; you have stolen my heart with one glance of your eyes, with one jewel of your necklace. How delightful is your love, my sister, my bride! How much more pleasing is your love than wine, and the fragrance of your perfume than any spice! Your lips drop sweetness as the honeycomb, my bride; milk and honey are under your tongue. The fragrance of your garments is like that of Lebanon. You are a garden locked up, my sister, my bride; you are a spring enclosed, a sealed fountain" (NIV).

[2] The first throng is composed of redeemed souls, and the other is composed of angels.

[3] In Canto 30 the angels were like sparks or gems bounding from the honey-colored river of light onto banks of flowers and back into the river. In Canto 31 the angels are like bees flying down into the rose and back up to their hive, which is the light of God.

[4] The white-robed angels have ruby-colored faces and golden wings,

When they descended into the flower, from row to row they carried some of the peace and passion that they acquired as they fanned themselves with their wings.[5] But the interposing of this great swarm between the flower and what was above it did not impede the view or the brightness; for Godlight penetrates through the universe according to the merits of its parts, so that nothing is an obstacle to it.[6] The looking and loving of this safe and gladsome realm that is filled with ancient and modern people was all aimed at one target.[7] O Threefold Light in the single sparkling star that delights their eyes so, look down upon our tempest![8]

If barbarians (from the region where every day is capped by Helice wheeling with her beloved son) were stupefied when they saw Rome and her mighty works, back when the Lateran towered above human accomplishments,[9] then for me—coming to the divine from the human, to the eternal from the temporal,

---

related to their appearance in Canto 30 as rubies (or hot topazes, which turn red) set in gold.

[5] Here angels are likened to bees again, and Dante seems aware that both in and out of the hive bees fan themselves with their wings. (They do this not only to fly, but also to regulate their body temperatures.) According to commentators, these metaphorical bees carry peace and passion with them like nectar, from the hive to the flower. If so, this is another of Dante's surprising reversals. My alternative reading is that Dante likened the peace and passion of the saints to pollen that the angels (bees) spread among the saints (flowers). Because real bees spread pollen, not nectar, this way, it strikes me as a more natural and appropriate metaphor and highly evocative and creative in its own right.

[6] In the Empyrean light and vision pass right through solid objects.

[7] The minds and hearts of redeemed souls from the Old Testament dispensation and the New Testament dispensation are all focused on God.

[8] Dante implores that triune God, likened here to a sun, to behold the dark and stormy conditions on earth.

[9] Visitors from primitive far northern Europe (where the two Bear constellations of Helice and her son Arcas are always visible in the night sky) used to be stunned by the grandeur of Rome and, supposedly, the Lateran palace in particular.

and from Florence to a people just and sane—how stupefied I was bound to be![10] Truly, between that and joy, I was content to hear and say nothing.

Like a pilgrim who feels himself refreshed as he gazes at the shrine he had vowed to reach, hoping he will be able to describe it, so I directed my eyes through the living light along the rows—now up, now down, and now circling all around. I saw faces consecrated to love, adorned by Another's light and their own smiles,[11] and gestures graced with every dignity. My eyes had soon taken in the general plan of Paradise in its entirety but had not paused on any part of it; and with renewed eagerness I turned to question my Lady about certain things that put my mind into suspense.

I expected her, but another responded: I thought I would see Beatrice,[12] but I saw an elder robed like those in glory. His eyes and cheeks were bathed in beneficent joy, his bearing kindly as a tender father's.

"Where is she?" I exclaimed immediately.

He answered, "Beatrice urged me away from my place in order to fully satisfy your desire; and if you look up at the third row from the top you will see her again, on the throne her merit reserved for her."[13]

---

[10] Dante compares himself to a gawking tourist, and manages to slip in one last thrust at the injustice and idiocy of Florence.

[11] These wonderful people are a joy to behold, and they are recognizable.

[12] In Canto 30 of *Purgatory* Dante turned to speak to Virgil, his guide, and wept when he saw that Virgil was not there. Dante is far wiser now.

[13] Beatrice had no high position or prominence in her first life; yet here she is seated in the third highest row. C. S. Lewis described such a Lady in Chapter 12-13 of *The Great Divorce*. In her first life her name was Sarah Smith and she had lived in humble Golders Green with her self-centered husband; but in Heaven she was a great saint. "Love shone not from her face only, but from all her limbs, as if it were some liquid in which she had just been bathing." Beatrice and Sarah Smith are brisk, beneficent, and free from sentimentality.

Without answering, I lifted my eyes and saw her crowned by the rays of eternal light that she reflected.[14] No mortal eye, even if it is down at the bottom of the deepest sea, is as far from the highest realm of thunder as my eyes were from Beatrice; but that made no difference to me, because her image did not descend to me through anything that dulled it.[15]

"O Lady in whom my hope is strong, who for my salvation endured leaving the imprint of your feet in Hell,[16] it is by your power and goodness that I recognize the grace and might in all the things I have seen. You have delivered me from slavery to freedom by all those paths, by all those means within your power.[17] Preserve your grand generosity to me, so that my soul, which you have healed, may be pleasing to you when it leaves my body."[18] So I prayed; and as distant as she was, she smiled and gazed at me.[19] Then she turned back to the Eternal Fountain.[20]

---

[14] Dante still sees the light of God only as it is reflected from the rose, not directly.

[15] In ordinary (inadequate) earthly terms, in the Empyrean eyes have automatic x-ray vision and telescopic vision combined. Dante can hear voices and see facial expressions from what can only be described spatially as thousands of miles away.

[16] In Canto 2 of *Inferno* Virgil explained to Dante that Beatrice had descended to Limbo to urge him to rescue Dante: "I was among the dead who dangle in an in-between, and a lady called to me—a lady so blessed and lovely that I begged to serve her. Her eyes were brighter than stars, and she spoke to me softly and gently in an angelic voice ...."

[17] In Canto 1 of *Purgatory* Virgil explained to Cato the reason for Dante's trip through Hell and Purgatory: "he seeks freedom."

[18] In this thankful tribute to Beatrice, Dante repeatedly uses the informal (rather than the formal) Italian word for *you* for the first time in *Commedia*. Relationships are personal now.

[19] It is obvious that in the Empyrean all perception is as unimpeded as vision.

[20] Beatrice gazed at God because, as Dante already observed, "the looking and loving of this safe and gladsome realm ... was all aimed at one target." The last paragraph of C. S. Lewis's heartwrenching book about his wife's death, *A Grief Observed*, ends with Dante's exact words. "How wicked it would be, if we could, to call the dead back! She said not to me but to the chaplain, 'I am at peace with God.' She

And the holy elder said: "So that you may culminate your journey perfectly—the reason prayer and holy love sent me to you— soar throughout this garden with your eyes; for looking at it will prepare your eyes to rise into God's Ray of Light.[21] And the Queen of Heaven,[22] for whom I am all aflame with love, will grant us every grace because I am her faithful Bernard."[23]

I was like someone who comes from Croatia, perhaps, to look at our Veronica;[24] and because his old desire is not quickly assuaged, as long as it is shown to him he keeps repeating in his mind, "My Lord Jesus Christ, true God, was your appearance back then like this?" That's how I was while gazing at the living love of the one who, in contemplation, had tasted that peace while he was down here below.

"Son of grace,"[25] he continued, "you won't know this joyful condition by keeping your eyes fixed down here; instead, look at the circles, clear up to the most distant one, until you see upon her throne the Queen to whom this realm is subject and devoted."[26] I lifted my eyes as if looking from a valley to a

---

smiled, but not at me. *Poi si tornó all' eterna fontana."*

[21] Dante is preparing to see Christ.

[22] The Queen of Heaven is Mary, mother of Jesus. In Canto 2 of *Inferno* Virgil revealed that, because of her compassion, Mary ("a gentle lady') had delegated Lucy to delegate Beatrice to delegate Virgil to rescue Dante. Now Dante has arrived at the fountainhead of that grace that has rescued him.

[23] St. Bernard of Clairvaux (1090-1153) was a great contemplative mystic, writer, preacher, and leader of the Cistercian Order of the Benedictines. He was especially devoted to Mary, and while still a mortal he reportedly had a true vision of God—which makes him the ideal guide as Dante approaches that same experience.

[24] The likeness called the "true image" (Veronica) of Christ was imprinted on a cloth occasionally displayed at the Vatican; according to tradition, Christ's face was wiped with that cloth on His way to Calvary. Many pilgrims traveled all the way to Rome to stare at this image of Christ's face. Similarly, Dante kept staring at Bernard's face.

[25] In the sense that Dante has been spiritually born again, he is the son of Mary's (ultimately God's) grace.

[26] Dante should stop staring at Bernard and look up at Mary in the

mountaintop, and just as at daybreak the eastern part of the horizon outshines the part where the sun set, so my eyes beheld a place at the rim outshining all the rest. And just as the sky is brightest where we on earth expect to see the shaft of Phaeton's badly driven chariot[27] —and on either side the light is dimmer—so that oriflame of peace was brightest in the center and burned less brightly on either side.[28]

Around that midpoint I saw more than a thousand festive angels with outstretched wings, each one distinct in its radiance and its performance. I saw there, smiling at their games and songs, a beauty that rejoiced the eyes of all the other saints.[29] And even if I had a wealth of words and an imagination to match, I would not endeavor to describe the smallest part of that delight.[30]

When Bernard saw my eyes fixed and intent on the flaming focus of his own love, he turned his eyes to her with so much love that he made mine even more ardent.

---

highest tier.

[27] Phaeton once drove the chariot of the sun, and because the shaft pole is at the center of a single-shafted chariot this metaphor means that at sunrise the sky is brightest at the very point where the sun will rise.

[28] The oriflame was the battleflag of ancient France (depicting a red flame on a gold background), reputedly a gift from the angel Gabriel. It was alleged that this flag made its army invincible, and thus it is a fitting symbol of the most beautiful and joyful part of the heavenly amphitheater. However, because the Church Militant has become the Church Triumphant, the battleflag has become a peace flag.

[29] Mary is surrounded by more than a thousand celebrating angels, and all the other saints rejoice in the beauty of her smile.

[30] As C. S. Lewis said in *Letters to Malcolm*, "Joy is the serious business of Heaven."

CANTO THIRTY-TWO

The Saints Assembled

Absorbed in his delight, the one who contemplated easily took on the role of teacher[1] and began with these holy words: "The beautiful one who sits at Mary's feet is the one who opened and pierced the wound that Mary closed and anointed.[2] As you see, Rachel and Beatrice sit below her among those in the third tier.[3] While I descend from row to row by naming

---

[1] Although Bernard was completely absorbed in his contemplation of Mary, he was free to instruct Dante about the seating arrangement in the circular amphitheater. This seems to me to demonstrate that just as the blessed souls can (in our terms) be in two or more places at once because they are no longer limited by space, they can also be doing two or more things at once because they are no longer limited by time.

[2] As the mother of humankind Eve sits right below Mary, the mother of Christ. Eve pierced humanity with sin and opened a wound; later, Mary medicated the wound and closed it (through her Son). Dante's phrasing includes two of his characteristic chronological reversals, and these two reversals are themselves reversed. The original beauty of Eve has evidently been restored (another reversal), and in another reversal Dante counts her as a Hebrew woman because all Hebrews (as well as others) are descended from her.

[3] Rachel lived in the Middle East roughly 3000 years before Beatrice lived in Italy. In Canto 2 of the *Inferno*, Virgil quoted Beatrice's statement that she was seated next to Rachel, and now the reader learns that this is part of a detailed seating plan. Rachel symbolizes contemplation (in Canto 27 of *Purgatory* Dante dreamed of Leah, who said of her sister Rachel "She finds joy in seeing; I find it in doing"), but that in itself hardly explains Dante's reason for bracketing the entire *Comedy* between images of this pair (in the next-to-first and the next-to-last cantos).

I propose that Dante links Beatrice to Rachel because Rachel is sacred history's most ardently loved woman. Thus Dante associates himself with Jacob, whose devotion is recounted in Genesis 29. (Jacob worked for Laban seven years to earn Rachel as his bride, but Laban substituted

them—down the rose, petal by petal[4]—you can see Sarah, Rebecca,[5] Judith,[6] and the great-grandmother of the psalmist who repentantly cried out "Have mercy upon me!"[7]

---

her weak-eyed sister Leah; so to attain Rachel Jacob worked for Laban seven more years.) I contend that Dante, a poet of the Courtly Love tradition, could not possibly have overlooked the parallel between Jacob's 14-year labor of love for Rachel and his own equally long labor that places Beatrice as high as Rachel in the literary pantheon of love. (For a good introduction to Courtly Love, I recommend *The Book of Courtly Love, The Passionate Code of the Troubadours* by Andrea Hopkins [San Francisco: HarperSanFrancisco, 1994].)

[4] Each petal in the rose is an enthroned saint. It seems to me that Dante's visual descent into the fragrant white rose is meant to remind readers of his earlier descent into the foul darkness of the Inferno. At the bottom of that pit Dante and Virgil saw and touched Satan himself, the frozen negation of love and beauty. In contrast, God is blazing above the rose like a sun.

[5] I have not encountered any commentator who explains the relationship of the three central women and their significance, but to me it seems clear. Sarah was the beautiful wife of Abraham (circa 2000 B.C.), mother of Isaac and mother-in-law of Rebeccah. Rebeccah was the beloved wife of Isaac, mother of Jacob and mother-in-law of Rachel. See Genesis 11-49. These three women were the grandmother, mother, and wife of the devoted lover Jacob, whose other name was Israel—from whom the twelve tribes of Israel descended. So they were the foremothers of Judaism.

[6] The book of Judith is included among the deutero-canonical books. Judith (whose name means Judaism or Jewish woman) was a beautiful and devout widow who single-handedly saved Israel by befriending the Assyrian general Holofernes, tricking him, and cutting off his head. Scholars find no time or place for the story of Judith to have really occurred, but Dante apparently believed that Judith lived between Rachel and Ruth, perhaps shortly after 1200 B.C.

[7] According to the Book of Ruth, Ruth was the great-grandmother of King David (circa 1100), a young widow from Moab who so loved Naomi, her impoverished Israelite mother-in-law, that she moved to Bethlehem to live with her. There Ruth followed Naomi's instructions, spent the night with Boaz (innocently), and married him. David wrote Psalm 51, which begins "Have mercy upon me, Lord, according to your unfailing love," when he repented for his sinful love for Bathsheba.

"From the seventh tier the line of Hebrew women continues on downward,[8] dividing all the flower's tresses; this forms a partition by which the sacred seating is parted[9] according to the direction in which a person's faith has looked toward Christ. Those who believed in Christ to come sit in one section; those who looked toward Christ already come sit in the other section, where empty seats intersperse the half-circles.[10]

"Just as on one side of the circle the partition is composed of the glorious seat of the Lady of Heaven and the seats below it, so on the other side the partition is composed of seats assigned to great, ever saintly John (who endured the wilderness and martyrdom and then two years in Hell)[11] and below him to Francis, Benedict,[12] Augustine,[13] and others, circle by circle, all

---

[8] Ruth was the seventh woman down from the top of the amphitheater. Beatrice was sitting to one side of Rachel and was not in the line.

[9] The word *chiome,* tresses, can also mean leafiness. The (rose petal) seats in the amphitheater were in two immense sections, and the thrones of Hebrew women formed a dividing line between the two sections where they met on one side. (A dividing line of Christian men is on the opposite side.)

[10] The completely filled section of the amphitheater is for those who died before the Christian era, and the unfilled section is for all those who die in the Christian era. Because the two sections are like mirror images of each other, we know that half the blessed souls were not Christians in their earthly sojourns.

[11] John was a cousin of Jesus and baptized Him in the Jordan. After living an ascetic life, John the Baptist was beheaded because of a woman; this is the second beheading referred to in Canto 32 and a reverse image of the first one. Then John spent about two years in Limbo—until the harrowing of Hell, when Christ took redeemed souls from Hell to Heaven. John died before Christ's death, and Mary died after it; yet she sits at the top of the vertical line of Hebrew (not Christian) saints, and he sits at the top of the vertical line of Christian (not Hebrew) saints. This somewhat surprising arrangement allows the two people who were most intimately connected with Jesus in His lifetime on the borderline between the pre-Christian and Christian epochs to head the two borderlines between pre-Christian and Christian saints.

[12] St. Francis (1182-1226), in the second tier, was praised in Canto 11 (one third of the way through *Paradise*) as the foremost guide of the

the way down here. Now marvel at the greatness of divine providence; for both of faith's vantage points shall fill this garden in equal measure.[14]

"Understand that those below the row that cuts through both dividing lines at their midpoints do not receive their permanently assigned seats through their own merit, but through Another's goodness; for these are spirits set loose before they could make choices.[15] You can easily tell that by their faces and their childlike voices, if you look well and listen.[16]

"Now you are perplexed, and in your perplexity you keep silent; but I will release you from the tight knot with which

---

Church. St. Benedict (480-543), in the third tier, is the great contemplative whose face Dante wished to see in Canto 22 (two-thirds of the way through *Paradise*), where he was told he would see it in the Empyrean.

[13] St. Augustine of Hippo (354-430), in the fourth tier, was the author of *The City of God* and *The Confessions*, but has hardly been mentioned until now, although his famous sentence at the beginning of the latter could perhaps be cited as the theme of *The Divine Comedy*: "Thou awakest us to delight in Thy praise; for Thou madest us for Thyself, and our heart is restless, until it reposes in Thee." In his book *Dante's Ten Heavens*, Edmund Gardner theorizes that this seating arrangement indicates Dante's opinion that theology is a sacred thing, but contemplation is higher, and the imitation of Christ is higher still. If so, in my opinion Dante ranked his own calling (to write about theology) below disciplined personal experience of God and purity of heart with sacrificial service to others. (Such callings are not mutually exclusive, as lives like that of the late Henri Nouwen seem to illustrate.)

[14] Now Heaven is likened to an immense two-section garden full of saints who are flowers. In Canto 23 Dante had a preview of this garden, in which Mary was a rose and the other saints were all lilies.

[15] The redeemed in the lower half of the amphitheater are not there by a combination of God's grace and their right choices, like all the others, because these were too young to make choices. They are there by grace alone.

[16] Although it is often assumed that in Heaven everyone will be at the prime of youthfully mature life, Dante portrays people there at the age they actually attained on earth. For Dante, who was a evidently a child-lover, the huge crowd of children in Heaven would have been a joyous spectacle.

your exacting thoughts have you bound.[17] Within this kingdom's immensity there is no room for chance, any more than for sadness or thirst or hunger,[18] because everything you see has been ordained by eternal law so that the fit is as exact as that between a ring and a finger. Therefore these early arrivers to the true life have not been ranked higher or lower here without due cause.

"The King through whom this kingdom rests in such great love and delight that no one could venture to desire any more[19] — who creates all minds in his own glad image — endows them differently, just as He pleases. Let that fact be enough for you.[20] (This is clearly and plainly recorded for you in the Holy Scripture about those twins whose competition began inside their mother's womb.)[21] As with their hair color, God's light

---

[17] Bernard realizes that Dante wonders why the souls of those who died in infancy and early childhood should be accorded varying degrees of bliss, since they had no chance to achieve varying degrees of goodness.

[18] See Revelation 7:13-17.

[19] In Canto 18 of *Purgatory* Virgil explained to Dante, "...love binds you naturally with bonds of pleasure." In *The Weight of Glory*, C. S. Lewis wrote "What would it be to taste at the fountain-head that stream of which even these lower reaches prove so intoxicating? Yet that, I believe, is what lies before us. The whole man is to drink joy from the fountain of joy."

[20] In Canto 3 of *Purgatory* Virgil advised Dante, "Limit yourselves, you of the human race, to discovering *what is*. For if you had been able to understand the *why* of everything, there would have been no need for Mary to give birth." Here Bernard does not untie the knot with logic; instead, he cuts right through it. Similarly, the Eagle in Canto 20 told Dante, "And you mortals, restrain yourselves from judging; for even we who see God do not know yet all the roll of His elect. Yet our limitation is sweet to us, because our good is perfected in this good: that what God wills, we also will." In Canto 21 Peter Damien told Dante to urge people not to presume to understand the workings of God's will, but to trust in God's goodness and fairness.

[21] In my opinion this image of infants in the womb is an overt suggestion of an underlying theme throughout *Paradise*, the innate longing in humans to "return to the womb" of their origin, the Mind of God. (The Empyrean is like the womb of the entire cosmos.)

fittingly crowns them with degrees of grace.[22] Therefore, they are graded without acquiring merit by their deeds, differing only in their inherent keenness of vision.[23] It was enough, in the earliest ages, for no more than their parents' faith and their own innocence to secure their salvation.[24] When the first ages ended, male children needed circumcision to add strength to their wings of innocence. But when the age of grace arrived, then without the perfected baptism in Christ such innocence must remain below.[25]

Once again in this image, Jacob is implicitly pivotal in Canto 32. Rebeccah's twin sons Jacob and Essau were unevenly matched even before they were born (see Genesis 25 and Malachi 1:2-3). Paul addressed Dante's knotty question in Romans 9:11-16: "Yet, before the twins were born or had done anything good or bad—in order that God's purpose in election might stand: not by works but by him who calls—she was told, 'The older will serve the younger.' Just as it is written: 'Jacob I loved, but Esau I hated.' What then shall we say? Is God unjust? Not at all! For he says to Moses, 'I will have mercy on whom I have mercy, and I will have compassion on whom I have compassion'" (NIV).

[22] As Dante and his readers knew well, Esau happened to have red hair and Jacob did not, just as Esau was firstborn and Jacob was not.

[23] God knows which souls are endowed with spiritual perspicacity (thirst for Reality) from the start. I find it significant that four months before his death, on January 20, 1320, Dante remarked in a physics lecture he gave in Verona, "from my boyhood I have been continuously nurtured by a love for truth." Evidently he did not take personal credit for this providential thirst for Reality.

[24] The first period of sacred history lasted from creation to God's covenant with Abraham. (See Genesis 1-17.)

[25] According to traditional Roman Catholic doctrine, circumcision was an imperfect kind of baptism and it was replaced by Christian baptism, without which babies who die are relegated to Limbo. At this point the poet has devoted far over a quarter of his total lines in Canto 32 to the vexing question of souls who die in childhood; now he attributes his conclusion, which many readers find morally repugnant, to Bernard. As Dante was well aware, on earth Bernard wrote that he didn't know what happens to the souls of children who die; and yet Dante takes it on himself to provide Bernard with that knowledge in Heaven. In my opinion this was not the result of carelessness or

"Look now upon the face that most resembles Christ; for its brightness, and that alone, can prepare you to see Christ."[26]

I saw such joy rain down upon her face (carried there by the holy Intelligences created to fly throughout such heights) that nothing I saw before had ever awed me so or showed me such a likeness to God.[27] And the same angelic Love that had once descended to her sang out "Hail Mary, full of grace" and spread his wings wide before her.[28] This sacred canticle was joined from all sides by the blessed court, so that every face was luminous with joy.

"O holy Father—willing to be here below for my sake, leaving the sweet place where you are destined to sit forever— who is the angel that looks into the Queen's eyes with such delight that he appears to be aflame?" So I turned again to instruction from the one who drew beauty from Mary just as the morning star does from the sun.[29]

And he answered "As much confidence and gracious joy as there can be in an angel or in a human soul is all in him; and we would have it so, for he is the one who bore the palm to Mary when the Son of God Himself chose to bear the burden of our flesh.[30] But follow my words with your eyes as I continue

---

callousness, but in order to lay out the strongest charge of all against orthodox Christian faith and to answer it with his theme: God is the source of all goodness, wisdom, love and justice. We must abide in simple childlike trust.

[26] Bernard instructs Dante to look back up at Mary. At this point Dante has ended three rhyming lines (83, 85, and 87) with the word *Cristo*. (He did this earlier in Cantos 12, 14, and 19.)

[27] The angels drench Mary with joy. She looks most like Christ because she is His mother, and also because as His mother she loves Him the most. On earth Dante had beheld countless awe-inspiring sights and works of religious art that attempted to portray Christ.

[28] The angel Gabriel sings the same words that he spoke to Mary on earth about 1300 years earlier. (See Luke 1:28.) He is probably the same angel who crowned Mary with light in Canto 23, when she appeared to Dante in the Heaven of the Stationary Stars.

[29] Bernard reflects the beauty of Mary just as the planet Venus (the symbol of love) reflects the light of the sun.

[30] Artists frequently depicted Gabriel carrying a palm frond to

teaching, and note the noble aristocrats of this most just and merciful empire.

"The two who sit up there nearest to the Empress, most blessed, are like two roots of this rose. The one next to her on her left is the forefather whose reckless appetite has caused the human race to taste such bitterness. On her right, see the ancient father of Holy Church to whom Christ entrusted the keys of this beautiful flower.[31] By this one's side sits the man who foresaw before he died all the grievous times of the lovely bride who had been won with the spear and the nails; and on the other's side rests the leader of the ungrateful, fickle, and rebellious people.[32]

"Behold Anna, seated across from Peter, so satisfied to gaze upon her daughter that she does not move her eyes when he sings Hosanna.[33] And across from the first father sits Lucy, who sent your Lady to help you when your head was leaning downward toward your ruin.[34]

---

symbolize victory when he informed Mary that she would conceive a son and name Him Jesus.

[31] The two fathers seated next to Mary are Adam on her left side and Peter on her right. As I see it, Adam caused the human race to be locked out of Paradise, and Peter was entrusted with the keys to open Paradise. (Adam sits in the pre-Christian section and Peter sits in the Christian section.)

[32] Seated at the right of Peter is John, who recorded in the book of Revelation terrible times the church was going to go through. Seated to the left of Adam is Moses, who recorded in the book of Exodus terrible times the Israelites had gone through. These two are matched because long after the griefs they both recorded, they enjoy together the bliss they both foresaw.

[33] Anna, the mother of Mary and grandmother of Jesus, is one of the tenderest images of mother love in *Paradise*. She has the joy of feasting her eyes upon her glorified daughter and Grandson forever.

[34] Anna sits on the right of her nephew John the Baptist (in the pre-Christian section), and Lucy sits on the left of John (in the Christian section). Lucy and Anna may be paired because Anna doesn't take her eyes off her daughter Mary on the far side of the amphitheater, and Lucy is the patron saint connected with good vision. Lucy is also the last saint Dante will see in Paradise before looking directly at God;

"But since the time for your vision grows short,[35] let us stop here, like a careful tailor who cuts out a garment according to the amount of cloth he has; and let us turn our eyes to the Primal Love, so that by looking at Him you may penetrate into His radiance as far as possible.[36] But in order to acquire the grace to avoid falling back down by expecting to rise with your own wings, you must pray for grace from the Lady who has power to help you. You must follow my words with such devotion that your heart is with my words."

And he began this holy prayer...[37]

---

thus she represents both the clear vision and the spiritual enlightenment that Dante desperately needed in the first sentence of *Inferno*

According to Canto 2 of *Inferno*, Mary summoned Lucy across the amphitheater and committed Dante to her care; then Lucy commissioned Beatrice to rescue him, which she did by recruiting Virgil. Virgil arrived just as Dante had given up his effort to climb the sunlit hill and was descending to the dark wood that he had been trying to escape.

[35] In *Letters to Malcolm* C. S. Lewis speculated about time and timelessness in heaven: "I certainly believe that to be God is to enjoy an infinite present, where nothing has yet passed away and nothing is still to come. Does it follow that we can say the same of saints and angels? Or at any rate exactly the same? The dead might experience a time which is not so linear as ours—it might, so to speak, have thickness as well as length. Already in this life we get some thickness whenever we learn to attend to more than one thing at once. One can suppose this increased to any extent, so that though, for them as for us, the present is always becoming the past, yet each present contains unimaginably more than ours. I feel...that to make the life of the blessed dead strictly timeless is inconsistent with the resurrection of the body."

[36] Instead of looking at the amphitheater any longer, Dante is instructed to look directly at God with the aid of Mary. (This is like looking directly into the sun rather than looking at reflections of its light.) But first Bernard would pray aloud to Mary, and Dante was to pray along in his heart.

[37] The storyteller has finally arrived at Canto 33 of the third book. One reason *Inferno* does not have exactly 33 cantos (symbolizing perfection) was because it was all about imperfection. Both *Purgatory* and *Paradise* have 33 cantos because they are about the attainment and enjoyment of perfection.

CANTO THIRTY-THREE

The Vision of God

"Virgin Mother, daughter of your own Son, most lowly and most uplifted of all creatures, the pivot of the eternal plan, you are the one who so ennobled human nature that its Maker did not disdain to be made by it. The Love that caused this flower to unfold under His warmth, in the eternal peace, was kindled in your womb. Up here you are the high noon torch of love for us, and down there you are a living spring of hope for mortals.[1]

"Lady, you are so great and have such authority that if anyone wants grace and does not turn to you his desire is trying to fly without wings. Your kindness not only helps a person who has asked for aid, but often issues freely before the request. In you there is tenderness, in you there is pity, in you munificence, in you everything good that exists in any creature.

"Now this man—who has seen the lives of the spirits one by one, from the deepest pit of the universe all the way up here— begs you, of your grace, for the ability to lift his eyes higher toward the ultimate bliss.[2] And I, who never longed for my own vision more than I do for his, offer you all my prayers (and I pray they are not inadequate) that with your prayers you will sunder the shadows of his mortality so that the Supreme Joy may be revealed to him.[3]

---

[1] Bernard's salutation to Mary employs a series of paradoxes: mother and daughter, lowest and highest, maker and made, noon sun and fountain. The Celestial Rose, where Mary is the most beautiful petal of all, blooms under the very Sun that was conceived within her womb.

[2] Joseph Gallagher points out that Dante had first descended a shrinking spiral where it is always night, until he came to Satan; then he ascended a shrinking spiral where day and night alternate, until he came to Beatrice. Now he has ascended through expanding circles where it is always a spring day, until he has come to God.

[3] This is Dante's final image of being freed from bonds. Ironically, he

"And I pray further, Queen, you who can do whatever you choose, that you will preserve his devotion after his great vision. Let your protection prevail over natural human inconstancy.[4] Behold Beatrice and all the saints clasping their hands with me in this prayer."[5]

Her eyes, so loved and prized by God, rested on her petitioner and showed how much she appreciates devout prayers; then they turned back to the Eternal Light—and we have to believe that no one else's eye sees into it more clearly. And I, nearing the goal of all desires, let the burning desire within me be quenched accordingly.[6]

Bernard gave me a signal and smiled to me that I should look on high; but I was already doing that,[7] because my sight, becoming clearer now, was increasingly able to pierce deeply into the Ray of Light that is Truth itself.[8]

---

was unexpectedly and permanently sundered from the shadows of his mortality immediately after completing *Paradise*. (If reports are true, he did not even have a chance to send the last 13 cantos to his copyist.) He suddenly died of malaria on September 14, 1321.

[4] In Canto 5 Dante acknowledged that he was changeable by nature.

[5] The redeemed souls agree with Bernard's petition for Dante to complete his quest and then to retain what he has gained. In this final mention of Beatrice, she reverently celebrates Dante's direct encounter with the true object of all his desire; his love for her has brought him beyond her, to God. (As C. S. Lewis postulates, "God will look to every soul like its first love because He is its first love.")

[6] Ever since Dante first tried to climb the sunlit hill in Canto 1 of *Inferno*, his ultimate goal has been seeing the Sun Himself. According to commentary in the Modern Library edition of the Carlyle-Wicksteed translation, "Dante, anticipating Bernard's permission, with the passion of his longing already assuaged by the peace of now assured fruition, looks right into the deep light."

[7] Some commentators say that Dante is inadvertently contradicting himself here because he could not possibly have seen Bernard (who was next to him down in the center of the rose) if he was already looking upward to the Light. But I find Dante's attainment of this ability at the end of *Paradise* no more unlikely than all the rest of his attainments in *Paradise*.

[8] Dante's improved eyesight is essentially "mindsight," and Dante's main purpose in writing *The Divine Comedy* was to improve the

From that point on, what I saw was beyond words, which fail at such a sight; and memory fails at such extremity. Like a dreamer—who sees things, and after the dream is gone its strong feeling lingers, but that is all he can ever recall of it—I find that what I saw almost entirely eludes me, although the sweetness of it still showers on my heart. So snow loses its imprints in the sun, and so the wisdom of Sibyl was lost on windborne leaves.[9]

O Supreme Light who rises so far above human comprehension, restore to my mind a little of how You appeared, and give my tongue enough power to leave behind just a single spark of Your glory for future generations; for by returning to my memory somewhat, and with a brief description in these verses, more of Your victory will be understood.[10]

I am convinced that because of the intensity of the Ray of Living Light that I endured I would have lost my senses if my eyes had turned aside.[11] And so I was emboldened, as I recall, to keep gazing until I saw the Ultimate Goodness.[12]

---

mindsight of his readers. As he stated to his friend Can Grande, "the purpose of the whole [*Divine Comedy*] and of this portion [*Paradise*] is to remove those who are living in this life from the state of wretchedness, and to lead them to the state of blessedness." Geoffrey Burton Russell claims "Throughout the *Paradiso*, it is not heaven itself that changes but the pilgrim, and, through him, the reader."

[9] In the *Aeneid* Virgil told how the legendary prophetess wrote an oracle on many tree leaves (according to John Ciardi, one letter per leaf) that were laid out in order; then she allowed the wind to scatter them, and the oracle was lost forever.

[10] In *A History of Heaven*, Jeffrey Burton Russell says, "The most important aspects of the concept of heaven are the beatific vision and the mystical union. In the beatific vision of God, the person's 'seeing' is his or her complete understanding and love of Christ. In this earthly life one can 'see' this understanding and love only 'through a glass darkly'; in heaven one sees 'face to face' (1 Cor 13:12). On earth one may have a transitory intimation of the mystical union; in heaven the union is intense, permanent, complete. In the heavenly union complete love and complete knowledge are one and the same."

[11] John Ciardi points out the logic of this seeming paradox, which he calls a parable of grace. By looking steadfastly into the Light of God,

O grace abounding, by which I dared to plunge my sight
into the Eternal Light until all my viewing was consummated![13]
Within its depths I saw ingathered, bound by love into one vol-
ume, the scattered leaves of all the universe;[14] substance and
accident and their relationship[15] all fused together in such a
way that what I am describing is a simple light.[16] I believe that

---

Dante is strengthened to do so; and man can lose his good by looking
away from God.

[12] Bernard's prayer to Mary for Dante is being answered: "for the
ability to lift his eyes higher toward the ultimate bliss."

[13] I think Dante employs a slight suggestion of erotic love here to
symbolize the intensity of the spiritual climax. According to Charles
Singleton, this high point of the entire *Comedy* occurs on line 81 of
Paradise because in numerology the numeral 81 signifies nine, Dante's
favorite number.

[14] According to Charles Singleton, the Italian word for "scattered"
includes a shorter word that means four, and the word for "ingath-
ered" includes a shorter word that means three; hence, according to
Singleton, Dante suggests the four material elements (fire, air, water,
earth), representing the universe, bound together in the triune Godhead.

[15] Dante restates his evocative concrete image of the book of reality in
the terminology of Aristotle, as developed and expounded by the
scholastic philosopher/theologian Thomas Aquinas. *Substance* (essence)
means the inherent identity of anything that exists—what the thing is. In
contrast, an *accident* (quality) means any specific nonessential charac-
teristic of that thing. For example, the *substance* of a certain green apple
is apple, and an *accident* of the apple is green; and if that color should
happen to change, the thing is still an apple. Thus the *substance* is
primary and the *accident* exists strictly in its relationship to the
substance. According to Aristotle and Aquinas, all the things of this
world are made up of substance and accidents, the former existing in
its own right, the latter only as an aspect of a substance. Dante sees the
substance, the accidents, and the relationship between the two as an
indissoluble trinity, an image of the Holy Trinity itself.

[16] According to Platonist John Bremer, "Dante seems to be offering a
poetical vision of what it would be like if the distinction of this world,
between substance and accidents, were transcended, if the two orders
of being, essence and accident, became one. His vision is that of radiant
energy, light." Perhaps to some contemporary readers this idea
suggests a kind of philosophical parallel to nuclear fusion.

I beheld the universal form of this knot, because as I tell about this I feel my joy swell within me.[17]

A single moment causes me more memory loss than twenty-five centuries have caused concerning the enterprise that amazed Neptune with the shadow of the Argo.[18]

So my mind hung in abeyance, staring fixedly, immovable, intent, its ardor increasingly enflamed by the sight. Anyone who sees that Light becomes a person who would not possibly consent to turn away to any other sight; for the good that is the object of all desires[19] is ingathered there in its fullness, and elsewhere it falls short of its perfection.[20]

---

[17] This is not another mortal knot to be untied; this is the transcendental unity of all things in the Mind of God. Like many who have had mystical experiences, Dante cannot recall the revelation well or explain it, but his extraordinary inner joy when he thinks of it assures him that he has really experienced it. (Thus "the sweetness of it still showers on my heart.")

[18] It took the world 25 centuries to forget as much about Jason's quest (in his ship the Argo) as Dante forgot about his sight of God in one moment. Of this sentence C. S. Lewis said, "Notice here the art. Mere numbers [25 centuries] do nothing in poetry. Even words like *immeasurable* do little. But the Argo puts us at once in the dawn of time, in the old untraveled world when the shadow of a ship was a wonder, and thence causes us to view the whole distance which separates it from the moment of Dante's vision."

The legendary adventurer Jason (whom Dante encountered in the eighth circle of Hell) might have lived closer to 2000 B. C. than to 1200 B. C., but Dante's figures are adequate for his purpose. In Canto 2 of *Paradise* he likened his quest to Jason's daring voyage to win the golden fleece, and now he contrasts them. He may even be suggesting that his amazement at the sight of God was as much greater than Neptune's amazement at the shadow of the Argo as the difference between one second and 25,000 centuries of seconds; hence his loss of memory. There is also a parallel between Neptune (in the depths, marveling at the shadow of Jason's quest far above) and mortal man (on earth, marveling at Dante's quest far above). In his introduction to the Ciardi translation, John Freccero claims "The figure completes the navigational imagery with which the *Paradiso* began."

[19] All human desires are basically for goodness.

[20] In *The Problem of Pain*, C. S. Lewis wrote of "that something which

From here on my language is even more deficient for what is in my memory than that of an infant who is still bathing his tongue at the breast.[21]

It was not that the Living Light, which is always what it was before,[22] had more than one appearance; but as my looking made my sight grew stronger, that single semblance changed in my changing eyesight. Within the deep and luminous essence of the Utmost Light three circles appeared to me as three distinct colors in one space;[23] one a mirror of the other, like one rainbow and another,[24] and the third was like fire that issued equally from the other two.[25]

Oh, but how inadequate speech is to express my idea, which in itself is so weak! Compared to what I saw, it is not enough to be called little.

O Light Eternal, You who abide self-contained, self-known, and—self-knowing and self-known—self-loving and smiling at

---

you were born desiring": "All the things that have ever deeply possessed your soul have been but hints of it—tantalizing glimpses, promises never quite fulfilled, echoes that died away just as they caught your ear. But if it should ever really become manifest—if there ever came an echo that did not die away but swelled to the sound itself—you would know it. Beyond all possibility of doubt you would say 'Here at last is the thing I was made for'."

[21] Once again, for the last time in his *Comedy*, Dante returns to babies, their inborn thirst for mother's milk, and language development. In addition to comparing his verbal inadequacy to that of a baby, I think Dante is implicitly comparing his spiritual thirst to a baby's physical thirst, comparing the Empyrean to a mother, and comparing the light of God (itself a metaphor) to milk. Several lines earlier, Dante wrote of sweetness still showering on his heart, an image of refreshing and fructifying rain; now he returns to the familiar image of being embraced and nourished, of his human thirst being quenched.

[22] Hebrews 13:8, "Jesus Christ is the same yesterday, today, and forever."

[23] A perfect circle is the shape commonly used to symbolize divinity and eternity.

[24] It was believed that when there are two rainbows the second springs from the first.

[25] The first circle is God the Father, the second is the Son, and the third is the Holy Spirit.

Yourself!²⁶ When my eyes had looked awhile at that circling²⁷ which had thus been fathered by You as reflected light, our image seemed to be depicted in it in its own color; and therefore my sight stayed completely focused there.²⁸ Upon seeing this new spectacle I was like a geometrician who tries to square the circle, and—think as hard as he may—cannot find the formula he needs.²⁹

I wanted to see how the image conforms to the circle and how it coincides, but my own wings were not enough for that— had it not been that my mind was struck by a flash that brought its wish.³⁰ Here force failed my lofty fantasy;³¹ but my

---

²⁶ The Son reflects the omniscient Father and understands Him; together they emanate the Holy Spirit, who is Love.

²⁷ According to Charles Singleton, the triune God is not motionless, but spinning: "All is active in God, nothing is passive."

²⁸ Dante beholds God as three circles in one. Next, he begins to see the second circle as a human form as well as a circle, and so he stares at it.

²⁹ "Squaring the circle" (constructing a square with the same area as a given circle) was a goal in geometry for many centuries; but it would have required discovering a correspondence between the radius of a circle and the side of a square with the use of no more than a straight edge and a compass. The task was eventually proved to be impossible, as Dante foresaw, like the task of intellectually reconciling the two natures of Christ—both fully human ("our image") and fully divine (a perfect circle). In Canto 31 of *Purgatory* Dante had seen Christ's two natures seem to alternate, as reflected in the eyes of Beatrice. Now he sees the two simultaneously, as Beatrice does; because he is still mortal, however, he tries hard to understand and cannot. (I suspect that one reason the square is the symbol of Christ's human nature is that He was the perfect manifestation of the four cardinal [human] virtues.)

³⁰ Dorothy Sayers says, "It is for the vision of God in *Paradise* that all the rest of the allegory exists." As if struck by lightning, Dante glimpses the human nature of Christ at one with His divinity. Christ has been identified as Wisdom (the desire of the intellect) ever since Dante read the verse over the gateway to Hell at the beginning of Canto 3 in the *Inferno*. and now Dante's desire has been fulfilled.

³¹ The force that propelled Dante's flight and then caused it to end is really the will of God the Father. His flight ended, Dante finds himself back on earth, where he is telling his story. (As used here, the word fantasy does not mean fiction.)

desire and will were being turned already, like a wheel in perfect balance,[32] by the Love that moves the sun and other stars.[33]

---

[32] As if in fulfillment of 1 John 3:2 ("...we know that when He appears we shall be like Him, for we shall see Him as He is"), Dante's desire and will are miraculously conformed to the will of God. As C. S. Lewis stated in *Letters to Malcolm*, "The angels never knew (from within) the meaning of the word *ought*, and the blessed dead have long since gladly forgotten it." (There is a rather poignant connection between *Letters to Malcolm* and *Paradise* that has not been noted until now. Just as Dante died before there was time for *Paradise* to be copied and read, C. S. Lewis died before there was time for *Letters to Malcolm* to be published and read. Both books were completed when their authors were unaware that they were on the very brink of the eternity they were describing.)

[33] As I see it, Dante ends his entire *Comedy* with one last tribute to divine light (Christ), power (the Father), and love (the Holy Spirit); and for the third time he ends a canticle with the word *stars*. Thanks to the grace of the First Mover, Dante has now had a foretaste of the circling bliss of all the universe and Paradise.

The Destination of All Desires

Moving toward the First Mover,
I pace my way;
Dazzled by Dante, drawn by love.

    On moving day
    I dual with Plato at his sunrise
    For a pass to ideal world before the fares go up;
    I have no real idea, but I'm eager to go.

Moving toward the First Mover,
I phrase my say;
Boggled by Aristotle, drawn by cause.

    On moving day
    I gasp at Aquinas, beyond my grasp,
    And know, will, and love what I have at hand,
    With the implicit packed up all ready to go.

Moving toward the First Mover,
I phase my stay
In hostels of providence, drawn by choice.

    On moving day
    I have lost both Occam's razor and Pascal's wager.
    But my bags are full of reason that reason does not know
    And when the moving hearse arrives I'll go,

Moving toward the First Mover.

FURTHER READING
ON *PARADISE*

For readable translations of Paradise *into poetry, with helpful notes, I recommend the following*:

John Ciardi, *Dante Alighieri: The Paradiso* (New York: New American Library, 1961). The third of three volumes, written in three-line rhymed stanzas. Ciardi explains that he is a not a Dante scholar, and his aim is readability rather than strict accuracy. Dante scholar John Freccero wrote the introduction.

Dorothy Sayers and Barbara Reynolds, *The Comedy of Dante Alighieri: Paradise* (New York: Penguin Books, 1962). The third of three volumes, written in terza rima.

Allen Mandelbaum, *The Divine Comedy of Dante Alighieri: Paradiso* (Berkeley, California: University of California Press, 1984). The third of three volumes, written in unrhymed verse without stanzas, with the Italian on the adjoining page.

Mark Musa, *The Divine Comedy: Volume 3* (Bloomington, Indiana: Indiana University Press, 1984). The third of three volumes, written in unrhymed tercets.

For widely contrasting studies of Paradise, I recommend:

Sheila Ralphs, *Etterno Spiro: A Study in the Nature of Dante's Paradise* (Manchester, England: Manchester University Press, 1959). In this brief but scholarly monograph, Ralphs considers the theological significance and interrelationship of some of the key words and images in *Paradise*.

Dorothy Sayers, "Dante the Maker," *The Poetry of Search and the Poetry of Statement* (London: Victor Gollancz, 1963). Sayers explores the central roles of light and movement in *Paradise* and also shows how Dante leads from the abstract First Cause of Greek philosophy to the actively personal God of Jewish prophecy.

C. S. Lewis, "Imagery in the Last Eleven Cantos of Dante's *Comedy*," *Studies in Medieval and Renaissance Literature* (Cambridge, England: Cambridge University Press, 1966). Lewis read this paper to the Oxford Dante Society on November 9, 1948. (On February 13, 1940, he had read the closely related essay "Dante's Similes" to the same group, and it appears in the same volume.)

Richard Kay, *Dante's Christian Astrology* (Philadelphia, Pennsylvania: University of Pennsylvania Press, 1994). An exhaustive scholarly study of the properties and meanings Dante ascribed to the planets in Cantos 1-22 of *Paradise*. Kay identifies and explains Dante's academic sources.

Barbara Reynolds, "Dante's Vision of Heaven," *Journey to the Celestial City: Glimpses of Heaven from Great Literary Classics* , ed. Wayne Martindale (Chicago: Moody Press, 1995). A clear nontechnical introduction and overview of *Paradise*, written by the co-author of the Dorothy Sayers translation.

John Pope-Hennessy, *Paradiso: The Illuminations to Dante's Divine Comedy by Giovanni di Paolo* (New York: Random house, 1993). This lavish presentation of an outstanding Sienese manuscript created in about 1445 contains 93 detailed, brilliantly colored illustrations. Pope-Hennessy's informative introduction and notes begin with the statement "This book is about the greatest of all poems .... Its language and its use of metaphor and simile are incomparably rich, and it is filled with visual observations with which we, over 600 years after its completion, can still identify."

For general introductions to The Divine Comedy *that are especially enlightening with regard to Paradise, I recommend:*

Dorothy Sayers, "The Meaning of Heaven and Hell," *Introductory Papers on Dante* (London: Methuen, 1954). Sayers prepared this essay for presentation at a summer school of the Society for Italian Studies.

Irma Brandeis, *Ladder of Vision: A Study of Dante's "Comedy"* (London: Chatto & Windus, 1960). The title chapter in this book traces and analyzes Dante's major theme—light and vision—from the double darkness of *Inferno* through the brightness of *Purgatory* and the supernal radiance of *Paradise*.

C. S. Lewis, "Imagination and Thought in the Middle Ages," *Studies in Medieval and Renaissance Literature* (Cambridge, England: Cambridge University Press, 1966). Lewis delivered this two-part essay to an audience of Cambridge scientists on June 17 and 18, 1956. For the benefit of people unfamiliar with the view of the cosmos held by Dante and his readers, Lewis explains it all in his inimitable style.

Mary Patricia Sexton, C.S.J., *The Dante-Jung Correspondence* (Northridge, California: Joyce Motion Picture Company, 1975). Sexton explores the connection between Dante and the tenets of Carl Jung, and her theme is Dante's extraordinary use of circles and spirals. Her main emphasis is upon Dante's concept of Heaven, which is explored in chapter 5, "The Psychocosmos of *Paradiso*."

Helen M. Luke, *Dark Wood to White Rose* (Pecos, New Mexico: Dove, 1975). Luke leads readers through the *Comedy* and shows how love culminates in *Paradise*. She observes, "It is a strange thing that most people are convinced that descriptions of bliss must be dull." She draws her insights from the scholarship of Dorothy Sayers and her own learning and teaching about the inner life.

For a variety of works closely related to Dante's Paradise, *I recommend:*

C. S. Lewis, *The Pilgrim's Regress* (London: J. M. Dent, 1933). This allegorical account of C. S. Lewis's spiritual pilgrimage was his first Christian publication. In it a man named John awakens in a woodland and realizes that he wants out. After an adventurous journey in which he learns many lessons, he approaches at last the true object of his deepest desire.

C. S. Lewis, *The Allegory of Love: A Study in Medieval Tradition* (London: Oxford University Press, 1936). Lewis's second book of prose established his reputation for academic excellence. It is a sober, rigorous study of both the courtly love tradition and allegory. Although it culminates with an analysis of Spenser's *Faerie Queen* rather than *The Divine Comedy*, it is useful for scholarly understanding of Dante in his cultural milieu.

C. S. Lewis, "Heaven," *The Problem of Pain* (London: Centenary Press, 1940). The final chapter in Lewis's first book of straightforward Christian apologetics is also his first description of Heaven, obviously influenced by *Paradise*. Heaven would prove to be the theme of most of Lewis's writing until his death in 1963; and *Letters to Malcolm*, the book he wrote when he was dying, ended with his final discussion of heaven.

C. S. Lewis, *The Great Divorce* (London: Bles, 1945). Lewis greatly preferred this profound little fantasy ("my Cinderella") to his more popular *Screwtape Letters*. He finds himself in Hell and travels to Heaven by bus. (The driver is the same angel that descended in *Inferno* to help Dante on his way.) George MacDonald is his teacher there. Lewis's wit, brevity, and moral certitude are similar to Dante's.

C. S. Lewis, "The Weight of Glory," *The Weight of Glory and Other Addresses* (New York: Macmillan, 1949). Published in England under the title *Transposition and Other Essays*. Lewis delivered this famous sermon in 1941, ten years after first reading *Paradise;* and it is like a summary of Dante's most important points. Lewis stresses that God wants us to strongly desire our own blessedness and joy, that our deepest desire is for Heaven, the Bible's teaching about Heaven, and the costly implications of the forgoing in our daily lives.

C. S. Lewis, *The Discarded Image: An Introduction to Medieval and Renaissance Literature* (Cambridge: Cambridge University Press, 1964). Lewis's extraordinary explanation of the medieval model of the universe (as it relates to the modern model) is a demanding but invaluable commentary on *The Divine Comedy.* Lewis says of *Paradise,* "[Dante] is like a man being conducted through an immense cathedral, not like one lost on a shoreless sea."

Harry Blamires, *Highway to Heaven* (Nashville, Tennessee: Thomas J. Nelson, 1984). First published in 1955 as *Blessings Unbounded,* the third in a good-natured satirical Christian trilogy loosely modeled on *The Divine Comedy.* The first two in the series are *The Devil's Hunting Grounds* (London: Longmans, Green, 1954) and *Cold War in Hell* (London: Longmans, Green, 1955).

Jostein Gaarder, *Sophie's World: A Novel about the History of Philosophy* (New York: Farrar, Straus and Giroux, 1994). Translated by Paulette Moller. A Norwegian fantasy novel for young people and adults. This forthright survey of the history of philosophy does not mention Dante, but it defines the philosophy of his mentor Thomas Aquinas as well as other predecessors and followers.

Jeffrey Burton Russell, *The History of Heaven: The Singing Silence* (Princeton, New Jersey: Princeton University Press, 1997). An almost lyrical investigation of the concept of Heaven, from its origin in about 200 B.C. through its "highest expression" in *The Divine Comedy.* Although this is a work of scholarship, Russell provides unusually joyful, loving, and readable prose.